PRAISE FOR *COWGIRL DREAMS*

"Some girls claim they were born as horses and only later grew up to be western women. Heidi Thomas gives us one of those passionate, persistent young women in Nettie Brady, and she's based this sparkling and enduring character on her own grandmother's story. *Cowgirl Dreams* is a heartwarming read for all ages and lets us all know why Ms. Thomas is not only a fine editor of other authors' books but shines as a skilled and compassionate writer herself." —Jane Kirkpatrick, author of *A Sweetness to the Soul* (Wrangler Award, 1995) and *A Tendering in the Storm*, winner of a WILLA Literary Award, 2008

"Nettie Brady defies anyone who challenges her right to become a rodeo rider. She'll gladly take the bone-jarring, gut-twisting ride of a wild steer rather than endure the stark boredom of women's work in the 1920s. Needlepoint isn't her thing—horseback riding, working cattle, and, yes, rodeo riding are what her life is all about. But family is important, too, and their disapproval makes for heart-wrenching decisions. Heidi Thomas does a magnificent job of pulling readers into another time, another place. *Cowgirl Dreams* is an ex read, full of heart and yearnings." —Mary E. Tri f *Rosemount, McClellan's Bluff*, and Spur foot

" … Brings heart, verve a the intrepid Nettie. A lively an almost forgotten West." —Deirdr ngish Professor, University of Montana, *My Russian*, and *One Sweet Quarrel*

"A fine drama of life as it was ninety years ago on a ranch in Montana." —Norma Tadlock Johnson, author of *Donna Rose and the Roots of Evil* and *Hazards of the Game*

"A triumph in every respect in this delightful celebration of life, is as inspiring as *Erin Brockovitch*, and as entertaining as *The Horse Whisperer*." —Geraldine Ahearn, reviewer, author of six books, Founding Member ABI Women's Review Board

"Lovely story . . . a real window into the challenges that women riders faced back in the 1920s." —Allison Fraclose, "Teens Read Too"

"A delightfully engrossing pleasure: a 'good read' . . . great satisfaction found in experiencing a well-told story." —Peter Olsen, reader

"A great coming of age story with a lesson in history, lots of adventures, a touch of romance and a great lesson in perseverance." —Svetlana Kovalkova-McKenna, reviewer

"Reminded me of the Little House on the Prairie series. Nettie, like those strong-willed girls who knew what they wanted, went after her dreams with determination and spirit." —Sharon Miner, Horse Book Reviews

"Captured me from the very first page and I couldn't put it down. Not many books can make me cry, but this one sure did." —Rulan Capper-Starr, Fiction Showcase

COWGIRL DREAMS
A Novel

HEIDI M. THOMAS

TWODOT®

GUILFORD, CONNECTICUT
HELENA, MONTANA
AN IMPRINT OF GLOBE PEQUOT PRESS

Names of real cowgirls have been used in the story, but the relationship to the main character is fictional: Marie Gibson, Fannie Sperry Steele, Prairie Rose Henderson, Margie and Alice Greenough, Birdie Askin. All other characters and events in this book are fictional, and any resemblance to persons, whether living or dead, is strictly coincidental.

To buy books in quantity for corporate use or incentives, call **(800) 962-0973** or e-mail **premiums@GlobePequot.com**.

A · TWODOT® · BOOK

Project Editor: Lauren Brancato
Layout: Joanna Beyer

Library of Congress Cataloging-in-Publication data is available on file.

ISBN 978-0-7627-9699-1

Printed in the United States of America

10 9 8 7 6 5 4 3 2 1

*I dedicate this book to my grandmother, "Tootsie,"
Olive May Bailey Gasser, a real Montana cowgirl.*

Acknowledgments

First and foremost I thank God for so richly blessing my life with opportunity and advocates. My dream would never have come true without the love and support of my dear husband, Dave. Thanks for putting up with years of frustration, writing, rewriting, and rejection. I am thankful for my family who bolstered me: my parents who read to me at an early age and encouraged my love of the written word; my dad who encouraged me to write the family stories and told me about his growing-up years with my grandparents; my brother Mark and sister-in-law Lynn (and Sarah, Jadyn, and Lee); sisters-in-law Marylou and Lonnie and their families (Dan, Laura, and Zoe) as my first-line cheerleaders. And without my critique groups, I would not be where I am today: Thank you, Hema, Kay, Ann, Jennifer, Teleia, Irene, Frances, Heidi M., and Erika (RIP, you were right); Sherry, Kari, Mystique, Janet, Jennifer, Pat, and Cristina; Joe and Sheri; and to all the students in my classes. Thanks to my high-school English teacher, Rick Cadieux, who encouraged me to pursue writing as a career; to all of my journalism professors at the University of Montana who taught me so much; to my fiction writing instructor at the University of Washington, Pam Goodfellow, and all my fellow students who gave such great feedback. Thanks to my sisters in Women Writing the West, to Lee Emory, to the Montana (Women) Writers Guild, and to the Skagit Valley Writers League for your support and encouragement.

CHAPTER ONE

The rangy, reddish-brown steer stared into Nettie Brady's eyes for just a second. Then it shook its massive head and blew hot, moist air into her face.

Nettie leaped back and glanced around the makeshift arena to see if anybody was laughing at her. A dozen parked Model Ts formed a black ring in the pasture where cows had grazed only hours before. Ranch hands perched on their vehicles in the late-morning sunshine as they waited for the next stage of the neighborhood rodeo to begin. One cowboy, ready to announce Nettie's debut, stood on the fender of his brand-new 1920 Coupe, a saddle blanket protecting its shiny black finish from his boots.

"Look out there, little gal. Let us get 'im eared down first." A cowboy grabbed the animal's ears and held its head close to the ground, while another man fastened a denim jacket blindfold over the eyes. Two more cowhands stood behind and splayed the hind legs tight with ropes so Nettie could mount. She took a step forward.

"This ain't no place for a girl." A bow-legged, leather-faced man wedged himself between her and the steer. "You belong in skirts, not trousers."

"What?" She'd borrowed her twelve-year-old brother Ben's denims, sneaked out of the house before her folks rose that morning, and come all this way, and now this old man wasn't going to let her ride? Nettie rose up to her full height. "Mister, I can ride as good as my brothers. And they're competing today."

"You're a girl. You're too young," the old cowboy persisted. "You get on outta here 'fore you get hurt."

"Yes, I'm a girl. But I'm almost fifteen." Nettie looked him straight in the eyes, anger boiling inside like a stewpot on a stove. "And I'm gonna ride that steer. You just wait and see." She stepped around him.

One of the cowboys holding the animal chuckled. "Ah, let her give it a try."

The leathery face scrunched into a frown. "You know you gotta ride till yer thrown or the steer stops bucking, don't ya? Ain't no ten-second whistle here t' let ya off easy."

Nettie squared her shoulders. "I know."

The old man snorted, mumbled something about "women in rodeos," and stalked away.

"Ready?" a cowboy asked.

Nettie wiped her sweaty hands on her pants, tugged on a pair of leather gloves, and turned toward the angry steer beside her. Was she really ready for this? Sure, she'd ridden calves and yearlings out in the pasture, but a nearly half-ton steer? And in front of a bunch of men?

One more hard swallow, one more deep breath of the manure and animal-sweat-laden air. She accepted a leg up onto the steer's bony back from one cowboy's cupped hands. He chuckled. "You don't weigh much more'n a feather to be ridin' this big ol' beast. You sure you wanna do this?"

She couldn't back out now. She had to show them she could ride.

"Yep." Nettie pulled her hat down tight over her auburn braids and wrapped the surcingle around her right hand, palm up. She flexed her thigh muscles through her borrowed denim overalls to make sure she had a death grip on the steer's sides. Then she gave a nod to the men holding the animal.

In the background she heard a few jeers and catcalls as the announcer bellowed out, "And now . . . ready to join the ranks of Montana lady rodeo riders . . . is . . . first-timer . . . Net-tieeee Brady!"

With just a moment of dread, she felt the curve of the animal's spine as he hunched, muscles tightening. The noise and the heat and the dust of the day disappeared. It was just her and nine hundred pounds of muscle and bone locked in combat.

The steer exploded off the ground. His loose hide rolled across his backbone. He twisted his front quarters up to one side. His hind legs kicked out to the other. A frothy bawl escaped his mouth. He switched directions, then again.

Nettie's right hand froze around the strap. Her knees dug a hold into the steer's ribs. She waved her left arm high, just like a real cowboy. Each twist and turn jolted along her spine, up to her clenched jaw.

Her mind and body worked together to anticipate each move. With every jump, the animal snorted ropes of saliva into the air. The wild body writhed beneath her, trying to shed his unwelcome load.

Each tug and jerk strained Nettie's arm muscles to the limits. Her shoulders felt as though they would pop out of their sockets. Numbing fatigue threatened to loosen her hold. She would not lose this fight. She'd rather die than fail in front of all these cowboys.

Seconds dragged like a roped calf to a branding fire. The whirlwind slackened. The steer gave a few more half-hearted twists. Cheers gradually penetrated her tunnel world. Thought returned to her hazy brain. The steer was winding down. She was still on its back.

He gave a last, disgusted kick and came to a dead stop, his head hung low. Two men distracted the animal while he continued to blow strings of saliva and butt his menacing horns toward them. She felt herself being lifted from the steer's back with a sensation of flying. Her oldest brother, Joe, reached out from atop his horse, carried her to safety, and let her down to the ground. Before she could spit the word "Thanks" through still-clamped teeth, her younger brother Ben was there hugging her.

"You did it!" Joe slid from his horse and clapped her on the back. "We knew you could."

The boys hoisted her onto their shoulders to parade her around the small arena. Car horns squawked. The watching men cheered. She had done it. No jeers now. Dizzy, unbelieving, she grinned and waved until they reached the outside of the arena and set her down.

But the crusty old cowhand who'd confronted her spat into the dust and called out, "That musta been an easy one. Let me ride him next!"

The answering ripple of laughter and whoops flushed Nettie's face, but despite her shaking limbs, she stretched herself taller, held her head straighter, and smiled. "Why, you couldn't ride a corral fence if it was standing still."

The listening men applauded. "You tell 'im, little gal!" someone shouted.

A giggle rose inside. She tossed her braids over her shoulder and strode away. She didn't care if those old-timers thought women shouldn't ride in rodeos. She had done it.

Powered by adrenaline, she floated through the crowd, her boots barely connecting with the dusty ground. Unbelievable. She really had ridden that steer, and stayed on him till the end. Her arms tingled, sweat stung her eyes, and her legs still quivered from the effort. She let out a whoop and skipped around behind the circle of cars.

The crowd cheered on the next rider. Nettie stopped and yelled, too. She wanted to hear those cheers for her again. Gosh, that had felt good.

Here at this rodeo, with horses and cattle and cowboys, with the noon sun beating down, with the dust and the noise—that's where she'd rather be any day of the week. She watched the next rider, a bronc buster atop a big bay, as he spurred high and waved his hat at the crowd.

"Good ride there, miss." A young blond cowhand doffed his hat, the white line on his forehead a contrast to his tanned face. "You lookin' to be the next Fannie Sperry Steele?"

Nettie smiled back at him, pleased to be compared to the champion woman bronc buster. "Yeah, I'd like that."

She stopped by the chuck wagon set up behind the pasture arena to get a drink of water and watched cowboys coming and going. Some, carrying tin plates, helped themselves to beans from a cast-iron kettle hanging over a fire and filled tin cups with coffee. Others brandished bottles of moonshine and called out wagers. "Betcha a buck Jim rides that sorrel down in half a minute." And the answer: "You're on. That cayuse'll have 'im on the ground in five seconds."

Nettie grinned and moved on to where Toby was tethered on the far side of the circle. Her horse whickered a greeting. She caressed his soft neck and laughed out loud. "I did it, Toby. I rode that steer." He turned his head toward her and bobbed it as if to say, "I knew you could."

Still giddy, Nettie mounted and rode over to where Red Jones watched the bronc riders from atop a black mare.

He touched the brim of his sweat-stained hat. "Good ride there, Toots." Just a hint of a smile creased his leathered face; he turned to spit a stream of tobacco juice off the other side of his horse.

Nettie blushed. "Thanks. Good rodeo." She watched the next young cowboy get ready to mount a big blue roan that looked strong enough to pull a plow.

"That's the new neighbor, Jake." Red spat again. Nettie shrugged. She hadn't met this one yet. Or wait, wasn't he the guy who'd compared her to Fannie Steele? The tall, wide-shouldered, slim-hipped cowboy dragged his saddle to the corner of the makeshift arena where the horse was blindfolded and eared down by several cowboys. Jake made several attempts to fling his saddle over the animal's back while it snorted, thrashed its head, and tried to kick. Finally successful, he pulled the cinch tight and stepped into the stirrup.

Nettie's shoulders tensed as he snugged his hat down low over his brow, wiped his mouth with the back of his hand, grabbed the halter rein, and nodded to the other men.

They quickly pulled the flank strap tighter to make the horse buck more, stripped off the blindfold, and released its ears. The big roan ducked and dived, tossing its head and front legs high in the air in repeated attempts to dislodge its rider. Jake first spurred high on the shoulders. Then as the horse came down to kick up its hind legs, he raked the flanks behind him. The ride settled into a rhythm, horse rearing and bucking, cowboy spurring forward and back.

Nettie understood the punishment Jake's body was taking. Her knees tightened instinctively, and she again felt the jar of each impact from her own ride.

Then, as Jake spurred high in front, his left rowel tangled in the rein. The roan jerked his head to one side, pulling the man's foot out of the stirrup. With the next jump the big horse faded to the right, and Jake crashed to the dusty ground. The bronc's hooves landed perilously close to his head.

Nettie gasped, "Get up." He must be hurt.

She leaned forward in her saddle and kicked Toby into a trot as if she could help Jake to safety. A mounted rider galloped to his rescue, but came from the far side of the arena. Nettie urged Toby on.

"Get up," she screamed again. The bronc reared and pawed the air.

Just as it seemed about to land on him, Jake finally rolled onto his side and stumbled to his feet. Nettie pulled Toby up, embarrassed now. This wasn't her job. What could she have done?

Jake limped into the middle of the arena to pick up his hat. He slapped it against his leg to dust it off and shook his blond head as he replaced it, a sheepish grin on his face. Then he glanced up at her and winked.

"Better luck next time," Red hollered.

Only then could Nettie relax. She felt her face flush hot. He probably thought she was a fool for dashing out into the arena like that. She turned her horse back to where Red watched.

"Quick reaction there, little gal." Red turned to Nettie. "Those draft-thoroughbred crosses make the durndest, er, 'scuse me, ma'am, best buckers. I dunno if that one'll ever be broke to ride. We'll keep him for our rodeo string." He dug his snoose can from his shirt pocket for a fresh wad. "Yup. Keeps the boys on their toes." Red worked the chew into a comfortable lump next to his gums and grinned, showing tobacco-browned teeth. "Cowboys just can't do nothing simple, like breakin' a cow horse. Gotta be a contest to see who can stay on the longest. You know how that goes."

She did. "The neighbors bring their best buckers, and roping horses, and compete against each other, just like today."

"You got that right, girlie." Red let a brown string of tobacco juice splat into the dust. "We're still mostly ridin' to work the buck out of our cowhorse strings."

As saddle-bronc riding ended, Red rode off to oversee the goings on. Nettie stayed to watch the bareback-bronc contest, then calf roping, where cowboys showed off their roping skills on some of Red's range herd. Finally, she rode Toby around the ring of cars.

She suddenly realized not a single woman had come to this neighborhood event. Well, they just didn't know what they were missing. Women certainly were an important part of rodeo life. Just look at Marie Gibson, for instance. Nettie adjusted the red neckerchief she'd been wearing ever since she'd seen a picture of Marie in the newspaper.

After she'd read an article about this Montana cowgirl, the dream of Nettie's own debut had filled her every waking moment. She yearned to see a real rodeo where she could meet this Marie Gibson. Especially after today.

Today had been Nettie's day. The excitement and exhilaration rose in her again as she relived the feeling of that ride. The pounding rhythm. The whipping twists. Her knees fastened like a vise on the steer's back. And the cheers. For her.

CHAPTER TWO

The evening shadows lengthened by the time Nettie and the boys arrived home. Almost dinnertime. A sudden pang of guilt assailed her. She'd put all thoughts of home out of her mind amid the excitement of the rodeo. A feeling of something left undone niggled at her.

"Let's hurry and do our chores. Maybe Mama and Papa won't be mad that I've been gone all day." Nettie quickly unsaddled, and while her brothers brushed down the horses, she scooted into the chicken coop to gather eggs. Then back to the barn to see if Joe and Ben needed any more help. Their brothers, ten-year-old Eddie and six-year-old Chuck, had wandered out to watch.

Just as she picked up the egg bucket again to head for the house, a shadow darkened the barn door. She looked up.

Papa frowned, arms folded, legs spread.

Uh-oh. She gulped, but put a big smile on her face. "Look at all the eggs we got today. They're laying great again."

Her brothers stood by the stalls, frozen in the hanging silence. Nettie shifted her eyes in a frantic search for some topic to take Papa's mind off whatever was eating at him.

He cleared his throat. "Where you been all day?" Nettie tried to swallow, but her mouth was as dry as August. "Uh, just out. With the boys. Riding."

Papa had an odd look on his face. "Uh-huh. Well, your mama's fit to be tied. You git on up to the house, now." He turned to her brothers. "What the heck did you think you were doin', taking your little sister . . . ?"

Nettie didn't wait to hear what he said next, but scurried out the barn door. Once out of sight, she slowed to a foot-dragging pace up the incline to the house. Did Mama and Papa really know where she'd been? She'd often been out with Joe nearly all day, riding. And they'd come home early enough to do chores. But Papa looked upset.

Nettie winced as she pulled open the creaky screen door. Baby Esther sat in her high chair, squishing her hands into a plate of mashed potatoes. Mama turned from the stove and stood, hands on hips, glaring down her nose.

Nettie cringed. "Hi, Mama. Here are the eggs." A lame excuse for diverting trouble, but she couldn't for the life of her come up with anything better.

"You." Mama stepped forward, her face dark red with anger. "You defied me."

Cold dread pooled in Nettie's belly. She'd never seen Mama so mad. "No, I—"

"Young lady, you were supposed to stay home today. Work on that pile of darning. You know Mrs. Connors wants it done by tomorrow, otherwise we don't get paid till next week."

The darning. She hadn't given it another thought after she'd decided to sneak out. Oh dear. Icy prickles of guilt stabbed at her. "But, Lola. Why couldn't she finish it?"

"Your sister had other chores to do." Mama stepped closer. "And, we had to hear it from the neighbor's hired man. You. Rode. In. A. rodeo." With each word, she jabbed her finger an inch from Nettie's face. "You know how I feel about that."

"But, Mama, I stayed on. I didn't get bucked off."

"Don't you sass me, girl." Mama's voice shook now. "And wearing pants in public, too." She closed her eyes a moment and sighed. "You will take that basket of socks, go to your room, and don't come out until they're all finished. No supper. No riding. For a month." She turned on her heel and stalked out of the kitchen. At the door, Mama stopped. "And, for heaven's sake, take that filthy red rag from around your neck and wash it."

Nettie's shoulders sagged. As she picked up the basket, she saw her nineteen-year-old sister, Lola, grin at her from the doorway to the living room. Drat. Now Miss Priss was going to lord it over her.

"Why didn't *you* finish the daggoned darning anyway?" Nettie made a face at Lola and stomped toward the bedroom they shared.

"Mama, Nettie's swearing."

Nettie stopped, her fists clenched. "I did *not*."

Mama slammed a pot on the stove. "You'd better not be. Now get busy. Lola, come help me with supper."

Nettie slumped onto her bed. No riding? Hot tears stung her eyes. Durn it anyhow. How could she have been so stupid to think she wouldn't get caught? Mama was so mad. But it wasn't as if Nettie had never helped out with the mending her mother took in. She did, nearly every day, too. And the one day she wanted to go with her brothers. . . . She pounded her pillow. It just wasn't fair. Nettie picked up the basket. Drat. "Darn it." She bit her tongue and looked around the room to see if anyone might have heard her. Her stomach growled. And no supper. Mama wasn't kidding either.

She sighed. Well, she had skipped out on her chores and defied her mother. Better get busy or she'd never get out of this room again. She slipped a sock over a wooden egg, exposing a gaping hole in the heel. Back and forth she stitched, weaving it shut.

Lola stuck her head around the doorframe with a self-satisfied grin.

Nettie's face burned. "Yeah, you love this."

"Well, it's all a part of learning how to be a lady."

Nettie snorted in disgust. "I'll never be a lady. You and Margie are the 'real ladies' in Mama's eyes. Fine. I don't see why I have to be one, too." She stabbed the sock with the thick needle.

"You're goofy, wanting to ride in rodeos." Lola's voice held a note of incredulity.

"It's just . . ." Riding that steer, the lofty feeling of accomplishment, of a job well done, washed over her. How could she explain this feeling to her sister? Or her mother? Her older married sister, Margie, wouldn't understand it either. "I just like being out in the fresh air and sunshine. It's free. It's exhilarating."

Lola shook her head. "You should've been a boy." She turned and left.

Nettie chewed at her lip. Why wasn't she a boy? She didn't care how many extra chores her mother might saddle her with. Riding was the most important thing in the world to her. That power and the soaring freedom that she had felt the very first time Papa hoisted her atop their plow horse Sam's broad back.

That feeling was why she got her chores done early every day, usually, so she could ride.

That feeling was why she'd dared Joe and Ben to let her sneak out to Red's rodeo with them. It was why she'd shucked her skirts and borrowed a pair of Ben's pants, marveling yet again at the sense of freedom they gave her on the back of her horse.

That feeling was why she gladly risked broken bones, her mother's disapproving looks—even her reputation—since Mama called women rodeo riders "loose women." And she was ready to do it again. With a sigh, Nettie rethreaded her needle.

Besides, if she could ride in some big rodeos, she might be able to win a few dollars. She stopped and gazed out the window. Hey, she could even contribute to the family. Then maybe Mama wouldn't think so badly of her. Nettie picked up another sock.

She once again heard the cheers, felt her brothers lift her high on their shoulders. *That* is what she wanted to do. More than anything in the world. Why couldn't Lola and Mama understand that she'd rather be outside, working with the horses and cattle?

Nettie groaned. With that look on Mama's face, she'd be lucky to get outside again by this time next summer. Maybe if she did a really bad job of darning, she wouldn't have to do it anymore. She wove the needle over and under, under and over, deliberately missing some threads.

After about an hour, Mama stepped into the room. "How are you doing?"

"Okay." Nettie kept her head down.

Her mother picked up a darned sock and inspected it closely. "No."

Nettie looked up, keeping the smile from coming. This was it. Now Mama would let her quit rather than being embarrassed to give the socks to Mrs. Conners.

Mama picked up the scissors and cut the woven patch right out of the sock. Nettie gasped. Then her mother picked up another, looked at it, and cut the darn out, too. "This is sloppy work. You'll do it all over." She flung the socks back into the basket.

"Mama." Nettie bit back a protest.

Her mother sighed and sat on the bed next to Nettie. "Listen, I know you hate this job. But it's important to be able to take care of our family. This skill not only keeps you and your brothers in socks without holes, it's earning us pin money, so we can buy something special when we go to town. Do you understand?"

Nettie nodded and hung her head. "Sorry, Mama."

Mama stood. "Okay, now do it right. Then come out and get something to eat." She left the room.

Shoulders sagging, Nettie picked up another sock. Darn, darn, darn.

CHAPTER THREE

After two weeks, Nettie itched to get outside and ride. She couldn't sit still one more day. "Mama, look." She held up her fingers, red and sore from poking the darning needle into them and handling the rough wool yarn. "Could I please go out and ride for just a little while today? My neck is all crooked and my eyes are probably permanently crossed." She focused on the tip of her nose to make a point.

For a moment, Mama just stared. Then a *humph* turned into a chuckle. "Did you get all the socks finished?"

"Yes." Nettie picked up a pair from the basket. "See, I've learned to do it all neat and tidy."

Mama nodded. "Looks acceptable. All right, you can go out for a ride this afternoon. After you finish your other chores."

By the time Nettie finished her garden duties, hauled water, beat rugs, and swept floors, the late afternoon sun slanted across the distant hills. She ran for the horse pasture, where she buckled a halter over Toby's head, hiked up her long skirt, and leaped onto his bare back. As soon as she was out of sight of the house, she urged him into a gallop. Her bare legs and feet gripped his smooth warm belly. She leaned into his neck, her fingers laced through his mane.

"Faster, Toby, go faster." She felt him respond as if he shared the same exhilarating sense of freedom. A giggle rose from her chest and erupted in throaty laughter.

They raced through coulees green with new grass, over low hills peppered with white, pink, and blue wildflowers until the horse's back was slick with sweat. Nettie's breath came hard, too, as though she'd been running alongside. She slowed Toby to a walk, then stopped under a lone cottonwood tree. Sliding to the ground, she caressed his neck and inhaled the warm, familiar scent of horsehair and sweat. Then she dropped the reins so Toby could graze, knowing he wouldn't stray far. Wiping her face with her red neckerchief, she flopped onto her back in the cool, prickly wheatgrass to gaze up at the fleeing wisps of cloud. With her sweat-drenched skirt spread wide around her to dry, she took in the aroma of the fresh breeze and green grass.

The warm air and sunshine banished all Nettie's resentments. She was finally free of Mama's punishing regimen. She supposed it could have been worse. It could have lasted a month, or even all summer.

Nettie closed her eyes and let rodeo applause echo in her head. It grew louder as she pictured herself in a white Stetson hat, red silk shirt, comfortable pants, and buttery-soft buckskin chaps. She would stride toward the chute and mount a coal-black bronc. He would be the meanest, toughest bucking horse ever seen. Nobody would be able to ride him, except her. Someone, like Colonel Zack Mulhall, would be there to see the ride and invite her to join his famous Wild West Show. Then she would dress up like Prairie Rose Henderson, who always wowed the audiences with her bright costumes: high-topped boots with bright-colored silk stockings, ostrich plume skirts over satin bloomers fastened just under the knees, and blouses covered with sequins. Oh, the scandal Rose caused.

Nettie giggled.

A breeze chilled her bare arms. She opened her eyes to see the sun sinking behind the tall buttes in the west. "Oops, better get home." She jumped to her feet, up again onto Toby's back, and urged him into a gallop.

～～

Nettie eased through the kitchen entrance while her mother's back was turned.

"Girls, will one of you please get the butter and the leftover roast from the icebox? Call your dad and the boys in, then we'll eat supper." Nettie's mother sliced thick hunks of heavy wheat bread on the big wooden cutting board and set it in the center of the table.

"I'll get it." Nettie didn't want Mama to chastise her for returning so late or banish her from riding altogether. Not when she'd just gotten her privileges back.

Lola sniffed the air and pinched her nose. "Pee-yew. You smell like a horse," she mouthed.

Nettie glared back at her sister and put her finger to her lips. "Don't you say a word," she hissed.

"Nettie's a cow-boy. Nettie's a cow-boy," Lola taunted in a sing-song.

Nettie held her breath, waiting for a reprimand from their mother, but Mama ignored them, busy with supper preparations.

Nettie turned her back and reached into the icebox that held a block of ice they'd cut last winter from Round Lake and buried in the ground under a layer of sawdust. Before getting this new, modern, insulated wooden box, the Bradys had kept their milk, butter, and eggs in the root cellar, hollowed out from the side of the hill, about fifty feet from the house.

Before, it seemed to Nettie that she had run out there a hundred times a day to descend the five steps into the cellar. What a luxury to have fresh, cold food right inside the kitchen.

She smiled to herself. Of course, she could always push Lola down into the damp, earthy-smelling hole when her sister teased her. Maybe nobody would find her until fall when Mama stored the jars of canned goods.

Nettie carried the food to the big pine table. This batch of butter she had churned herself. That was one chore she didn't mind too much. In fact, a time or two she'd put the cream jar in her saddle panniers and rode Toby until she had butter. Of course, Mama hadn't approved of that method. But she could at least daydream about riding like the

15

wind—sitting on the back step, rhythmically turning the handle of the daisy wheel that agitated the sweet cream with wooden paddles inside a gallon-size glass jar.

"Thank you, dear." Mama put a stack of plates on the table. Lola set them out at their places, occasionally giving Nettie a smirk, which she ignored. The pump handle creaked just outside the door. Water sloshed into the trough where Papa and her brothers washed the field grime off their faces and hands before they came in.

She smiled at Eddie and Chuck, already seated, gazing wide-eyed at the platter of venison. Baby sister Esther, just one year old, sat in her high chair and banged a spoon. Nettie grinned, still feeling a rush of good-will euphoria from her ride. Sometimes these demanding little brats could be very sweet. She circled the table, patted Eddie's shoulder, ruffled Chuck's dark hair, and planted a kiss on Esther's milky-soft cheek before sitting beside Mama.

Papa came in at last and sat at the head of the table. He glanced at his family gathered around him and bowed his head to say grace.

As each family member grabbed slices of bread to make their supper sandwich, he cleared his throat and looked straight at Nettie. *Uh-oh.* What had she done now? A spark of dread spiraled up her spine as she waited for his words.

"Toby was pretty sweat-up, I noticed. You shouldn't be ridin' him so hard. He's gettin' a little old for that."

She ducked her head to stare at her plate. Oh no. Poor Toby.

"You can thank Joe. He wiped him down this time, but don't forget to do that yourself from now on. You hear me, young lady?"

"Yes, Papa." Nettie's face was on fire. Lola tittered. Nettie bit back an angry retort and ignored her. She looked at her brother across the table. "Thank you, Joe."

He dipped his head in reply.

A cold pang of shame gripped her. She had been so intent on getting into the house without being noticed that she had forgotten to care for her horse. How could she have neglected Toby, her best friend?

"Antoinette, you pay attention to what your father says, now." Her mother's mouth was set in a thin line.

Nettie's growling stomach instantly became a hard rock. She could only pick at the suddenly bland-tasting bread. Why, oh why couldn't she stay out of trouble? She took a deep breath. *Dear Lord, help me try to do better from now on.*

After supper, she and Lola cleared the table. Nettie grated flakes from the hunk of homemade soap into the dishpan. Then she poured steaming water over them from a large kettle left to heat on the coal stove. She scrubbed the dirty plates in the suds and stacked them on end in another dishpan.

Lola poured more hot water over those to rinse. "Why do you always risk getting into trouble, especially after that rodeo blunder? You're just asking for it." She picked up a dish to dry and put it away in the blue gingham-skirted cupboard.

Nettie gave Lola a sidelong look and gritted her teeth. "What do you know about it? All you ever want to do is sit around the house and make moon eyes over that Floyd Marshall."

A gap as big as the coulee in the north pasture had grown between them since her sister had attracted a boyfriend. They didn't talk and giggle anymore like they used to. Besides, Lola had never loved horses the way Nettie did.

"I know plenty you don't." Lola wrinkled her nose and stuck out her tongue.

"Like what?" Nettie made her tone as sarcastic as she could.

"Girls!" came Mama's sharp voice from the living room. "Any more of that and you'll be scrubbing floors until midnight."

Lola lowered her voice to a whisper. "Like kissing, and . . ."

CHAPTER FOUR

Nettie tried to be a good girl all week. Really tried to help Mama without making her ask. But, good grief, she didn't get out to ride Toby once. She fidgeted at the sewing machine as she tried to sew neat patches on denim pants. She was trapped. *Don't know if I can keep this up.* She blinked sweat out of her eyes. *I'm not cut out for housework.* She would almost prefer to be back in school, even though she'd finished eighth grade and wouldn't be going on to high school.

When Joe came in from morning chores to get a drink of water, she motioned him into the living room. "Aren't you riding today? Can't you do something to get me out of this? I'll do your chores for you for a week."

Joe grinned at her. "Oh, sure. That's a big sacrifice. You love feeding the horses and milk cow. Besides, last time you sneaked out to ride, Ben and me got in trouble too."

"That's why you're getting permission." Nettie cocked her head. "It would be just one less thing you'd have to do in the morning."

Her brother swiped his hand through his thick brown hair. "How about for a month?"

"You'll do it?" Nettie beamed up at him. "Yes, a month, anything."

She stood in the doorway as Joe went into the kitchen where Mama was cooking. "I'm going to the Fergusons' today to work their horses. All right if Nettie rides along?"

Mama laughed at Nettie's hopeful expression. "Well, you've worked hard all week. I guess you can go help your brother, have some fun. But don't forget your chores tonight."

Nettie didn't wait to hear another word, but left the unpatched overalls hanging from the machine by one leg.

"Hey, hey, hey. Come back here." Mama put her hands on her hips and scowled. "At least finish that patch job first."

Nettie groaned. "Don't leave without me, Joe."

"All right. Hurry up. I'll get the horses saddled. Meet you at the barn."

❧

Nettie laughed aloud as she urged her horse into a gallop, leaving Joe behind, and delighted in the feel of the wind and the muscled power beneath her. The morning was glorious, the rolling prairie green and fresh with new grass. And she was free, blessedly free.

"Come on, slow down. You'll have Toby all worn out before we get there," Joe yelled and rode harder to catch up.

"Oh, now, you're sounding just like Papa." Nettie laughed, but slowed to a more sedate trot. "Where's your sense of adventure?" Toby's head bobbed as if he agreed.

"I'll show you when we get there." Joe's grin gleamed white in his sunburned face. "I'm gonna work you so hard you'll be too tired to even hang on to your saddle horn."

"Phooey. I'll never be that tired." Nettie dug her heels into Toby's sides and she was off again at a hard run over a small rise and across a meadow polka-dotted with white daisies.

After an hour's ride, they reached the corral where Jim Ferguson had brought in a half-dozen steers from the pasture. Nettie dismounted, loosened Toby's cinch, and climbed on top of the pole fence. Ferguson gave her a brief nod, and before the rancher went about his other duties, he gave Joe instructions to train a newly broke gelding for roping.

Her brother opened the gate where the big bay was penned with a smaller white mare. As Joe saddled and mounted him, the reddish-brown gelding stiffened, then sidestepped gingerly as though walking

19

on eggs. Ears flattened, the horse looked around the corral pen with wild eyes like he was looking for an excuse to buck.

Joe pulled the reins taut. "I'm going to take him for a ride to calm him down some before I start roping off him. He's still a little green."

"Can I come?"

"Sure. If you'd like to work that mare, you can come along. She's not as rambunctious, but still needs to be ridden down a bit."

Nettie needed no further encouragement. She saddled the mare, mounted, and followed Joe away from the corrals. They rode over gentle swells and through coulees filled with lush new grass, letting the skittish horses have their heads in a full gallop for a short time to take the edge off. Nettie leaned forward, riding neck-and-neck with Joe's gelding. He turned and gave her a grin.

She wasn't sure why Joe'd helped her come along today. But her seventeen-year-old brother seemed to understand her. *I have to do such a good job of riding he'll always want me to help.*

Nettie basked in the spring air, still as tender as the grass, the penetrating sun just hinting at the withering heat to come in the summer months. This was heaven on earth. "God's country," as Papa called it. She gave a happy laugh. Nobody to tell her to "take it easy" or "slow down" or darn the darn socks. Wouldn't it be great if she could get a job at the Fergusons' too?

⁓

Back at the corral, Nettie and Joe were ready to start their task. Their charges were less excitable and seemed ready to take direction. She released the mare for the time being and went on foot to help Joe and one of Ferguson's cowhands who had arrived while they were gone.

Joe nodded at the cowhand. "Howdy, Slim."

Nettie watched the lean, dark-haired cowboy as he walked up to them. He was taller than Joe, more muscular through the chest, and looked to be a few years older.

Slim grinned and ducked his head toward Nettie, then turned to Joe. "Goin' to the dance at the Hay Lake School tonight?"

"Yeah, I figured on it." Joe swaggered a bit.

Nettie felt a little flutter in her midsection. "A dance? We're going?" She double-stepped to catch up with the young men. Slim half-turned and gave her a wink. She felt her face flush. Hmm. Maybe Slim would ask her to dance.

Joe glanced at her. "Uh . . . well, Mama didn't say you could."

She stared at him, wide-eyed. "What do you mean? She didn't say I *couldn't*, did she?"

Her brother stepped back until he was out of earshot of the other man. "Now, don't be getting on me about this. You know Mama's expectin' you home to help with evening chores."

She turned to face him. "What on earth's gotten into you, Joe? I thought you were on my side."

He gave her a squint-eyed look and turned to follow the cowboy.

Nettie glared at his retreating back, fists on hips. Then she grimaced. The chores. She shifted from one foot to the other, guilt warring with desire. Well, surely getting the eggs a little later wouldn't hurt anything this once. And Lola was home to help get supper.

Resolutely, she strode to where the two young men were setting up the chute. She'd show him she was just a good as they were.

On foot, they drove the yearling steers into an adjoining long, narrow alley with a gate on each end. From there, Slim would release the animals one at a time so Joe could train the gelding as he practiced roping. Joe scratched a line in the dirt about forty feet out into the corral in front of the gate, then swung onto the bay again on one side of the chute. Nettie mounted Toby and waited on the other side, her hand tight around the reins. She had to do this right.

"Ready?" Joe looked across at her.

She shot him a grin. "Of course."

Slim released a yearling from the chute. Nettie leaned forward in the saddle, ready to ride. The steer charged into the arena. As soon as it crossed the line, Toby launched himself forward and Nettie rode alongside Joe after the steer.

Nettie's job was to keep the steer running straight and to prevent him from turning away from Joe, the head roper. Nettie would follow up by roping the animal's heels. They had done this many times together, practicing on Papa's calves at home just for fun. The two of them made a good team, and Nettie was confident that Toby knew his job. This was more like the "real" thing, what the rodeo teams did. If she could prove herself in these training sessions, maybe she and Joe could ride and rope together in some rodeos this summer.

Overtaking the animal, Joe swung his rope, but the bay hesitated and fell back a step. The steer veered to the left, Toby still close on its heels. Joe's loop sailed on past its head as it skirted away in front of his horse.

"Dadgummit. You gotta pull back when that happens." Joe's voice was gruff.

"Since when?" Nettie couldn't believe her ears. "It was your bay that made the mistake, not me." He'd never snapped at her like this before. "You're treating me like a little girl. I'm almost fifteen." She scowled at him and turned Toby around. Just because he had a man's job now and he had to show that other cowboy he was all grown up.

Joe rode back into position and squared his shoulders. "Let's try 'er again."

Slim released another yearling. This time the bay kept going and the rope settled around the steer's horns. Joe drew back on the gelding's reins to turn the steer around to the left so Nettie could throw a loop around its heels. The animal flipped on its side.

"Not bad." Slim spat tobacco into the dust.

Joe shook his head. "The horse needs a little work yet."

Nettie resettled her hat. *Oh, sure, now he's admitting it's the horse.*

They repeated the process with the rest of the steers, one at a time. Joe's bay still seemed unsure of himself, and Joe had to coach him through the stops and the holds. But as they repeated the drill, the horse gradually began to anticipate the steer's moves, which let Joe concentrate on roping.

"All right. This is more like it." Joe grinned now. Nettie relaxed. She loved this kind of work. She and Toby were as one, the horse moving with the steer, always aware of where Joe and his mount were. It didn't seem to matter now to Joe or the cowhand that she was a girl, working alongside them. That was as it should be, as far as she was concerned, as long as she could hold up her end of the job.

After Joe finished working the bay, he tipped his hat back and wiped his forehead with a handkerchief. "Whew. That about wore me out."

Slim nodded. "Yup. It's hard work. Need to take a break?"

"Sounds good." Joe took off his hat, wiped his forehead.

"I'm not tired," Nettie spoke up. The sudden bursts of speed, ride after ride, stirred her adrenaline anew. "Can I do it again?"

Joe glanced at Slim. "We might as well go ahead and work that mare now." He looked at her. "Then we'll call it a day."

Disappointed that she wouldn't be involved in this part, Nettie unsaddled Toby and watched from the corral fence. Joe and the cowhand used the same techniques with the white mare as with the bay to train her for steer wrestling, or bulldogging, as the cowboys called it. Slim rode into position on the mare, with Joe as hazer. The steer broke from the chute, the two riders thundering close behind. In just a few seconds Joe had the steer crowded next to the other cowboy's horse. Slim leaned over to grasp the steer by the horns and, twisting its neck as he slid off his horse, he wrestled it to the ground.

Boy, he was strong. Nettie whooped and applauded. "Good one."

At the end of the day Ferguson joined Nettie on the log fence. "Good job, guys. Both the bay and the white look like they're going to make good stock." He jumped down into the dusty corral to shake Joe's hand, then tipped his hat at Nettie. "Come on in for some supper."

Nettie and her brother stopped at the well to wash the grime of the day from their faces. Now that they were alone and Joe didn't have the cowboy to impress, she tried again. "So, can I please come with you tonight?"

Joe glanced around to see if anyone was listening. "Now, if it was up to me, I wouldn't care a lick. But you been in trouble with Mama a lot lately, and we didn't ask permission for you to go. You know how she's been watchin' you. It's still light enough, you can be home before dark."

Nettie gulped. "You knew about the dance. Why didn't you ask her?" She tried not to let the tears show as she turned to go inside, then stopped to glare at him. Why didn't he want her to go along? *I suppose I should go home and do chores.* Maybe she could come back then. No, Mama wouldn't want her riding back in the dark. Surely her mother wouldn't mind, just this once. Nettie'd been good for a long time now. Fighting her conscience, she turned on her heel and stomped into the house.

She ate in silence, barely listening to the men talk. Afterward, Joe changed into the clothes he'd brought along and rode off with a group of Ferguson's cowhands without even a wave.

Nettie steamed at his attitude. Well, she'd show him he couldn't boss her around. She stepped into the kitchen. "Mrs. Ferguson, I didn't bring a skirt with me for the dance. Do you suppose . . . ?"

A new surge of happiness flowed through her as she rode off to the schoolhouse with the Fergusons. Her weariness vanished, along with any thoughts about Mama. Next to riding, Nettie loved dancing best. She'd grown up learning at the periodic schoolhouse dances, although usually dancing with Papa or other girls. She could hardly wait. Maybe she would even get asked to dance tonight. Maybe that handsome cowboy Slim . . .

Nettie tied Toby to the rail fence in front of the one-room schoolhouse. Several horses already stood dozing, their heads bowed. Each, as though choreographed, cocked a hind leg and rested it on the tip of its hoof. Some riders had left cinches loosened, while others had removed their saddles and left them resting on the ground nearby. Lantern light spilled softly from the door and windows, illuminating a couple who had just driven up in a Model T Ford.

She stepped inside. Her booted feet seemed to take on a life of their own as she listened to the festive lilt of fiddle, accordion, and guitar. "Buffalo gals, won't you come out tonight . . . and dance by the light of the moon." Her toes tapped on the wood floor and her heels rocked. She swished the borrowed skirt.

Then Joe, in the midst of a group of tittering girls, caught sight of her and rolled his eyes. Uh-oh, was he mad at her? She watched with apprehension as he tipped his hat at his admirers and walked toward her. Handsome in his crisp white shirt, he came around the perimeter of the room, where desks had been shoved against the walls.

"Now, sis, I ain't gonna take responsibility for this."

"You don't have to. It's all on me. C'mon, Joe, can I have just one dance, before you go off and dance with everybody else?"

Her brother shook his head and muttered something about "stubborn as a mule," then pulled her onto the floor. They joined several couples already in full swing. Her heart soared, and her feet followed. Her brother was a fine dancer, much in demand. She counted herself lucky he'd consented to dance even once with her.

When the fiddle player launched into a waltz, "If You Were the Only Girl in the World," Joe escorted her back to her seat, gave her a little bow, and headed back to the group of older girls now sitting along the wall.

Nettie found a seat on the other side of the room. She looked around for Slim. His dark hair was slicked back from his handsome face, and the rolled-up sleeves of his dark blue shirt showed his sinewy arms. She smiled in his direction, but his attention was on an older girl who filled out her blouse a lot more than Nettie. Soon the two were dancing cheek to cheek.

Her shoulders sagged. Darn, she had hoped he would ask her at least once. Or some of the other Ferguson hands. *They all think I'm too young.* Well, she wasn't too young to haze for them, so why wouldn't they dance with her? She sniffed. Fine. Ol' Slim wasn't all that good-looking anyway.

Nettie got up and joined a group of other girls without male partners who were dancing off in one corner. She didn't really know any of them. They must be visiting from another community. But why not? She liked to dance, so might as well dance.

At midnight, the band broke for supper and couples paired off to share box lunches. She expected Joe to go eat with the Ferguson girl he'd been dancing with most of the evening. But then Nettie saw her leave the dance with her folks. Joe approached her with a chuckle. "Well, I guess I got me a gal to escort home. Ready to go?"

The soft warm air smelled of new grass, and crickets chirped their own moonstruck love songs. Nettie imagined a slim-hipped, square-jawed cowboy who would one day escort her home from one of these dances. Would he be swarthy and mysterious, or golden-haired and good-humored? Whichever it was, they'd be partners. He'd have to let her ride with him every day. She drifted in the moonlight, eyes closed, rocking in her saddle. She could almost see the couple they might become, riding side by side out to check their herd, galloping after a stray calf during a roundup, or perhaps cheering each other on as they both rode in a rodeo.

Yes, maybe someday, someone would notice the tiny, copper-haired girl who could sit a horse as well as she could step a waltz. She wouldn't always be Joe's kid sister, the girl who loved to pretend she was a boy. Someday, her handsome fellow would plant a soft kiss on her lips, and she would be transported on wings of music, soaring among the stars in a dark velvet sky.

Joe stayed at the barn, where he slept summers, and Nettie trudged the hundred yards to the house, tired but still humming a dance tune. She opened and closed the squeaky screen door as carefully as she could, then stopped cold in the middle of the kitchen. Lanterns burned bright all over the house. The skin on Nettie's arms tingled as though she'd just walked through a cobweb. Uh-oh. She must be in big trouble.

Lola bustled from Mama's bedroom through the living room and into the kitchen, carrying an armload of blood-stained sheets.

The spider-web feeling crawled over Nettie's body. "Wha . . . what happened?"

Lola stuffed the sheets into a big copper kettle filled with cold water. "Not now. I'm busy."

"But the blood . . ." Had one of the boys cut himself?

Lola sighed. "I sure could've used your help earlier. But no. You had to sneak off again."

Nettie stamped her foot. "Lola, tell me what's happened."

"All right. I'll tell you. Mama's had a miscarriage."

"A mis—what?"

Lola looked at her with a sneer. "Mama lost a baby."

"A baby." Nettie's bones felt chilled. She hadn't even known Mama was expecting again. "Oh, dear, is she . . ." The thought *going to die* flitted through her head. " . . . all right?"

Lola nodded and shaved laundry soap into the kettle. "She's fine. Pains started about suppertime. Of course Papa was only underfoot so I made him take the boys and skedaddle." She glanced at Nettie with narrowed eyes. "So here I was, all alone."

"Uh. I, well . . ." Nettie couldn't think of a single comeback. "Can I see her?"

"She's asleep now, finally, but you can go in if you want."

Nettie tiptoed into Mama's room, where a single candle burned. She sat by the bed and peered into her mother's wan face, waxy and slack in sleep. If only she'd come home, she might have been able to help. Fear flickered inside. Why did Mama keep having babies if it hurt her so bad? *Why do I have to keep doing things that hurt Mama?*

Gently, Nettie took her mother's hand and whispered, "I'm sorry, Mama."

Mama's hand squeezed back ever so softly. Tears coursed down Nettie's cheeks.

❧

The next morning, Mama sat in her rocker, still in her nightgown and wrapped in a blanket despite the heat. Lola sat nearby, working on the week's mending jobs.

Nettie stroked her mother's hair. "Mama, are you feeling all right? Do you need a doctor? Should I ride after Mrs. Jones?"

"No, I'm just fine." She gave Nettie a weak smile. "I just need to sit and rest for a little while. Would you make me a cup of chamomile tea?"

Nettie went to the kitchen and made the tea for her mother. Pouring it into the china cup Mama only used on special occasions, she brought it to her. "Can I do anything else? Are you sure you don't want Mrs. Jones to come?"

"Thank you, honey, no."

Nettie stood watching from the doorway for a while, uncertainty gnawing. *It was my fault Mama lost the baby. She had to work too hard. Somehow that caused it.* She turned away, grabbed a white shirt from the clean laundry pile on the kitchen table, and sprinkled water onto it from a root-beer bottle with holes poked in the cap. Her hands felt shaky. Mama hadn't said a word about her sneaking off to the dance. She must not be feeling well, for sure.

Nettie swallowed hard. She rolled up the shirt and added it to the basket of laundry to be ironed. Lifting the heavy flatiron from the pantry shelf, she set it on the kitchen stove, added more coal, and stoked the fire.

She brushed sweaty hair from her forehead, picked up the sprinkler bottle, and dashed a few drops on her face. Even with the stove burning hot on this already-hot July day, Nettie preferred hefting the four-pound iron to the endless stitching she'd endured the past several weeks. And she felt like she needed to help today.

She swished her long skirts with both hands to create a breeze. If only she could wear pants again. These skirts were always getting in the way. When she was on her own, she wouldn't wear skirts unless she had to. And she'd never again pick up a needle. No matter how tattered her clothes might get. No sirree. *But, for right now, I need to be a better daughter.*

Flipping the legs of the fold-up ironing board into place with a snap, she wet a finger with her tongue and touched it to the bottom of the iron with a sizzle. It was ready.

Later that afternoon, Mama was back on her feet, starting to clean the kitchen as if nothing had happened.

"Shouldn't you be resting, Mama?" Nettie folded the last of the ironed shirts.

"Oh goodness, no. I'm just fine." Her mother picked up the water pail to refill. "There's too much work to be done. I can't just sit around idle."

Nettie strode forward and grabbed the bucket. "I'll get more water for you." As she pumped and water splashed into the pail, tears came unbidden to her eyes. Was Mama sad about losing the baby? Was she angry with Nettie?

She carried the water into the house, where her mother was trying to sweep. A grimace passed over Mama's face and she reached for the back of a chair to steady herself.

"Mama, go sit down." Nettie took the broom from her mother and finished sweeping, then mopped the kitchen. While the floor dried, she went to the living room where both Mama and Lola sat mending. She picked up a sock and started the weaving process.

Lola snickered. "What on earth's gotten into you today? You're working like a house afire and nobody's even had to ask."

Nettie bit her lip. "I just wanted to help, because of the baby. And, I'm sorry I sneaked off to the dance instead of coming home."

Mama turned toward her, a look of surprise on her pale face. "Oh thank you, honey. You've been a great help today. But it's happened before. It's just part of life. There's nothing you could've done to prevent it."

As Nettie breathed a sigh of relief, Mama continued, "But, my dear, you know that you were wrong not to come home when I specifically asked you to. I expect you to be more careful with your decisions from now on."

Nettie nodded, tears blurring her vision.

Her mother never mentioned the baby again.

CHAPTER FIVE

One morning in mid-August, Papa pushed back from the breakfast table. "Well, the Browning Fair and Stampede is the end of this week."

Nettie looked up from her plate. "What are you saying, Papa? Do we get to go?"

Her father smiled. "Yes, you've all been working purty hard, especially you, Nettie. I know how much you wanted to go to the last one. But you've earned this trip."

Mama nodded.

Nettie jerked upright in her chair and gave a loud whoop. Joe, Ben, and Eddie joined in.

"Oh, thank you, Papa and Mama." Nettie's summer burden of guilt lifted, leaving her feeling as light as a wisp of wheat chaff. Even though Mama had never again mentioned Nettie's sneaking off to the dance, Nettie just knew that's why they hadn't gone to the Fourth of July Browning rodeo. It was because she had disobeyed and Mama had worked too hard and lost her baby.

Up before sunrise on Thursday, Nettie hurried through her breakfast. Hardly able to contain her excitement, she ran to help pack the wagon box. Papa had already filled canvas water bags and loaded a tent.

Her feet barely touched the ground. Since they'd be gone a total of five or six days, they would have to take along all the food they needed. She grabbed the sourdough starter for pancakes and biscuits, loaded it into the wagon, then ran back inside.

"Hey, wait just a second. Why don't you take more than one thing at a time?" Mama stood in the kitchen, a bemused look on her face. On the table were boxes of salt-cured side pork and dried antelope meat, bags of beans, and loaves of bread.

Nettie stopped. She was acting like a flighty colt. Not a good way to impress her mother and change her mind about rodeoing. She really wanted to try riding a steer again, but with Mama going, too, probably not.

"Shouldn't you stay home and rest, Mama?" She loaded a bag to take to the wagon.

Mama laughed. "No, honey. I'm just fine. I don't need to be coddled. Now, I don't particularly enjoy rodeos, but it is a big social event, too. I'll get to visit with some women I haven't seen all year."

Well, darn. Browning had a real arena with chutes, and she'd heard Papa say the rodeo organizers even offered prize money to the winners. To ride. To win. To make money at it. Nettie set the sack into the back of the wagon and stopped to gaze into the clear sky. *Gosh, wonder if I'll ever get to compete in a real rodeo.*

At last Papa hooked up the team. Mama shooed the younger children onto the wagon seats while Joe, Nettie, and Ben mounted their horses. Lola had gone to visit Margie.

Thank goodness. Nettie didn't want her around anyway, since she thought rodeos were a "colossal bore."

Shy little Chuck climbed aboard without a word, but ten-year-old Eddie protested at having to sit with "women and babies." He wanted to ride a horse, too, but there weren't enough to go around. Esther whimpered until Mama settled the toddler on her lap with a sigh of exasperation.

Nettie dug her heels into Toby's sides. She was finally off on the two-day, fifty-mile trip to Browning, on the Blackfoot Indian Reservation. She loved going there to see the colorful Indian dances, but had never been to the rodeo.

Nettie gasped as they rode over the rise. Model Ts, horseback riders, wagons, and teams overwhelmed the little reservation town. More tents than usual, along with dozens of Indian teepees, and outhouses dotted the prairie like mushrooms after a rainstorm, and outnumbered the houses in town.

Off to one side of the rodeo arena, she saw a Ferris wheel and heard barkers invite visitors to "step right up" to whatever wares they were selling in their striped tents. To the west beyond the dusty little town, the majestic Rocky Mountains rose up in white-capped splendor.

As she approached the rodeo grounds, Nettie's gaze moved from one group of horsemen to the next cluster of spectators, her anticipation growing. Next to the arena, cowboys formed long lines outside the tiny booth that served as a rodeo office to pay their entry fees and register for events. She dismounted, tied Toby to the corral fence, and followed her brothers to the end of the line. Joe would enter saddle-bronc riding and Ben, steer riding. Papa and Mama left to find old friends to visit, taking the younger kids along.

Nettie breathed deeply of the dust-and-must aroma of horses, sweat, and manure and felt at home.

She had never seen so many people in one place at the same time. A flutter of shyness flickered through her. For a moment she was glad she wasn't allowed to ride today. There were just too many people watching. But then the itch that had taken root on the back of that steer a few months ago scratched at her as she watched the cowboys check their saddles and cinches, hitch up their denim overalls, and strap on their spurs.

"Hey, little gal, what're you doing in line? You're not gonna ride, are ya?" An older cowboy snorted a laugh as he walked by.

Nettie turned to the cowboy. "Maybe I am. What's it to you?" She'd show him. She'd just sign up to ride a steer, too. She flounced her divided skirt and turned back to the line.

But wait. It cost money to enter. "Ben, how much to ride a steer?"

"Five bucks."

Darn. She only had a dollar's worth of her Christmas quarters saved. "Can I borrow four dollars from you?"

"No." Ben frowned. "Five's all I got, for my ride."

"Joe?" She looked at her older brother.

He shook his head. "Me neither, sis."

Nettie gave an exasperated sigh, walked back to where Toby was tied, and swung onto his back to ride around the outskirts of the arena. Maybe she would find someone she knew. Maybe Red Jones would lend her the money. She'd show that old coot!

Several neighbor ranch hands waved or called out a "hello" as she rode past. One drunk stranger leered. "Hey there, purty gal, stop and talk to me." She blushed and spurred Toby onward, not finding Red anywhere. How would she be able to pay him back, anyway? At the rate she saved her Christmas quarters, it would take years. Unless she could get a job.

At the chutes, she heard the rodeo producer yelling directions. "Get those kids off the back of the chutes before somebody gets hurt. Tell those people at the end they'd better get off the fence. Some bronc's gonna run into it and pile the whole bunch of 'em on the ground. Men, get your flank straps on your horses. Better put a neck rope on that horse in chute two. Bill, get me a chaw of snoose."

She rode up to the man. "Can I help, or make an exhibition ride? I'd like to earn some money for the entry fee."

He looked at her as if she'd spoken in a foreign language. "Hey, little gal, you git on outta here 'fore you get hurt." He went back to barking orders.

Teeth gritted, Nettie rode on. The musical rhythm and hum of activity rose in pitch and intensity as the rodeo start time loomed near. Nettie felt the vibration rise from the earth through Toby's frame. He danced little sideways steps as if he, too, felt the itch.

She'd sure like to try riding a steer again. But she didn't have any hopes of earning the money or paying it back if she borrowed it. But she just *had* to find a way to ride. Maybe if she just got in line for the steers. Nettie rode to where the cowboys were lining up. Nope, each man had a number pinned to his back. She squared her shoulders against disappointment.

Okay. When she got home, she'd find a way to earn some money at Jones's or Fergusons' or even ask for a share of the mending money. Then if she could win and pay the money back, maybe Mama would let her ride in a rodeo again.

Besides, this was the biggest rodeo she'd ever been to, and she could probably learn lots by just watching.

At last the announcer bellowed through his bullhorn, "Lay-dees and gentlemen, welcome to the Browning Stampede. We're gonna have us a swell time today. Here's the lineup of events . . ."

Nettie leaned forward on Toby, urging on the saddle-bronc riders. The first few cowboys rode tough mounts that proved to be high, crooked, sunfishing horses. She applauded their rides along with an enthusiastic audience.

The next bronc burst from the chute, uncoiled his bunched muscles in a fury, and after three jumps, turned a somersault over the top of his rider. A hushed gasp came from the audience as the cowboy was carried unconscious from the arena. Nettie gnawed at her lip. What had happened? Was he all right? She hated to see anyone get hurt.

The cowboy next to her gave a low whistle. "Whew. That looked bad. Hope the saddle horn didn't hit him in the gut. Or his chest."

"Oh my gosh, yeah." Nettie hadn't thought of that. Cowboys brought their own saddles for the event, and not many could afford a second hornless one. She hoped her mother hadn't watched that man get hurt.

She waited, along with a now-quiet audience, while pickup riders cleared the corral. The announcer picked up his bullhorn. "Ladies and gentlemen, not to worry. That cowpoke'll be all right. He's come to and rarin' to go again." Nettie raised up in her saddle and cheered along with the crowd.

He cleared his throat. "Ridin' next, we have a young cowboy by the name of Joe Brady, on Wild Fire."

Nettie's palms were suddenly cold and sweaty. *Oh, please let him have a safe ride.*

Joe's horse broke out of the chute, ears laid flat. The bronc ducked its head, bellowed like a mad cow, and went into a series of fast, high, crooked jumps. Then the animal seemed to break in two in the air, landing hard and twisting out of shape. Her brother looked surprised when he slipped loosely on the horse's back for a moment.

Nettie clenched her fists. Oh no. He was about to be bucked off.

But then Joe's instincts must have kicked in. He straightened up, grinned, and absorbed the next jumps. Spurring high and waving his hat in the air, he ended a good ride, his grin still in place when the whistle blew at ten seconds.

Nettie cheered until she was hoarse and loped Toby over to her brother when he walked out of the arena. "Good job." She slid off her horse to give Joe a big hug. Her whole body vibrated with an overwhelming pride.

"Whooee! That one was dynamite." The emerging man in Joe drew up to his full height. He swaggered a bit and grabbed Nettie to swing her around as she giggled. Then he let out an almost self-conscious boyish laugh.

Nettie tied Toby to a rail and climbed up on the pole fence behind Joe to take a teetering seat on top. They watched a couple of rides where the bronc refused to buck, just broke into a lope around the arena. The next horse had barely cleared the chute when the cowboy crashed to the ground.

"Nicky don't ride so good." A grizzled cowboy sitting on the rail nearby chuckled.

"Oh, he rides good, he just don't ride too long." Another old-timer dipped a finger into his snoose can for a fresh chew. Nettie laughed along with them.

Just then, she heard Mama's voice behind them. "That was a very good ride, Joe."

Papa clapped him on the back. "Way to go, son."

He turned to grin at them. "Thanks."

Nettie looked at Mama. *She's actually proud of Joe.*

That's it. Nettie *had* to ride and win. Then Mama would approve of her.

"And now, ladies and gentlemen," bellowed the announcer, "we have a treat for ya. This li'l lady . . ."

Nettie whipped her head around to look for the woman rider.

" . . . wowed the Prince o' Wales himself up at the Saskatoon Rodeo with her bronc ridin' skills. From Havre, Montana, on Black Widow, h-e-e-ere's Marie Gibson."

Marie. Nettie's heroine.

Mama gasped. "Oh, heavenly mercies. A woman."

The horse escaped the chute, nostrils flaring, teeth flashing, eyes darting. Nettie studied the woman rider. *She's dressed like man, in trousers.* Marie Gibson's body moved with the bronc. Nettie gaped. *She's so small on that big horse.*

Ever since she'd read about her in the newspaper, Nettie had imagined Marie as bigger, taller, someone to look up to.

The outlaw mare reared back, front legs clawing the air. Hooves slammed against the ground, raising dusty swirls. Writhing, twisting, grunting, the bronc unleashed another buck and another.

Nettie dug her fingers into her thighs, afraid that any second she'd see Marie crash to the ground. If Marie got hurt . . . why, oh why had Mama shown up right now?

Her trouser-clad bottom smacking hard against the saddle, the tiny woman rose and swooped with every explosive movement, her left hand waving freely in the air as though taunting the odds. The mare soared, all four hooves off the ground for just a moment, then horse and rider returned to earth with a bone-jarring, teeth-rattling thud, only to rise again, and again.

Nettie could barely breathe. She pictured the horse's hooves leaving huge holes in the earth. How much longer could this woman stick with that bronc?

Then Marie started to slip as they spun around the arena. Bile rose up in Nettie's throat. *Oh no, she's going to fall.* She stretched herself taller on the pole fence to get a clear view.

But the woman clutched the reins with one hand, pulled herself straight in the saddle, and settled again into the rhythm of the twisting flesh and bone beneath her.

A roar swept down from the stands. A whistle blew. The horse kept bucking, if only half-heartedly. The petite woman jumped from the back of the once-raging beast before the pickup man could reach her, and raised her high-crowned hat in the air in triumph. The crowd roared.

"Whooee." Joe yelled and slapped Nettie on the back. She snapped out of her trance and exhaled, her open mouth dry with dust.

"Whew!" Her admiration for this woman enveloped her and left her reeling. "What a ride. Did you *see* that?"

"That's what you could be doin'." Joe's grin was white against his tanned, dusty face.

"If only . . ." The longing was a living thing inside.

"Women riding broncs. What's this world coming to? Only loose women get involved in rodeo." Mama clucked her tongue. "Meet us back at the wagon at six for supper." She turned on her heel and stalked off.

Adrenaline buzzed through Nettie. She climbed off the fence and jumped on Toby. That spectacular ride. By a woman. Marie Gibson had ridden just as well as the men, heck, better than some of them. Now, more than ever, determination pulsed in Nettie's heart. She had to find a way to be a cowgirl like Marie.

Nettie circled Toby around the outskirts of the arena, thinking back on the rides she'd just seen. Like a moving picture show, she saw the cadence of each buck and crowhop, every cowboy who was thrown, the ones who rode to the end. It was the rhythm. She could feel it, watching them. She could do that.

Rounding the back of the chutes, Nettie saw her. Marie thrust her booted foot into the stirrup, swung up onto the back of a pinto, and waited just inside the gate for the next bronc rider to finish.

Nettie rode up behind to watch. Marie was going to serve as pickup man. This ought to be interesting. How would this small-framed woman—not much bigger than Nettie herself—be able to help a bigger man off his horse? Nettie slipped Toby in behind so she could see better.

The eight-second whistle blew. Nettie heard a collective gasp from the crowd. The rider's spur was tangled in the rigging. The horse flung him around on its back like a rag doll.

Marie's pinto leapt toward the wild, thrashing bronc. Without thinking, Nettie nudged Toby forward, racing alongside Marie toward the rider in trouble. When they reached the bucking bronc, Marie's horse went to one side and Toby instinctively ran to the other, just like when Nettie'd been hazing for Joe. Confined between the two horses, the bronc stopped bucking and broke into a run. Marie reached out. The cowboy grabbed hold of her arm with one hand, and with the other tried to yank his foot free. Marie started to slip from her saddle, but managed to stay upright, and the rider slid to the ground and raised both arms in triumph.

"Whooee. Nice save," the announcer yelled. "Let's hear it for the ladies."

The crowd stood and applauded. The cowboy then gave a little bow and with a flourish, indicated Marie and then Nettie. "Thank you," he mouthed.

Marie turned to Nettie. "Thanks. Good work."

Nettie ducked her head, too tongue-tied to reply.

A couple of cowboys herded the bronc out of the arena, and the two women rode back out through the gate.

Nettie's hands shook. She could barely hang on to her reins. Excitement boiled through her veins. What had just happened?

Marie swiped stray hairs off her sweating face. Dark brown ringlets fell from beneath her wide-brimmed, high-crowned hat and brushed against her buckskinned shoulders. "Whew." She looked at Nettie. "Great teamwork, young lady. Thanks for your help. I'm Marie Gibson."

"Yes. Yes, I know, Mrs. Gibson. I just came to tell you what a great ride you made today, and, and all of a sudden, there we were, out there." Nettie felt like she'd just awoken from a dream.

"Yeah, wasn't that somethin'?" Marie grinned and shook her head. "I seen you around the corrals watching today. You're quite a hazer. What's your name? Are you ridin' in the rodeo?"

"I'm Nettie Brady, and I'm not riding today. Oh, how I wish, oh, Mrs. Gibson, I've so been wanting to meet you, ever since I read about your ride for the Prince of Wales. Your ride today was just wonderful." She averted her eyes, her cheeks hot. She was acting like a ten-year-old.

"Pshaw. Forget the Mrs. stuff, just call me Marie. The ride was all right. But you and me together out there. That was great. You're a natural."

"Thanks." Nettie's insides quivered. "Sometimes I help my brother, Joe, when he trains horses for our neighbor. You might've seen him ride, just before you. This is Toby. My dad got him for me when I was seven. Toby's my best friend. I did ride a steer in a little ranch rodeo near Sunburst just a couple months ago. And I really want to do it again. Can you tell me how?" She paused and watched Marie's face for a reaction. How embarrassing. Here she was, blurting out all these things to a stranger.

"That's great. That's exactly how you get started."

Nettie heard the announcer broadcast the next ride, and the bronc rider they'd helped came out of the arena, untied his horse from the corral fence, and walked up to her. "I say, young lady." He spoke with an unusual clipped inflection. "You helped save my life today."

Nettie thought she must have had a strange look on her face, for he laughed and slapped his thigh. "The English accent gets 'em every time." His tones relaxed somewhat into a more familiar cowboy drawl.

Marie chuckled. "Nettie Brady, meet my husband, Tom." Nettie leaned down from Toby to shake his hand.

He grasped hers, bent over, and kissed it. "Thank you, Miss Brady, for saving my poor English hide."

Now Nettie's face felt like it was on fire. "Oh, you're welcome. Toby and I just did what we needed to do. And you can call me Nettie."

Marie reined her horse around. "Say, we're headed over to the campsite for some beef and beans. Why don't you come join us?"

"Oh. Thanks. Sure." Nettie could hardly believe her good fortune. Just being close to this woman, she could feel the raw bold power that emanated from her. Maybe she could absorb some of that.

Marie urged her horse forward. "Where you from?"

"We have a homestead about twenty miles north of Cut Bank and fifteen miles east of Sunburst." Nettie adjusted her red neckerchief to the same angle as Marie's.

"Ah, the beautiful Sweet Grass Hills," Tom intoned behind them.

"Yeah, we ride through Cut Bank on our way home to Havre. I've been up in your area." Marie reined her horse to a stop amidst a group of tents and dismounted. Nettie followed. The tantalizing odor of barbecued beef wafted from a spit.

A cowboy sliced meat and ladled beans from a large cast-iron kettle hanging over the fire and handed each of them a heaping tin plate. "Great ride today, Marie."

"Thanks, Cookie. I was happy with it." Marie led the way to a plank table where a group of cowboys sat, and they settled on rough log stools beside the men, who were all retelling the stories of their rides.

"Yup, and I thought I'd made a good ride till this here little lady done showed me up proud." One young cowboy laughed and speared a forkful of beef.

"Yeah, how're we gonna keep our pride when the women ride better'n us?" Another man squinted at Marie from beneath his battered hat.

"Aw, pffft." Marie waved off their comments. "I just make you work a little harder, that's all." They all laughed and went back to eating and talking.

That's the way Nettie wanted to be, so strong, so sure of herself, so accepted. These men didn't seem to resent Marie competing against them.

Marie turned to Nettie with a smile that made her porcelain doll–like face glow. "So you'd like to ride in rodeos?"

"More than anything else in the whole world."

"But?"

Nettie shrugged. "My mama. She's scared I'll get hurt. She thinks I should learn to be a proper lady, and she says she needs my help with the little ones."

Marie leaned forward, her brown eyes intent on Nettie's face. "Hmm."

Nettie could hardly believe it. This famous cowgirl must be interested in what she had to say. A bees' nest seemed to have been stirred up in her stomach. But the woman's smile encouraged her to go on.

"I get in so much trouble all the time because I sneak out to go riding."

Marie gave a hearty laugh.

The cowboys guffawed. "Sounds like we got another Marie on our hands."

"Well, rodeoing certainly gets in your blood," Marie said. "And it can be quite rewarding for a talented rider like yourself."

That quivery feeling shimmied through her again. "Really?" *Me? A talented rider?*

Just then Mama's voice came from over Nettie's shoulder. "That's all well and good, but what a dangerous pursuit for a woman. You could get kicked, stepped on, broken bones, even killed."

Nettie turned to see her parents and brothers standing behind her. Her excitement plummeted as if she'd just been bucked off a bronc.

Mama stood, arms akimbo. "You, young lady, were supposed to join us for supper at six. We've been looking all over for you for an hour. I was afraid you *had* been trampled."

Nettie gulped. Oh no. She'd forgotten. Darn. In trouble again. *Oh, Mama, please don't embarrass me in front of this real live champion cowgirl.*

Mama looked Marie up and down. "I apologize if our daughter has been bothering you. You should've sent her on her way."

Marie just grinned. "Oh no, she's been no bother."

"Besides, she saved my bacon out there today." Tom exaggerated his accent. "She's a right professional rider."

Nettie jumped up from the log seat. "Mama, Papa, this is Mrs. Marie Gibson, a famous cowgirl. You saw what a great ride she made today. And her husband, Tom. Marie, my parents. And my brothers, Joe, Ben, Eddie, and Chuck. And the baby's Esther."

"Oh. You're married." Mama looked surprised.

Marie stood up and offered her hand. "Nice to meet you, Mr. and Mrs. Brady. You too, young sirs." She chucked the baby under the chin. "You folks can call me Marie. Please, sit and join us. Have you eaten?" Marie's voice and language had suddenly changed.

The group of cowboys shifted to make room. "Oh, I don't think—" Mama started to protest.

Papa interrupted with a chuckle. "Well, we did have to miss our supper, lookin' for this girl."

Nettie felt her jaw drop as he sat, followed by her mother. The cook put filled plates in front of them.

Mama looked Marie in the eyes. "So, why do you pursue this dangerous profession?"

"I love it. There's nothing else I'd rather do." Marie poured coffee for Mama and Papa.

Mama shook her head. "But just look at what almost happened to your husband today."

Nettie held her breath.

"Anybody you know ever get snake bit? It's dangerous just walking across the prairie." Marie's face had an earnest look. "Or just living through the winter, like this last one. Some people I know didn't make it."

Nettie could see by her mother's pursed lips that she was chewing on that thought. A small flicker of hope kindled in her. Marie sure could make a persuasive argument.

"It can bring in some good money, too. I won a hundred dollars today." Marie gave her curls a little shake.

"Make money? But how can that be?" Mama furrowed her brow. "You don't always win, do you?"

"Often enough." Marie leaned forward again, her face closer to Mama. "And Tom won two hundred dollars."

Mama took a bite of beans. "Do you ride all year 'round? Travel all the time?"

"No, we have a ranch with a small coal mine near Havre. We work those in the off-season."

Nettie's excitement rose with that thought. So, not all women did as Mama said they should. That would be the perfect life, owning a little ranch and riding in rodeos, too. She straightened her back. That was it. That's what she wanted to do. Now, she *had* to get a job at Fergusons' or somewhere.

"I don't know." Mama still sounded skeptical. Her brows beetled. "That seems such an uncertain way to make a living."

Marie leaned toward Mama. "No more uncertain than farming. We'd have to sell fifteen calves to make as much as we won today. I can help make up the difference with my rodeo riding."

Nettie looked around for help from the rest of her family. Why didn't they speak up? Papa just sat beside her mother, a bemused half-smile on his face. He was no ally. The boys loved to rodeo, too. Where were they? But Joe and Ben had moved off to the side to talk with a couple of cowboys.

"Do you have children?" Mama's shoulders were braced.

"Two boys, nine and eight."

Mama sat silent for a moment, disapproval written all over her face. "And where are they when you're on the road?"

Marie chuckled. "They're home with their grandparents. They usually come along during the summer, but they have some bum lambs they're busy taking care of right now."

Mama silently scraped the last of the beans onto her fork with a knife. Nettie grimaced. She knew her mother wouldn't approve of leaving her children, but of course, she wouldn't want them exposed to rodeo either. Darn. This was not a winning argument as far as Nettie could see.

But to her surprise, her parents sat for a couple more hours, exchanging homesteading stories and listening to Tom Gibson's English accent as he related rodeo tales.

Nettie wasn't sure what kept her mother's attention, but maybe Mama felt something in common with the cowgirl, even though they didn't share a passion for rodeo. But even if Mama didn't, Nettie sure did. She wanted to talk to Marie some more about riding.

Later that night, after Nettie squeezed beside her siblings into her bedroll, she heard her parents still talking just outside the family tent.

"That Mrs. Gibson is really quite a lady, despite her rough occupation. She's so pretty, too." Her mother sounded surprised. "And I certainly was amazed at what Nettie did today. I just don't understand the lure of this pastime, though. It's bad enough to spend two days riding in a wagon just to come and watch cowboys being thrown to the ground. But to think of actually being the one thrown."

A glimmer of hope flickered again. Mama had actually praised her. Nettie couldn't hear her father's reply. And maybe Mama did like Marie just a little. Maybe, just maybe . . .

She soon drifted off to the sound of their murmurs, her mind filled with pictures of her riding up to the Prince of Wales, accepting a trophy, then counting piles of greenbacks at the kitchen table under her mother's admiring eyes.

~ — ~

The next morning, as Nettie helped her parents pack their tent and load the wagon, ready to head for home, Marie and Tom rode up. "We just stopped by to say good-bye and tell you how much we enjoyed meeting you all," Marie said.

"We enjoyed it as well." Mama reached out to shake the other woman's hand.

Disappointment clouded Nettie's vision. She wasn't ready to say good-bye to her cowgirl hero. She blurted, "You have to go home the same direction as we do. Why don't we all ride together?"

"You're absolutely right," Tom said with his delightful English accent.

"Why, of course." Marie smiled. "We'll all have some time to get to know each other better." She looked at Nettie's parents. "You don't mind, do you?"

Mama cleared her throat. "Ah. No, of course not."

Nettie bounced in her saddle to a nameless tune in her head. She barely noticed the heat and the dust that rose from all the departing wagons and riders. She'd have two whole days to talk with Marie on the way home. Just too exciting for words. She rode as close to Marie as she could and watched how comfortably the cowgirl sat her horse, chatting, gesturing, and looking around the sun-parched prairie. Nettie wiped her face with her red neckerchief, then retied it to hang from under her collar, the same as Marie's.

"Hello there, Buckskin Mary," a rider called out to Marie as he trotted by.

"Hello, yourself." Marie chuckled and waved.

Nettie looked quizzically at her companion. "Buckskin Mary?"

Marie laughed. "Oh, it's just a nickname I can't seem to shake. So, is Nettie your whole name or short for something?"

"Mama named me Antoinette," Nettie made a face, "after a French lady she read about, but everybody just calls me Nettie. Mama only uses Antoinette when I'm in trouble. I've always thought it was just too high-falutin' for a cowgirl."

They topped a hill and stopped a moment to look back at the wagon and other riders.

Marie turned to look into Nettie's eyes. "Well, isn't that something? I think our mamas must have read the same book. My first name is Antoinette, too."

"Really? Oh, I'm sorry. I didn't mean . . ." Nettie wished she could swallow her words. Now she'd insulted her heroine.

Marie nudged her horse forward again. "Aw, shucks, I use my middle name for the same reason, too fancy. But ya know, it doesn't really matter what you're called, it's what you do that makes you unique."

Nettie felt her face glow with pleasure. *Unique. I know what that means. I'm special. I'm me. Nobody else. Just me.*

Antoinette. They had the same first name. What else did she share with Marie Gibson? "Do you ride steers, too?"

"Oh, yes indeed. And bulls." Marie let loose a giggle and looked around to see where her husband was riding. "Let me tell you a story. When I was up in Saskatoon, this other lady who was just starting out in rodeo made me a bet on which of us could ride one of those big Brahma bulls they'd brought in special from India. Well, Tom had told me earlier, in no uncertain terms, I wasn't to be riding those huge beasts. Too dangerous. So first I said naw, I wasn't interested. But then, the promoter called me 'yellow.'"

Nettie gasped. "What did you do then?"

"Well, I'm not one to stand by and let that happen. So I said I'd do it. The other woman went first. Only lasted a couple seconds. Had to be carried out, unconscious. By now I'm thinking maybe yellow wasn't so bad after all. But it was too late. I was already mounted, and out the chute we went. I think I only lasted a few seconds longer than that other gal, but at least I walked away."

Wow. Nettie's admiration grew even more. "I've heard how dangerous those bulls can be. You were so brave." And Marie had stood up to that producer, too.

Marie paused, then whispered, "But Tom wouldn't speak to me the rest of the day."

Nettie raised her eyebrows. Her new friend was even braver to go against her husband's wishes. Mama would never have dreamed of doing something like that. *I'd like to be able to. If I ever get married.*

"Speaking of the devil, I'd better go back and talk to him about the rodeo down in Wyoming next month." Marie trotted her horse back to where her husband rode beside the wagon along the rutted trail.

Warmth radiated from Nettie's core. She rocked with Toby's easy rhythm and fingered the red neckerchief. Meeting Marie Gibson was the most important thing that had ever happened in her life.

❧

A day and a half later, when they reached Cut Bank, the Gibsons again made ready to say good-bye and ride on. Nettie jumped in. "Why don't you come stay with us and rest a day before riding back home to Havre?" She didn't look at Mama for fear she would see disapproval on her face.

"Gosh, we'd hate to impose," Marie began.

But Papa spoke up. "Why, shore. You can't make it all the way home today. Might as well come bunk with us. It's only another twenty miles."

Tom grinned. "I'll even help with chores."

That evening after Esther and the two younger boys had gone to bed, Nettie joined her parents, older brothers, and the Gibsons around the big pine table in the kitchen, playing cards. The mood turned festive as Tom Gibson brought out a jug of moonshine and poured a generous dollop into the adults' coffee cups. To Nettie's surprise, even her mother took a few tiny nips of the "evil liquid." Since Prohibition had taken effect earlier this year, Mama hadn't even allowed homemade wine to be served in her home. She was always one to follow the letter of the law. Papa just scoffed at it and kept a jug of his own out in the barn. But tonight, both her parents laughed more than usual and their faces seemed softer. Glad her mother was letting her hair down for once, Nettie relaxed, too.

Marie shuffled the cards and began dealing another hand. "I don't s'pose there's a ranch rodeo around here somewhere this Sunday?"

Nettie's brother Joe picked up his cards. "Yeah, I think Jim Ferguson was plannin' to buck out a few of his string."

Marie pursed her lips and looked thoughtful. "Well, now. I wonder if we might impose on your kind hospitality to stay long enough to take in that event?" She cocked her head and smiled at Mama. "I'd sure love to visit with you a little longer, and as long as we can take in a little rodeo . . ."

Nettie saw her mother exchange looks with her father. Papa raised an eyebrow, and Mama gave an almost imperceptible shrug. Nettie's heart pounded. They couldn't possibly say no. Could they?

Then she heard her father say, "We'd be honored." Before Nettie could even think, she leapt into the air, yelling "Yippee!" Now they'd surely have to let her go along.

CHAPTER SIX

Nettie sat on the front stoop snapping beans. She stretched her bare feet out and wiggled her toes in the warm sunshine. Grinning, she sang softly, "Marie Gibson is staying in my house."

Marie and Mama were taking a midmorning break and drinking coffee in the kitchen. She could hear them talking about Marie's two young sons and their ranch. Mama's voice wafted through the open door. "Marie, you seem like a very down-to-earth woman. How do you justify your rodeo riding with your family life? I've always had the impression women rodeo riders were, well, not of the best reputation."

Marie chuckled. "Well, there may be some of those but mostly they're women much like me. We just love it: the challenge, the excitement, the victory."

Nettie stopped in mid-snap and leaned toward the door. Her shoulders tensed. Maybe Marie could convince Mama to let Nettie ride at the Fergusons'. *Oh, please let her say yes.*

"Women who have families? Responsibilities?" Mama's voice held a note of disbelief.

"Have you heard of Lucille Mulhall?" A cup clinked on a saucer.

"From the Wild West Show?" Nettie heard her mother get up from the table and move around the kitchen.

"Yes. Lucille is Colonel Zack's daughter. She was like your Nettie out there, already riding her first horse at age two. I heard her daddy tell she cried to get up on the horse and then cried even harder when he took her down."

Mama laughed aloud. "That sounds familiar. I remember Nettie doing something like that, too." A kettle clanked on the stove. "I'd better get this roast in the oven for dinner."

Nettie closed her eyes and remembered that feeling of power and strength the first time she'd ever ridden a horse. That's when she knew.

"Oh, let me help. I'll peel the potatoes." Marie added to the kitchen sounds.

Nettie heard her mother chuckle and relaxed a little. "Yes, that Lucille sounds like Nettie, all right. She's been sneaking out to ride and rope calves since we moved here when she was six. In fact, she stowed away in the back of the wagon when Charles and the boys first came up here to build this house."

Nettie winced. Mama had not been happy and Nettie's punishment was to take care of the chickens. She hadn't minded that a bit, though. And she'd proved to Papa she could be of help—even if she was only six—getting him tools he needed, even frying the fish he and the boys caught in the lake.

Marie's voice again. "Ah, I thought she'd be capable of something like that. A lot like me. A lot like Lucille."

"Did Lucille ever learn to cook and sew and how to be a wife and mother?"

"Oh, yes. In fact, I read an article about Lucille that said she could break a bronc, lasso and brand a steer, and shoot a coyote at five hundred yards. She could also play Chopin, quote Browning, and make mayonnaise."

Mama laughed. Water splashed into a pan.

Marie continued. "At first, Lucille's mama, being a refined and genteel lady, much like yourself here, thought her daughter would learn more about life than horses and cows at a finishing school in St. Louis."

Nettie bolted to her feet. The pan of beans scattered on the porch. What was Marie telling her mother? Now Mama would get it into her head that Nettie should go off to some highbrow school back east to learn how to be a proper lady. She closed her eyes and balled up her fists.

"But that made Lucille terribly unhappy. She only lasted a year. She was born a cowgirl. That's what she loved, and she was determined to reach the top of her chosen profession."

"Hmmm. Big mistake. I would've given anything to have the opportunity to go to a school like that." Mama's voice was a wistful murmur.

Nettie gulped. Yes, she could see her mother enjoying that kind of experience, drinking tea from tiny cups, walking straight and tall with a book on her head, speaking "proper" English. The thought made her shiver.

"Say, that roast looks mighty fine. You know what might go well with it? Yorkshire pudding." Marie imitated a tiny bit of her husband's English accent.

"Hmm. I've read of it, but never tasted it. Would you make some?"

"I'd be honored. Let's see, I'll need some eggs."

Nettie sneaked a look through the door but couldn't see her mother's face. She returned to the step and idly picked up a few spilled beans. She didn't need no ol' finishing school. She could talk to most anybody, too. She'd completed eighth grade. She read books and newspapers.

Marie swished the whisk in a bowl. "It all comes down to the good foundation you've already laid, the virtues you've taught her. She's a mighty fine girl. You can be very proud of her."

Nettie suppressed a squeal.

"I suppose." Mama didn't sound totally convinced.

Marie pressed on. "The main thing is, with rodeo, I'm doing something I love. And look at how well Nettie rode with me in Browning. I can tell she loves it, too."

Mama gave an audible sigh. "I do want her to be happy."

Nettie's eyebrows raised. *She does? Then why does she stop me from doing what makes me happy?*

"I learned how to ride and rope and handle cattle and work with my husband on our ranch. Nettie may need to do that, too, when she gets married." Marie's voice had an earnest tone.

Nettie rolled her eyes. *Well, I'm not planning to get married, not for a long time anyway, but maybe that'll help convince Mama.* She suppressed a giggle. Marie was turning out to be a real friend. Nettie scrambled to pick up the rest of the scattered beans and took them into the kitchen.

Mama turned from the stove. "Just in time, Nettie. Thank you. Would you please wash those? I have some bacon frying and we can chop it up and add it to the beans."

At noon the men tromped into the house, ready for a hearty meal. Mama set the roast on the table and asked Papa to carve. "And look at the wonderful treat Marie made. It's called Yorkshire pudding."

"Ah, my favorite," chortled Tom. "She makes the best puddin' this side o' the Thames. Give it a taste." He scooped a spoonful onto Papa's plate, then one for everyone else.

"Mmm." Papa stopped in mid-chew. "Mmm. This is de-licious."

"Yeah," came echoes from Joe and Ben and Eddie.

"Did Marie give you the recipe?" Papa wanted to know.

"Of course." Mama cocked her head a little to one side and smiled. Marie winked at Nettie.

Has Mama been won over by a pudding?

❧

Sunday morning Nettie dressed in Ben's old denims and had her chores done and the fire blazing in the cook stove before anyone else was up. She filled the coffee pot with water from the bucket and set it on the stove. When the pot began to boil, she tossed in a handful of coffee grounds, spilling half onto the floor. With a quick glance around, Nettie grabbed the broom and hurriedly swept them under the stove. Then she got out the sourdough starter and mixed the pancake batter. She'd show Mama she wasn't just a tomboy, that she knew how to cook, too.

Her mother came sleepy-eyed into the kitchen and set Esther into her high chair. "My word." She blinked. "You're up early. And look at you, got breakfast started already. I was up so late visiting with Marie I didn't even hear you get up." She yawned. "My, that woman has done it all." Mama sat down at the table. "Her husband is a good man, much like your papa. And they did meet through rodeo."

Hmm. That's a point in my favor. Nettie bustled around the kitchen, pouring her mother a cup of coffee. She flipped a flapjack onto a plate and set it in front of her mother.

Mama poured syrup over the pancake and tasted a forkful. "Mmm. That's very good. Here, Essie." She offered a bite to the toddler.

Nettie breathed a sigh of relief. *She likes it. I did it right.* "Mama. I would really like to go to the rodeo today."

Mama stared into her coffee cup for eternal seconds and shook her head with a wry smile.

Nettie's hand gripped the ladle. *Uh-oh. Here it comes.*

"Well, you know it's against my better judgment to let you get involved in such things." Mama adjusted the hem of her bathrobe over her knees. "And we just attended a rodeo."

Nettie turned toward the stove, determined not to let the tears prickling in her eyes leak out.

"But then again, you are almost fifteen years old. You'll probably be getting married in a couple of years. So I suppose it's time I allow you to do a few things on your own."

Nettie whirled around, her mouth dropped open.

"Providing they're responsible decisions, of course." Her mother looked at her and smiled.

"What? You mean . . . I can go?" A bubbling like spring runoff rushed through her.

"Well, you've shown me just this morning that you can act like an adult."

Nettie grinned, forgetting her new status. "Whoopee." Then she turned serious. "Mama. If I go, then can . . . may I ride?"

Mama sighed and closed her eyes. "Let's just take one step at a time. Why don't you just watch for today. Maybe another time."

Nettie swallowed her disappointment. *At least I get to go.* She jumped to her feet. "Are you going to be there?"

"No, no. I had enough of the heat and dust in Browning." Mama stood and refilled her coffee cup from the blue tin coffeepot on the stove. "I just want to stay home with little Esther today. And Papa has to work in the field."

"Okay." Nettie rushed toward the door, breakfast forgotten. Then she stopped and turned. "Mama. Thanks." On impulse, she leaned over the high chair and kissed the top of her little sister's head. "Someday we'll go to rodeos and maybe I'll teach you to ride, too." It would be something they could do together.

Mama huffed. "Don't you start putting ideas in her head, now."

⌁

As they all rode away, Nettie glanced back at her mother standing on the steps, holding Esther. Mama probably didn't want her to ride because she was afraid of Nettie getting bucked off. Oh well; she was going to a rodeo with Marie Gibson.

But Mama was not going to be there. *Maybe I could ride anyway.* The more she thought of it, the better the idea seemed. Nettie barely felt the hard leather saddle as she trotted along beside Marie. Remembering the consequences of disobeying, little quivers of delight mingled with shivers of fear and guilt. She shouldn't do it. What if she did get bucked off? But what if she could prove to Mama that she was not just a fragile little girl and could ride as well as Joe and Ben? And maybe even Marie. If this professional cowgirl impressed her mother, then Nettie must work very hard to become as good, to win Mama's approval. There wouldn't be a chance to win any money today, but it would be good practice.

At the Fergusons' corrals, a small crowd of cowboys from around the neighborhood had gathered, ready to combine a little fun with work. Nettie, her brothers, and the Gibsons rode up to check in with Jim Ferguson.

Red Jones leaned against the corral talking to the rancher. "Got yerself a new string of broncs, huh?"

"Just bought 'em. We'll see which ones're worth breakin' to ride. The rest I'll sell for the rodeo circuit."

Joe greeted his boss. "I see you brought in a bunch of steers from the pasture to rope and ride, too."

"Yeah, thought that'd add to the festivities. You all ridin' today? I'll put your names in the hat to draw your mounts." He jotted down their names. "You, too, huh, li'l miss?"

"You bet I am." Nettie stretched herself to her full five-foot, two-inch height, then held her arm out with a flourish. "And this here's my friend, Marie Gibson, the famous rodeo rider."

Ferguson brushed the brim of his hat with his fingers. "Pleased to meet ya, ma'am. I've heard about your ridin'. It's good to have a Montana girl in the 'bigs.' Welcome to the Ferguson spread."

Marie nodded to him. "Thanks. Nice place ya got here." She turned to Nettie. "Well, let's see what these cowboys are up to."

"Women ridin' with men." The old-timer who had given Nettie such a hard time at the Jones rodeo glared at her and Marie from under his hat brim.

Marie stopped midstride, dug into her pocket, and drew out a wad of dollar bills. "I'll bet ya two to one Nettie and I stay on our mounts as long as those men."

"Right, sister." The grizzled cowboy pulled out his own money. "I'll take that there bet."

"Count me in," another man laughed. "Easy money." Several more put cash in the pile and someone gave it to Ferguson to hold.

Marie tugged at Nettie's arm. "Let's go show 'em how it's done."

❧

The steers bawled and pawed at the dirt, sending clouds of dust over their backs. The horses snorted wildly and broke into a circling run around the small pen. Now and then one would break out of the bunch looking for an escape over the top rail.

Nettie joined the cowboys sitting on the fence, hooting and hollering encouragement to the riders. Her excitement rose with each ride she watched. The closer the time came for the steer riding, the more nervous fluttering built in the pit of her stomach. She had more riding on this performance than money.

Nettie jiggled her foot and squirmed on her perch as Joe and Ben put on a good show.

When Marie mounted the roan she had drawn, Nettie's heart drummed. She leaned forward, studying Marie's relaxed body stance as the bronc kicked high and swooped low. The cowgirl seemed to adapt a natural rhythm to the horse's bucks and twists and turns. She stuck with the roan until one of the pickup men swept her off its back. Unlike the bigger, organized rodeo at Browning, today there was no buzzer. Riders stayed on until they were thrown or the animal stopped bucking, whichever came first.

"Woohoo!" Nettie waved her hat. A good ride. Could she do that?

Then it was Nettie's turn. She had drawn a small but wiry steer. The cowboys eared him down and kept him blindfolded until her rigging was in place and Nettie was mounted. Mouth dry, she adjusted herself on the steer's back, getting just the right grip on the surcingle.

As she sat waiting for the gate to open, a strange calm came over her. The gate swung out. The steer charged into the arena. The smells of sweat and manure, the sounds of whinnying horses, bellowing steers, and yelling cowboys all faded. The people and the corral fences around her seemed far away, in a mist. But she saw and felt with clarity where she was, moving with the mass of bone and muscle beneath her. Each spine-rattling jump she absorbed with more ease than the one before. She heard nothing but the steer's snorts and the thud of its hooves on the hard pasture ground.

Before she knew it, the steer had come to a stop, panting and blowing. The ride was over, and the noise and dust and heat infiltrated her awareness. Joe swept her onto the back of his horse just as the steer took off running. The cowboys were yelling for her now. Ben and Eddie jumped up and down. Where was Marie? Had Nettie ridden well enough to earn her praise?

She couldn't stop smiling. She had done it again. Ridden a steer to the end without being thrown. She raised her arm in a victory salute and whooped, then slipped down next to the pole fence.

And there stood Marie Gibson with a big, wide grin on her face. "Well done. You're a natural born rider." She flung an arm around Nettie's shoulders and walked out of the arena with her.

Nettie's emotions soared like the hawk that swooped through the blue afternoon sky. She tasted her newfound freedom, a whole new world opened to her. "Thanks, Marie. For helping me." Stopping abruptly, she threw both arms around her friend. "Oh, thank you, thank you, thank you."

———

"You rode?" Mama glared across the supper table at Nettie.

"You should've seen her." Marie passed a dish to Mama. "You could hardly tell where the steer ended and the rider began. Your daughter has a talent, and I think she can go far in rodeo."

Nettie saw her mother wince, but Marie continued as if she hadn't noticed. "And she won twenty-five dollars."

"Twenty-five? Dollars?" Mama's tight face turned into a puzzled frown.

"Yes, Mama. I stayed on the steer till the end." Nettie gave a tentative smile. Marie hadn't mentioned winning the money in a bet and that she'd given Nettie her half as well.

Papa looked into Nettie's eyes long and hard, then gave an almost imperceptible nod. "Good job, honey. We're proud of you."

"Well." Her mother pushed the word out in a puff. "Twenty-five dollars, huh? We certainly can use the extra money."

~~⌒~~

Before Marie mounted up to leave the next morning, she pulled Nettie aside. "There's still a good month to six weeks on the rodeo circuit. I asked your mama if she thought you might come with Tom and me."

Nettie's mouth dropped open. Go on the circuit? With Marie? She couldn't speak.

Marie held up her hand. "Now, don't get your hopes up too high. Your mama said she'd have to talk it over with your pa. But I just wanted you to know."

"Oh, gosh." Nettie grasped Marie's sleeve. "Oh. Thank you. I don't know what to say."

Marie grinned. "Well, just mind your manners and maybe I'll be seein' you again soon. I put in a good word for ya." She stuck her boot into the stirrup and swung up on her horse. "*Adios.*"

Unbelievable. Nettie could only stand and stare long after the Gibsons had disappeared from sight. She might get to rodeo! Maybe. Hands shaking, she rushed to do her chores.

Throughout the day, Nettie waited for Mama or Papa to bring up the subject. Without being asked, she strained the milk, washed the dishes, swept the floors, and made all the beds. She skipped through these chores with a strange, almost weightless feeling. Then, she settled in the rocking chair and picked up the darning basket.

Lola stopped in midstride as she carried a bundle of folded clothes to the bedroom. "Well, I'll be . . . I never. What's gotten into you, little sister?"

"Nothing." Nettie wove the needle through the cross threads on the sock.

"Oh-ho-ho. You never do this stuff till you're forced to. I know you. Something's up."

Nettie wrinkled her nose at Lola's smirk and said nothing. All afternoon, she sat and stitched until her back ached and her fingers were cramped. But inside, she felt as bouncy as the inflated pig's bladder the boys played with after butchering. Would Mama really say yes? This time next week, she could be on a train, traveling to rodeos all over the state. She tried not to think about the possibility, but visions of cheering crowds crept into her thoughts.

Mama worked out in the garden all day and said not a word when she brought in a bucket filled with potatoes and tomatoes for supper.

Finally, Nettie could stand it no longer. She went into the kitchen. "You want me to help you peel spuds?"

Mama turned. "Sure. I thought I'd fix some fried potatoes for supper."

Nettie washed the bucketful and began to peel. When would Mama say something? This waiting was so painful. Had Mama talked to Papa? Surely he would be on her side. Should she ask? She glanced at her mother out of the corner of her eye. Mama was busy slicing the potatoes into a pan of sizzling bacon grease.

"So, uh, did you—what did you think of Marie?"

Mama stopped cutting and pursed her lips as if thinking over her response. "She seems like a nice woman."

"Yeah, isn't she? And did you see her ride in Browning? She was just swell."

"Yes. She is quite good." Mama resumed her slicing. Nettie bit her tongue. Land's sake. Mama was so exasperating. Her toes itched and her fingers twitched. She couldn't wait any longer. "Mama?"

"Yes?"

"Mama, did Marie ask you if I could go rodeo with her? Did you talk to Papa? Is it okay?" Nettie couldn't help herself. It all came blurting out.

"So she told you, huh? Is that what this has all been about today? I noticed you were awfully industrious with that darning needle." Mama smiled. "It's not that I don't appreciate it. I do. You know I always welcome your help." She gazed out the window for a moment, reached up and shook out a fold from the blue-dotted flour sack curtains. "But, honey, I just can't, in good conscience, let you go out on the road alone. It's much too dangerous."

Nettie's buoyant hopefulness collapsed under the weight of her mother's words. "But I wouldn't be alone. I'd be with Marie and Tom."

"Nevertheless. The Gibsons couldn't be held responsible for your safety all the time."

"What does Papa say?"

"Your papa agrees. We just can't let you go."

For a moment, Nettie felt an almost uncontrollable urge to guffaw. This had to be a huge joke. This couldn't be happening. Her dream was just about to come true. "Even though I could be earning money. To help you and Papa?"

"Rodeo is no life for a young girl, honey. You need to be preparing for a home of your own some day. Not traveling all over the country, risking your life, and your reputation. I've set aside that twenty-five dollars you won and that can go toward more education. Maybe a finishing school wouldn't be such a bad idea."

The enormity of what Mama said hit her as though a horse had just stepped on her chest. It was no joke. "You're serious."

Mama nodded.

Tears stung Nettie's eyes and a reddish haze rose up to cloud her vision. "You've ruined my life!" She pivoted on one heel and slammed out the door.

Nettie ran full-tilt to the pasture where Toby grazed. She straddle-hopped the barbed wire, catching the hem of her skirt. She ripped it free, left a strip of cloth hanging from the barbs, and kicked the fence-post. "Drat. Drat. DRAT!" Her dream was over. She would never be happy. Send her to school? Not ride in rodeos? They just didn't under-stand. They didn't care. She flung her leg over Toby's bare back and urged him into a gallop across the pasture. The wind dried the tears that flowed now, scalding and angry.

If only she could keep going and ride to Havre. She sniffed and lifted her head. Wait a minute. She hiccupped. Maybe she could. "Yeah. That's what I'll do." She knew where Mama stashed the sewing money. After all, she'd earned that twenty-five dollars.

CHAPTER SEVEN

Nettie glanced at the clouds prematurely darkening the evening horizon. She pushed Toby hard, knowing she shouldn't, but she wanted to make it as far from home tonight as possible. She hadn't even bothered to pack, just stuffed saddlebags with oats for Toby, an extra saddle blanket, and a water skin from the barn and flung her saddle onto Toby's back. She was going to Havre, come heck or high water.

She'd only been riding for three hours, choosing to bypass Sunburst in favor of following the back roads, where she'd be less likely to run into someone she knew. Or be found. But dusk swooped in much quicker than she'd anticipated. The clouds looked black and ominous. It was August, for goodness sake. They hadn't had any rain for weeks. Surely it would just blow over.

A sudden gust of wind caught her hat and nearly took it off. Lightning cracked across the sky. Raindrops the size of saucers plopped into the dust. Nettie peered ahead in the dwindling light. Up ahead, a line of green foliage bisected the prairie. Ah, Willow Creek. Maybe she could find shelter under the willow trees.

By the time she and Toby reached the dry creek bed, the rain came down in torrents. Nettie dismounted, led her horse into a low spot under sheltering branches, and sat with the extra saddle blanket over her head and shoulders, Indian-style. Now she regretted not packing something to eat. Oh well, maybe she could share some of Toby's oats later. Relatively warm and cozy, she leaned back against the bank and closed her eyes to the soothing drum of the rain.

A roaring sound filled Nettie's dream. A train thundered toward her, its whistle shrieking. She opened her eyes. Toby tossed his head and neighed, a shrill sound above the roar. But wait. No trains out here. Nettie leapt to her feet. The rain fell in sheets, blown sideways in the wind.

She struggled to tighten the cinch, but her fingers were cold and slippery. The roar grew louder. Suddenly her mind grasped the sound. *A flash flood!* Gasping, Nettie grabbed Toby's reins. *Have to . . . get out . . . creek bed.*

A wall of water crashed against them. Nettie lost her footing. She screamed, choked on a mouthful of water. The torrent swept her away. *Toby! Where's Toby?* Flailing against the current, she tried to spot her horse. *Gone. Where?* Her head went underwater. Her lungs about to burst. *Dear Lord, help me. I'm going to die!*

Then Nettie's feet touched bottom. She gave a push. Just as she took a huge mouthful of water, her head surfaced. She coughed and choked, still churning her arms and legs. Her hand hit something. A dark shape loomed beside her. Nettie grabbed hold. Toby's mane. She wrapped her fingers in the horsehair and hung on.

She felt his powerful shoulders move as if he were galloping. Then a bump. Toby rose out of the water and dragged her up the bank, blowing and snorting. He stopped. His sides heaved. Nettie hung from his mane, unable to unclench her fingers. Finally her grasp released and she sank to the ground, sobbing.

It seemed as though she lay in the mud for hours, not able to force her trembling limbs to move. She'd been wrong to run away. This was her punishment. She'd almost drowned. Toby stood by her side and nudged her with his nose. Then he whinnied. An answering whicker caused Nettie to sit up. The horizon was a faint, dark line in the lightening dawn and the rain had stopped.

"Land sakes, girl. What happened to you?" A gruff, raspy voice came from the shadows.

"Hu-hu-who?" Nettie gasped out.

A large formidable-looking woman lumbered toward her, leading her horse. Gray stringy hair poked out from under a greasy hat, and a ratty buffalo robe covered her shoulders. Nettie couldn't help but stare.

"Ma Dunbar." The woman reached a hand out and pulled Nettie to her feet. "C'mon, girl. It's all right. Let's get you up to the house and get you dry." She led the way to a dilapidated two-room shack piled high inside with old harness, saddles, and wagon wheels.

Over a bowl of hot chicken soup, Nettie blurted out her story. "I just wanted to go compete in a real rodeo, and Mama wouldn't let me." She sniffed, feeling extra sorry for herself.

Ma Dunbar nodded her shaggy head. "Well, young 'un, I kin certainly understand that." She took Nettie's bowl and filled it again. "But let's face it, that wasn't the most responsible thing you coulda done, ridin' off with nary a lick o' supplies. And nobody knowin' where you was goin'."

Nettie blinked. "I was just so mad. I had to get away from there. Mama'd tie me to the sewing machine if she could. She just doesn't understand."

The big woman chuckled. "Yah, sounds a lot like my husband, Pete. He wanted me to move to his homestead and cook and do fer 'im. Huh-uh, I says. If'n you wants a wife like that you kin just go . . . find somebody else. I'm stayin' right here on my own homestead."

Nettie felt her eyes widen. Now this was a woman she could like.

❧

When Ma Dunbar drove her creaking old wagon up to the Brady house, Toby trailing behind, a flurry of activity met them. Papa and the boys were unsaddling their horses, and Mama stood by the barn with a bundle of wet blankets.

"We've been out all night lookin' for you." Papa had that stern look on his face, the kind that Nettie knew meant she was in big trouble.

Nettie hung her head. "I was upset. I just started riding, and, and I got caught in the storm. Mrs. Dunbar rescued me from the flood."

Mama dropped her load of blankets, stepped forward, and with tears in her eyes, wrapped her arms around Nettie in a tight hug. "I was so afraid. Are you hurt?"

Expecting a reprimand, Nettie shook her head. "No, I'm fine." A wave of guilt washed over her. What she'd done was wrong, so wrong. "Mama, Papa. I'm really sorry I caused you worry. I know I acted like a child, and it wasn't responsible." She hung her head. "I'll stay home and try to make it up to you."

Papa nodded. "All right then." He turned to Ma Dunbar. "Thanks for bringing her home."

"Yes, thank you, Mrs. Dunbar. You saved our daughter's life. Will you stay and have something to eat?" When the woman declined, Mama took Nettie's arm in hers. "I'm glad you're safe. Let's get you inside. I have some warm oatmeal fixed." She paused. "Thank you for your apology. Lola's wedding is coming up in September, and we have a lot of work to do, so I could use your help."

❧

On a warm late-September Saturday morning, Nettie stood sweating in the stuffy little teacherage at the Hay Lake schoolhouse. The voile bodice of her pink blouse kept coming untucked from her satin skirt. At this rate, she would look like she'd bathed and slept in this stupid dress. After having had a taste of wearing denim pants and men's shirts, donning any kind of dress—especially a silky, shimmery one like this—was so uncomfortable, so binding.

She wove the buttonhook around another tiny pearl button on the back of her sister's wedding dress and tried to pull it through the satin loop. "Pull in your stomach again. I can't get this hooked."

"Hurry up," Lola muttered through gritted teeth. "If I hold it any longer I won't make it to the altar alive."

Nettie squared her shoulders. Well, if her sister hadn't insisted on this stupid wedding gown with a million little buttons up the back, she wouldn't be having this problem. She jerked at the offending button with the hook. Not for her, when, if, *she* ever got married.

Their older sister Margie bustled in, smelling of lilac water. "Oh, Lola, you look so beautiful. Here, Nettie, let me help. I've had more practice with these things."

Nettie let out her own pent-up breath. Yeah, let the experts handle this "ladylike" chore. Fancy wedding dresses. What a waste of money, especially since her folks didn't have any to spare. Good thing Lola's fella was pretty well set. He'd bought the dress. Floyd Marshall seemed to worship the ground her sister walked on, would do anything to make her happy. That was all well and good, but did that mean he was spineless, that he'd let Lola walk all over him? Nettie hoped not. She wouldn't want a husband like that. *If* she ever did decide to marry.

Margie finished with the buttons and arranged the veil. Lola's cheeks were flushed, her eyes glowing. But Nettie just couldn't summon up a lot of excitement for all this falderal. Especially since she'd rather be at a rodeo somewhere with Marie and Tom, anywhere but here. Nettie sighed. Rodeo season was almost over, and she'd missed her chance. What a fool she'd been to run away. After that stunt, even if Mama and Papa had said it was okay, she would've felt too guilty to go. Oh well, next year for sure.

"Okay, it's one o'clock. Time to go." Margie stepped toward the door that led from the teacher's quarters into the schoolroom where the wedding would take place. Nettie tucked in her blouse and smoothed the skirt. She felt like a dress-up doll she'd seen in a catalog. She walked to the door, wobbling a little in her high heels. Hoo-boy, what if she tripped and fell?

With all the desks removed and its walls adorned with pale yellow cornstalks and braided wheat stems trimmed in lace, the Hay Lake schoolhouse had been transformed into a wedding chapel. Crepe ribbon adorned the windows, and someone had chalked "Lola and Floyd Forever" inside a heart on the blackboard.

The room overflowed with about fifty friends and neighbors, and the teacher plunked an out-of-tune Mozart composition on the old upright piano. A minister had ridden the nearly twenty miles from Cut Bank to conduct the ceremony. He waited up front behind the teacher's desk with the groom, best man Joe, and Ben.

Margie stepped through the door of the teacherage first and gave the teacher a nod. The music changed, and Margie led the way to the front. Nettie followed her slowly down the aisle to stand and wait for the bride. After a few *oohs* and *aahs*, a hush settled over the crowd.

As Lola walked forward on Papa's arm, Nettie blinked in surprise. Gosh, her sister really was beautiful in that dress. She looked happy, too. So did Mama, all decked out in a smart-looking navy dress with a white scalloped collar. Her mother dabbed at her eyes with a lace-trimmed handkerchief.

Nettie sneaked a look at Floyd. His face wore a wide grin as he stepped forward to take his bride's hand. Floyd really wasn't such a bad sort. Nice enough, although he never expressed any interest in rodeo. Well, anyway, he'd probably take good care of her sister. Nettie turned to face the minister.

"Dearly beloved . . ."

Before Nettie could gather her thoughts about what the minister said, the ceremony was over and she was walking down the aisle behind the newlyweds. Gee, all that work for weeks and weeks, and it was done in a matter of minutes.

After changing out of her frillies into a somewhat more comfortable corduroy skirt, she exited the schoolhouse and followed the crowd down to the Hay Lake reservoir. Nettie was drawn by the smoky tang of beef barbecuing over an open pit fire. A knot of men clustered around Dexter Garrish as he sliced the juicy meat onto huge platters with a flourish. Her stomach growled.

Plank tables held loaves of homemade bread, bowls of salads, and cold-beaded pitchers of lemonade. There were steaming baked potatoes, plates of cookies, pies, and cakes. It wasn't often that everybody got together. Nettie grinned. Any good excuse for a party.

She made her way through the line of people dishing up their plates.

Looking for a place to sit, she saw Jim Ferguson turning the handle on a wooden ice cream freezer. "Who's next?" he called out. "Wanna turn at makin' ice cream?" Immediately he was surrounded by a group of eager young helpers.

Nettie smiled. That used to be her favorite part of a picnic too, when she was about ten. She was too old for those kinds of activities now. But she really didn't want to join the groups of women either. All they wanted to talk about were kids and recipes and boring stuff like that. If she told them about her rodeo experiences, they'd probably just look at her like she was from a foreign country. She stood on the periphery of the festivities, momentary loneliness rising up inside. Oh well, enough feeling sorry for herself. Time to eat.

Nettie sat by herself in the shade of the pavilion and continued to watch the little knots of people that gathered to eat and talk and laugh.

Lola and Floyd stood beaming by the food tables, receiving hugs, kisses, and congratulations. After the ceremony, the new bride had changed into a lacy high-necked blouse and blue gingham skirt. How grown-up she looked.

Floyd bent toward Lola's face and gently wiped a smudge of frosting from the corner of her mouth. She smiled up at him, her face aglow. Nettie paused. It might be nice, having someone that sweet.

She just hadn't given much thought to men and marriage. Married. She shuddered. Such a stodgy idea. And yet, she thought of Marie and Tom. They seemed like such good friends. Maybe if Nettie could find someone like Tom . . . but no, she had a lot of rodeos to ride in, a lot more places to see before she even thought of settling down, if she could ever get out from under Mama's skirt.

Following the afternoon of eating and games and visiting, Nettie helped light lanterns. Others set the chairs around the walls and moved the teacher's desk outside to clear a dance floor. The musicians took their places at one end of the schoolroom, and the newlyweds danced the obligatory first dance alone. Then other couples surged onto the floor to join them.

Nettie sat. *Nobody's going to ask me to dance.* Even her brothers had chosen partners.

"Kin I have this dance?"

She looked up to see Porky Conners, red-faced and sweaty. *No, not Porky.* With an inward sigh, she pasted on a smile. "Sure."

Why not? It might be the only chance I get.

After the third dance with Porky, Nettie slipped out the door. Rubbing his sweat from her hands onto her skirt, she gulped the fresh air as though she'd been drowning. Porky was a nice enough kid, she supposed. But he was just one of the boys she'd gone to school with. And he was big and round and sweaty and awkward. Not exactly her dream cowboy. Her guy would be somebody tall and handsome enough to take her breath away. She huffed through pursed lips. Nobody like that for miles around. If only she could get to some rodeos, she might have a chance to meet someone. Then she snorted in disgust. *For heaven's sake, what am I thinking?*

She shivered in the chilly night breeze and turned her face up to the clear, diamond-speckled onyx sky. The music behind her spun a melancholy tune, a dance for couples in love. Not meant for her. She strolled toward the bonfire, where a group of six men passed a jug. She stood off to one side, near enough to gather warmth from the fire, but just out of their immediate notice. She longed to join them and listen to their colorful man talk. And why shouldn't she? Nettie breathed deeply and took a step forward.

Immediately the conversation stopped. "Uh, sorry for the language, ma'am," one cowboy said. "You oughtta go on over with the women, so's we don't offend your ears."

"Hey, I have a dad. And brothers, you know. I've heard a few cuss words before."

Red Jones let out a guffaw. "Aw, what the heck? Let 'er stay." He took another swig from the jug. "Y'all 'member my ol' horse, Brick? He musta weighed twelve hunnerd pounds er more. Yessir, he was a mean one, all right."

Nettie grinned and settled into the circle. She loved these stories.

At the end of Red's tale, the group erupted in guffaws, and the jug went around again, the men ignoring Nettie. She eased back out of the circle into the darkness. If she'd been a boy . . .

﹌

October's dry leaves scurried to escape the cold blasts of incoming November. Too late to go rodeoing now. Nettie sighed, thinking of lost opportunities. But in the spring, no matter what, she was going.

Nettie helped her mother can the venison Papa shot. She added the jars to those of pickles, beans, corn, and tomatoes in the root cellar. Standing back, she admired the shelves stacked with emerald, amber, and crimson glass containers of vegetables and berries. What a lot of work helping Mama do all this, but it looked so pretty and it sure would taste good this winter.

Late one afternoon, Nettie curled up in the rocking chair near the warm cook stove and thumbed through the Sears, Roebuck and Co. catalog. Esther crawled on the floor below her and played happily with an empty thread spool.

"What's Santa going to bring you, huh, Essie?" Nettie reached down to smooth the soft brown hair.

"Thanta?" her sister cooed.

"What a sweet little girl you are." Even though Esther annoyed Nettie at times, she really was pretty special, for a baby. Not that Nettie wanted any of her own. She'd had enough, just helping take care of little Chuck and this one.

At the table, her mother punched down bread dough, spread a white dishtowel over the pan, and set it on the cupboard near the stove to rise again. "What about you, honey? What do you see that you'd like?"

"Oh, Mama, just look at these boots. Aren't they the prettiest things you ever saw?" Nettie pointed to a pair of black leather boots stitched in green. What she wouldn't give to have a pair like that, something like Marie's. She would look so sharp, riding in a parade before a rodeo.

"Very pretty. Hmmm. Ten ninety-five. A bit expensive." Her mother sat beside her, took the catalog, and flipped through the pages.

Nettie's excitement dissolved. Mama and Papa would never be able to afford such an extravagance. She'd probably just have to wait until she was able to earn some more money of her own, maybe next spring if she could get away to a rodeo or two.

"Oh, look, a brass banquet lamp, two dollars and thirty cents. Wouldn't that look nice in our living room?" Mama glanced at the worn wooden kitchen table, shook her head, then ruffled through the pages. "Men's suits, nine ninety-five. Your dad needs a new suit. We might as well get him one for Christmas, huh?"

Nettie could barely nod. Well, the decision was made for sure. Papa and the boys would get clothes. She'd have to make do with Joe's old cast-off work boots. Every other year, Papa bought a new wool three-piece suit, and the old "dress" suit became his work clothes. He liked wool, said it was warm in the winter and cooled him in summer. And the jacket always had plenty of pockets for his watch and Bull Durham tobacco.

"Oh, my goodness, look at these short skirts. Nearly up to the knees. I'm sure glad we don't see them here in Montana." Mama clucked her tongue. "You better not get the idea to dress like that."

She got up to stoke the fire. "We'll go to Cut Bank next week to get our winter supply of groceries. Then we'll send off our Sears order for whatever we can't find in town."

Nettie waited until her mother's back was turned, then dog-eared the boot page. If the hints didn't work, she'd have to find a way to get the money on her own, even if she had to do extra darning.

Midmorning, the Bradys' wagon rumbled over the Cut Bank River Bridge. The steel girder structure spanned a narrow trickle of water, its edges rimmed with a thin crust of ice from the frigid early-November temperatures. It was really more of a creek, but the townsfolk called it a river.

The little community of five hundred had swelled since Nettie's last visit. It hummed with activity, ranchers in town from all over to stock up on supplies before the first blizzard hit.

She saw a team and wagon approach as they crossed the bridge into town. A large, formidable-looking woman occupied most of the seat. Ma Dunbar. The woman who'd saved her from the flood.

"Hello there, Mrs. Dunbar," Nettie called out as they met.

"Howya doin'? You look a little drier than last time I saw ya." Ma cracked a toothless grin, snapped the reins, and passed them by.

After a moment of embarrassment, remembering her runaway mishap, Nettie reflected on this strange woman. Ma Dunbar hadn't let her husband tell her what to do. She lived her own dream, on her own terms. Nettie grinned. Now *that* was a strong, independent woman. She knew her mind and no man was going to tell her what to do. *Hmm. I wonder if I could be like her.* Then again, the woman was all alone. That might not be so nice.

Papa hitched the team to the rail that ran along the main street in front of the gray, weathered facades of the drugstore, the saddle shop, and the general store. Nettie followed her parents, holding onto little brother Chuck's hand. Their shoes clunked over the creaking boardwalk, joining the rhythm of the men and women they met, exchanging greetings at this once- or twice-a-year meeting.

"Howdy, Lamar, how was your crop this year?"

"Charles, Mrs. Brady, good to see you. My, what a fine lookin' family."

Nettie searched the knots of people, looking for a familiar face. Maybe she'd see Ann Poole, a girl she'd gone to school with briefly before the Poole family moved to town. Nettie pushed the thought aside. Ann probably wouldn't even remember her.

Nettie stepped into the dimly lit interior of the general store, the Cut Bank Merc, their first stop. The mustiness of old wood and the mingled fragrances of kerosene, pickles, and leather assailed her nostrils. She trod on floorboards worn smooth from years of boot leather and gazed at the vast array of barrels, tubs, bins, and boxes that lined every shelf. Even the high ceiling hung heavy with hay rakes, pitchforks, and shovels.

Here Mama and Papa could buy fifty-pound bags of flour, gingham for dresses, and coal for the heating stove, as well as feed for the chickens, hammers, and nails. Even a new deck of cards for long winter evenings.

Nettie carried Esther and kept a tight hold on Chuck's hand so her mother could do her shopping. A twinge of resentment prickled at her. She really would rather have wandered through the store by herself instead of taking care of the little ones. Even ten-year-old Eddie was allowed to look by himself. But she knew better than to protest. It was best she did what Mama wanted. For now.

As they browsed, her six-year-old brother stopped in front of the display of red-and-white-striped peppermint sticks and horehound drops in the candy case. He tugged at her hand and pointed. "Can I have some peppermint?"

Her mouth watered. She could almost taste the bittersweet tang of the horehound. "Just wait, Chuckie. If you're good, maybe Papa will buy us some."

After what seemed like hours of riding herd on the little ones, they finally left the merc laden with packages. Papa stacked everything in the wagon. "While you all go to the drugstore, I'll go over to the saddle shop to pick up some leather for harness repair," he said.

"Sure, and to swap stories with Mr. Eliason. I know you." Mama chuckled. She took out her list again. "I need to stock up on mustard plaster, menthol, and camphor, in case anyone gets sick this winter. Nettie, would you please watch the kids again? Here's some money for a soda or something while you wait."

Nettie groaned inwardly. She'd much rather be at the saddle shop with Papa. She hesitated on the sidewalk. Well, why not? After Papa had disappeared inside, she tugged on Chuck's hand and carried Esther into the shop, with Eddie following. Inside, she stopped to take a deep breath of the rich, earthy leather aroma. The heck with fancy perfumes. Hand-tooled saddles and bridles lined the aisles, inviting dreams of a fancy outfit of her own.

Then she saw Papa standing by a shelf of polished boots. She froze. Her heartbeat sped up. Maybe he was buying her a pair for her birthday. She wasn't supposed to see that.

At that moment Chuck whined, "I'm thirsty."

"Shh." Nettie pulled him behind a tall shelf so Papa wouldn't see them. "Okay. Let's go." She herded the children to the drugstore and ordered phosphates for the little ones. But she stuck the quarter for her own back in her pocket. She'd save that toward going rodeoing with Marie next spring. She'd need every bit of spare change she could save by then. Six long months until rodeo season. But only three weeks till her birthday. Nettie could just see herself strutting in those green-stitched black boots.

When Papa came back, he handed each child a peppermint stick and a small bag of horehound drops, much to Chuck's and Esther's delight. Nettie licked her own peppermint stick and savored the cool feeling it left in her mouth. She'd have to agree with Chuckie anytime. She didn't think she'd ever outgrow her enjoyment of these sweet treats.

At last Papa and Ben were ready to take the team to the livery stable. Papa swung up onto the high seat. "We'll meet you in the hotel restaurant."

Later that night Nettie gratefully settled into bed with Esther in the hotel room they all shared. It had been a busy and exciting day, just seeing the sights and hearing the sounds of town. While it was fun to come to town, Nettie was eager to get home again to ride Toby.

Lumpy mattresses and communal beds aside, a gentle snoring soon filled the room. Nettie drifted off, thinking of her horse and a pair of black cowboy boots with green stitching.

CHAPTER EIGHT

The heady, roasted aroma of coffee roused Nettie from a drowsy slumber. December 17. Her fifteenth birthday. *I wonder what kind of presents I'll get. The boots? I hope, I hope.* She picked up her diary and pen from where they'd dropped on her chest as she'd dozed off earlier and slipped from her warm bed. Good thing Lola wasn't here. She'd probably have sneaked a look at Nettie's journal.

Frost etched leafy designs on the window, and she could see her breath. Shivering, she pulled on a heavy wool sweater and a pair of Joe's hand-me-down wool pants over her long johns. She jammed her already sock-clad feet into boots that were scuffed and wrinkled as an old man's face, also well broken in by her older brother. It sure would be nice to have some new ones.

She shuffled out of her room, through the living room, and paused at the kitchen door to soak up the warmth that radiated from the snapping fire in the cook stove. Mama dipped pancake batter onto the griddle as fatback popped and sizzled. Nettie gulped in the tantalizing smells. Her younger brothers, Ed and Chuck, were already seated in their places. Esther pounded a spoon on her high chair. In the middle of the table was a frosted cake with fifteen white candles surrounded by several wrapped packages. *Hmm, is one of them big enough for boots?*

"Happy birthday, dear." Mama turned from the stove and handed her a cup of steaming coffee. "Sit down. Breakfast will be ready in a minute."

Nettie took the cup and warmed her hands around it. She inhaled the fragrance before taking a sip. Mama had given her coffee without her asking. *Maybe this means she thinks I'm growing up.*

Nettie joined her brothers and sister at the table. The boys grinned and looked from her face to the presents. Esther shouted, "Bir'day, bir'day."

Nettie giggled, leaned over, and kissed the toddler's forehead. "Yeah, it's my birthday. Tell your sis 'Happy birthday.'"

Joe, Ben, and Papa banged through the door, letting in a gust of cold air. Papa deposited the milk pail on the counter. "Is today a special day?" he teased and tousled her hair.

Joe set a bucket of coal beside the stove. "The birthday girl is finally up." He grinned at her. "Must be nice to be able to sleep so late." Nettie wrinkled her nose at him.

Mama lit the candles on the cake. "C'mon, everybody." At her cue, the whole family launched into an off-tune "Happy Birthday."

Nettie grinned.

Mama whisked the delicacy off the table and replaced it with pancakes and bacon. "Okay, you all have to eat some breakfast before you get any cake, you hear?"

Nettie jumped up, grabbed a knife, and cut the cake. "Nettie. What are you doing? I just said no cake." Mama's voice rose in an exasperated tone.

Giggling, Nettie passed slices to the rest of the family. "It's my birthday. I should be able to eat cake first, if I want."

Mama sighed. Then she smiled. "Well, I suppose we can break the rules for once."

Nettie gobbled down the cake, almost too excited to taste it. What could be in those packages? She tried to keep a grin off her face and act matter-of-fact, like a grownup, but inside it was as though she were still Eddie's or Chuck's age.

Finally, when everyone finished eating, Mama stacked the pile of gifts on the table again. Nettie picked up a bundle wrapped in a piece of soft leather. She untied the leather string and unfolded it. Inside was a new lariat. She raised her eyebrows at Joe. "Isn't this the rope you won at—?" She stopped as he smiled broadly. It was. The rope he'd won at the last rodeo. She grinned back at him. What a brother. A new rope to go with new boots.

The next package held a halter, hand-woven by Ben. "Ben, this is beautiful. And you made it? Wow."

Eddie stood up and stretched as tall as he could next to her chair. "I made this leather quirt all by myself, too."

Nettie put her arm around him. "This is so nice." What a lot of work her brothers had gone to, just for her. All these things, with a new pair of boots, would make up a very nice outfit.

"Good job, boys." Papa looked at his sons with pride. Chuck came around the table. He grinned and ducked his head as he presented her a picture with bright-colored squiggles. "That's you, on Toby."

She bit her lip. How sweet. "This is a great picture, Chuckie. Thanks. I'm so proud of all of you." What a special family she had.

The next small package held a blue satin hair ribbon. "Oh, how pretty."

"That's from Esther."

Nettie blinked. Strange, how this little bit of fabric made her want to tear up. She didn't usually cotton to frilly things.

"And this one's from us." Mama handed Nettie a box. Nettie held her breath. Was it big enough? It looked a little small. Surely it would be the boots.

She ripped open the paper, ignoring her mother's frown. Mama liked to save wrapping paper to reuse. *That's okay. This piece has been well-used already.* Nettie opened the box and sniffed. It didn't really smell like leather.

Inside were several paperback western romances. Books. She loved books, but Nettie wanted to cry. No boots. Didn't they know how much she wanted those shiny black boots with fancy green stitching?

She looked up Mama's beaming face. Her mother usually looked askance when she caught Nettie poring over the *Ranch Romance* magazines and dime novels at the Cut Bank Merc. Studying a textbook or reading a cookbook was all right, but usually Mama considered this "paperback trash" a waste of time.

Nettie put on what she hoped was a bright smile. "Thanks, Mama, Papa." She did love to read. Her mother must be softening a little. "These are great. I can hardly wait to read them."

She finished her breakfast and tried not to think of boots.

❦

There were no boots for Christmas either. Papa got his new suit. Nettie's disappointment weighed heavy. *He could've gotten another year out of his old one. My boots cost about the same.*

The boys each unwrapped new denims and work boots. Nettie thanked Mama for the hand-knitted sweater she received. *I would've liked a pair of denim pants. Even new work boots.* She quietly squirreled away the quarter from her Christmas stocking. She'd have to buy them herself. Maybe she could talk to Mrs. Conners, ask if she could do some extra darning or mending to earn her own money. She grimaced.

Two days later, the sky turned slate gray. The horses milled about in their pen. Every now and then they stopped to sniff the air, then broke into a gallop with manes tossing, 'round and around. The wind increased its strength with every breath of the angry storm clouds billowing over the horizon. Nettie felt kinship with those clouds. By evening, the temperature had dropped drastically.

Before pitching the next forkful of musty-sweet hay into the feed trough in the corral, Nettie paused to watch the horses trot toward her. She took in the sharp, dry tanginess of the air that promised heavy snow. *Great. Now I have to be cooped up inside during a snowstorm while the boys brag about their new denims and boots.*

Papa rounded the corner of the barn with the milk pail. "It's gonna hit us hard. I left the calf in with the milk cow, so we don't have to worry about milking. Oh well, we've been lucky so far this year, only a skiff or two. Isn't it a blessing it waited till after Christmas?" He switched the heavy pail to his other gloved hand. "Don't forget to close up the chicken coop good and tight."

Nettie hurried to finish feeding the horses, then stepped into the warm, ammonia stench of the chicken house next to the barn to gather eggs. The hens clucked at her as she filled their water bucket, poured an extra pan full of feed, and gathered the eggs in the fading light. She pushed the door shut against the rising wind and pulled the wooden bar down in preparation for the storm. A sudden blast tugged at her hair, clawed at her face, and brought tears to her eyes, making her wish for a woolen scarf. She cradled the bounty in the hem of her coat and ran to the house. Still shivering, she carefully counted out twelve fresh eggs.

Nettie joined her family as they scurried in and out, pressed by anxiety. Mama grabbed a last pair of socks from the clothesline. Joe emptied the ash pan from the cook stove while Ben filled the coal box behind it. Papa poured the milk into the funnel-shaped strainer to clean tiny specks of straw and dirt from it.

"Guess we're ready." He filled a fresh cup of coffee and sat down at the kitchen table.

Mama chuckled. "At least I got the clothes in before it hit this time." Nettie remembered sudden blizzards coming up in years past, and not finding the long johns and socks that blew off the line until springtime when the snow thawed.

Supper was almost festive. They sat in the warm kitchen, ate by kerosene light, and listened to the wind's eerie wail. It wrenched at loose boards and tried to fit its frosty fingers into any available crevice. But Nettie and her mother had already stuffed rags into cracks between boards and around the window frames.

Nettie helped Mama put the youngest to bed around the stove in the living room and covered them with extra quilts. Papa set stones on the stove to heat for the rest of them. Later, each would wrap a hot rock in flannel rags for warm feet in the cold bed. Then they gathered at the kitchen table to play gin rummy. After awhile, Mama and Papa gave up and sat by the stove, sipping tea. Nettie and the boys continued to play.

"Hey, I'll bet my Christmas quarter on the next game," Nettie whispered and pulled out the shiny coin. Maybe she could glean a little extra money for her stash.

"You're on." Joe fished his out of his pocket. Ben followed suit. Eddie scowled, but not to be outdone, he finally put his on the table, too.

But Joe won Nettie's quarter right off, and she panicked. No. This would never do. She'd lost half her savings already. But the next round she won Ben's, then Eddie's.

"No," he yelled suddenly. "That's not fair. That was my first-ever Christmas quarter. Give it back."

Papa strode to the table. "What are you kids doing? Stop your bickering."

Mama set her teacup down with a rattle. "Give it back. Gambling for money is evil." She glared at Nettie. "And it certainly isn't ladylike. Don't you ever do that again."

─ ◆ ─

The blizzard settled in. Snow piled into drifts around the house. For three days, no one ventured outside for fear of being blown away or lost between the house and barn.

"Will the horses be all right?" Nettie fretted at the window.

"They're in the barn. We gave 'em extra hay. They'll be fine." Papa leaned back in his chair. "Yup, you could freeze to death in that short distance. You know the Jorgenson place, part of Red's spread now? Well, the way Red tells it, it was the winter of ought-seven. Blizzarding like God was shakin' out his feather bed with a vengeance and howlin' over his lost sinners."

Nettie shivered.

Papa took a sip of his coffee. "Seems after 'bout the fifth day, ol' man Jorgenson developed a powerful thirst, and he just had to get out to his still in the barn, not far from his house, mind you."

The boys leaned forward to hear the rest.

"Red says it had to've been fifty below with that banshee wind."

Nettie wrapped her arms tighter to her chest.

"Well, when the storm finally stopped, Red and his boys went over to check on the Jorgensons." Papa paused dramatically. "They found him just five feet from his kitchen door. Froze to death."

Mama sniffed. "See what happens when you give in to vile cravings? Liquor is the devil's brew."

Nettie rolled her eyes at her mother's rant. Poor Mr. Jorgenson. How could a person get so disoriented and give up so close to home? If only he had taken a few more steps. If only someone had opened the door and shone the lantern out at the right time. She got up and scratched a hole in the frost on the window to peer out into the swirling whiteness. *I sure hope Toby is all right. Did I leave him enough feed?*

As the days wore on, the festive feeling dwindled. The three younger boys scuffled, Esther whined, and their mother snapped at them all. Mama kept finding more cleaning or sewing chores for Nettie. Joe withdrew to the room he shared with his brothers. Papa paced and muttered about hoping the cows were safe in a coulee and finding something beneath the snow to eat. Nettie itched to get out to the barn. To see Toby and smell the familiar barn aromas. The closeness of the house and everybody in it and the rising stench of the slop bucket had begun to get to her.

On the fourth day the wind let up a little. Papa and Joe finally went out to the barn, tying a rope to the house door to follow back. If only Nettie could've gone too. She stood at the window, able to see nothing beyond the drifts, but hoping her watchful eye was enough to bring them back safely. After what seemed like hours, they thumped through the door followed by an icy blast.

"The horses are fine. We fed them and chopped ice on the water tank." Joe set his hat with a few eggs on the table. "And the chickens sure were happy to see us."

Papa pulled off his heavy wool hat, shaking snow onto the kitchen floor. Concern shadowed his face as he scratched his head. "Found that late calf from the milk cow frozen outside the barn. Came back to find her mother, I reckon. Sure hope the rest of the cows had sense enough to hole up in that coulee down by the lake."

Nettie bit her bottom lip. Oh, poor little Ginger. When things got rough she'd headed for home. Just like Mr. Jorgenson. Her eyelids stung. Nettie hadn't even thought about the poor cows out in the midst of the storm. She turned away so no one could see her face.

Two days later the sun lit up the world in white diamonds. The low hills blended into the coulees as if in a rolling sea of snow. Nettie couldn't tell where the lake was except for the white flatness at the base of their little hill. The snowdrifts sloped to the eaves of the house and rolled and dipped as far as the eye could see. There was no going anywhere but to the barn through the almost tunnel-like path Papa and the boys had dug.

Nettie bundled up against the sharp cold and followed the snowy pathway. She couldn't stand another hour in the house with rambunctious boys and an irritable toddler who wanted to get into everything. In the barn, she inhaled the welcome odors of hay, manure, and animals. She grinned. That was preferable to house smells any day.

The five saddle horses greeted her with low nickers, stomping in their stalls and tossing their heads. She fed each one a handful of oats, then stopped at Toby's stall. His ears pointed forward and his soft lips fluttered as he blew a hello.

"Hi there, boy, ya miss me?" Nettie reached up to stroke his velvet muzzle and ran her hand over his furry winter coat.

"I missed you." This is what she'd longed for those last long, cooped-up days. She buried her face in his neck and inhaled his distinctive scent. Mmmm, it seemed forever since they'd been able to run across the prairie, his mane and her hair blowing free.

Toby nuzzled her pocket. She giggled and fed him another handful of oats.

"Your 'toenails' are getting kinda long, boy. It's been awhile since we've been out riding." She grabbed the long-handled clippers and trimmed the excess growth from Toby's hooves. He stood patiently, nudging her back occasionally. Then she bent his leg at the knee and braced his foot between her knees to file the hoof smooth with a rasp. It sure was good to be out in the barn with her pal.

Finally, Nettie trudged back to the house, the cold snow crunching underfoot. She glanced toward the horizon over the mounds her brothers had shoveled. She stopped and frowned, squinting across the blue and purple shadows cast by the late afternoon sun. Someone was riding through the deep snow toward their place.

At that moment Papa stepped out on the stoop and shaded his eyes with his hand. "Well, I'll be . . . some crazy hombre is out ridin'."

It was Tex, a middle-aged bachelor who lived by himself in a little line shack and took care of a small herd for the Fergusons just a few miles south of the Bradys. His horse plowed through the deep drifts, snorting with the effort. Nettie watched him approach with a growing sense of envy.

"Howdy, Tex." Papa greeted the visitor. "What brings you out? Everything all right?"

"Aw, couldn't stand the silence no more." Tex dismounted in the lee of the barn, shuffled his feet, and cast his eyes downward. "Thought I'd come over and see how you all was a-doin'."

"Just in time for supper." Papa beckoned him toward the house.

Tex scrubbed a hand over his week-old stubble. "Much obliged."

After rubbing down and feeding his horse, Tex ambled in. The cowhand inhaled the aroma of canned beef and noodles cooking. "Yeah, I was a-gettin' tired of beans, myself." He grinned, then lapsed into a cough.

Glad for company to break the monotony, Nettie relished Tex's stories over supper. "Do you like living there all alone?" she asked.

He laughed. "Heck, yeah. I can do what I want, when I want. Nobody a-naggin' at me for nothin'."

Nettie smiled at the cowboy. How she envied his life. He could go riding whenever he wanted to. All he really had to do was take care of Fergusons' cows. That's what she would do someday: have a place of her own, own a few cows, go rodeoing whenever she wanted. In those green-stitched black boots.

After supper, Papa brought out the cards for an evening's play. Jokes and laughter ricocheted across the table, but ended with Tex's dry, raspy coughing spell.

"That doesn't sound too good," Mama said. "Here, let me make you some fennel tea. Be sure to rub some liniment on your chest before you go to sleep. Do you want a mustard plaster?"

"Aw, it's nothing, just a little too much cold air." Tex laughed and went out to the barn to sleep in the hay with his horse.

The next day he was off for the Fergusons'. "Goin' to ride the grub line." The cowboy grinned. He planned to stop in at every neighbor along the way, for food, drink, and company. Such was a bachelor's life.

As she and her family waved good-bye, Nettie already missed the camaraderie and laughter Tex had brought. It would probably be awhile before they saw another hardy soul brave these snowdrifts.

For the next week the Bradys settled back into their routine.

The wind wailed in the night. Nettie burrowed under her blankets, trying to shut out its screams. Funny, it sounded just like a baby crying. Then she sat upright. It *was* a baby. It was little Esther.

Nettie's breath caught in her throat. She could hear the old pine rocker squeak. Her mother crooned softly. Esther coughed, a deep, hacking sound that ended in a rasping gasp for air. Oh dear, had her baby sister caught something from Tex?

Heart pounding, Nettie slipped on her heavy woolen robe and padded out to the kitchen, where a single candle sputtered. She smelled menthol. "What's the matter with Essie?"

Mama's red-rimmed, puffy eyes rose to meet Nettie's. "I think it's the influenza. I've rubbed her chest with lard and mustard, and had the kettle steaming all night, but she's not settling down to sleep at all."

Nettie leaned close to her little sister and smoothed a hand over her forehead. She looked at her mother in alarm. "She's burning up."

Mama nodded.

"Here, let me rock her for awhile. Why don't you go to bed. I'll call you if I need to." Nettie took the feverish bundle tenderly in her arms.

Mama didn't argue. She stumbled a bit as she rose from the chair and choked back a cough of her own. "I'm fine." She waved aside Nettie's startled look. "Just tired."

"Now, now, Essie. It's your big sis. You'll be all right." Nettie stroked the little girl's damp, matted curls as she whimpered, and began to sing to her softly, "Hush, little baby, don't you cry." She stood and walked from the steam-clouded windows in the kitchen into the living room and back. Then she sat awhile and rocked. Her sister cried. They walked some more. Esther coughed and wheezed. Exhausted, Nettie sat again, on the verge of tears herself. What more should she do?

Nettie awoke in the gray half-light of dawn. Her arm was numb under Esther's weight. When she looked down at her sister's still form, she stiffened. *Oh, dear Lord, no.* Then she saw the small chest rise and fall. Her shoulders sagged in relief. The toddler had finally gone to sleep. Nettie lifted her carefully, carried her to the crib in Mama's room, then crept back into her own bed. *I'll just lie down for a few minutes.*

When she woke again, the sun shone through the windows, but the house was quiet and cold. Nettie pulled on her wool sweater and pants and tiptoed out to the kitchen. The coal box was empty. Just then the door opened. Her brother trudged in with a bucketful. "Mornin'." Joe slipped off his overshoes and tromped to the stove.

"Where is everybody?" Nettie handed him the box of Farmer's wooden matches. He shrugged. "Still asleep, I guess."

That was odd. A chill ran through her. It was nine o'clock. Papa was always out in the barn by six and Mama usually mixing dough for the day's batch of bread.

With trepidation, Nettie peeked around the doorjamb into her parents' darkened bedroom, where the curtains were still drawn. A stale, close smell hovered in the room. Her mother pushed herself up on one elbow in their brass bed and coughed. "Oh, my. I've overslept. What time is it?" Papa stirred next to her, but only groaned and turned over on his side. Esther whimpered in her crib.

Nettie stepped in to pick up her sister and peered into her mother's pale face. "Are you sick, Mama?"

"No, no. I'm fine." Her mother shivered as she slid out of bed and caught herself with one hand on the windowsill. "My. A little dizzy. Didn't get much sleep, that's all." Her brow furrowed. "How's Essie doing?"

"Well, she finally went to sleep, but her breathing is still kind of rattly." Nettie swayed the toddler to and fro in her arms. "I don't think she's quite as hot, though."

Nettie sat in a chair by the table with Esther. Mama banged around in the kitchen, starting the coffee and the pancake batter. Then she paused. "Papa's not up yet." She frowned and went back through the living room into their bedroom. A moment later she was back to dip water from the pail into a basin. She wrung out a washcloth. "Now *he* has a fever. Oh dear." She returned to the bedroom to bathe Papa's face.

Then Nettie saw her round the corner to the boys' room, where Ben, Ed, and Chuck were still in bed. Nettie could hear coughs and groans greet their mother and looked up to see Mama leaning on the doorframe. "They're all sick." Her arms dropped to her sides.

"Mama, I think you are, too." Nettie strode to her side, Esther balanced on one hip. "C'mon, you need to get back in bed." She'd never seen Mama look so pale.

"No, no. I've got to make some tea. Would you get my packet of herbs off the shelf in the pantry? The water must be hot by now." Mama would not give up until she had served each patient the steaming herb concoction, rubbed each chest with menthol in goose grease, and applied her eye-watering mustard plaster.

Nettie caught her mother's arm as she leaned heavily on the table. Mama was just being stubborn now. "Okay, Mama, now it's your turn. Let me put a mustard plaster on you. Have some tea yourself and please go to bed. I feel just fine. I'll look after everybody. And Joe is okay, too. He's out feeding the horses."

Mama coughed. "It was that Tex. He brought us the influenza."

Nettie bit her lip. That's right. Tex had a nasty cough. But they'd all had such fun. Was there a price to pay for that?

Nettie's world transformed into fetching and fixing. She made fennel tea by the gallon, kept soup hot on the stove in case someone regained an appetite, bathed feverish brows, and rocked Esther. Dirty clothes piled up until she was forced to melt a big copper pot of snow and set diapers to boiling on the stove. She emptied chamber pots into the now-reeking slop bucket by the door until Joe could take it to the outhouse.

Day became night, and she lost track of time. Despite her fatigue, she lay awake nights, fearfully listening for a cough or a cry.

Joe finally broke a trail to the coulee by the lake to feed the cattle some hay. It had taken him all day to accomplish this chore after he took care of the animals in the barn. The thermometer hovered around zero. When he staggered in at suppertime, exhaustion etched on his face, Nettie rushed to feel his forehead. *Thank goodness it's cool.* She didn't know what she'd do if he got sick, too. The animals depended on him, as the rest of the family relied on her now. They both had to stay strong.

Joe raised his eyebrows at the bowl of soup she set in front of him. "Is that all?"

Nettie shot him a look. "When did you think I had time to cook a big meal?"

He shrugged, but dug in enthusiastically. He ate not only his, but a Papa-size portion, too, sopping it up with a thick slice of buttered bread. He finally came up for air. "Everybody's still sick, huh?"

Nettie, at the table across from him, leaned her head on her hand and nodded. She was too tired to eat. Her eyes drooped. All she wanted to do was sleep. Esther's cry broke the spell.

The days blurred one into the other for the next week. More snow fell, and Joe was forced to dig his way out again to feed the cows. Papa thought he felt better one morning, got dressed, and made three steps outside the door before his knees buckled. He lay in the snow, coughing, until Joe and Nettie helped him back inside. Her throat closed in a sudden spasm of fear. What if they hadn't been there to find him?

Mama tried to get up, too. "You need some help with all of us." She allowed Nettie to lead her to the rocker, but soon admitted that she was too weak to sit up very long. "Just put Esther in bed with us, and get yourself some rest or you'll be getting sick, too."

Nettie rocked her sister, listened to her raspy breaths, and willed her own breathing to help Esther. "Poor little Essie. Tomorrow I've got to ride to town for the doctor. He'll know what to do."

Finally worn out from coughing and labored breathing, Esther fell asleep. Nettie tucked the toddler into bed next to her mother and eased herself into her own bed, not bothering to get undressed. The wind shrieked and buffeted their little house, but Nettie burrowed into her blankets and fell into a dead sleep.

Still in a half-dream state, Nettie awoke to an eerie stillness. Watery gray-yellow sunlight tried to penetrate the frost-swirled window. Then she heard the creak. She sat up with a start and listened. It was the rocker, sighing in steady rhythm over the squeaky floorboards. Nettie padded to the door.

Mama sat, her face so pale it seemed translucent. Nettie could see a blue vein pulsing in her mother's temple. She rocked, back and forth, back and forth, cradling Esther on her lap. One small bare foot protruded from the plaid wool blanket. So blue.

Staring at some infinite point, Mama looked through Nettie, not acknowledging her. The rocking continued. Nettie thought she should cover Essie's foot, but found herself reluctant to move. She shivered as though an icy finger had run up her spine. The baby was too still.

It was as if someone else's feet moved her from her spot to kneel beside the chair. With a trembling hand, she brushed her fingertips across Esther's cold, stiff cheek, then lowered her head to her mother's lap. Her hot tears fell on her sister's body. *No, no, no.*

Mama stopped rocking. Her hand found Nettie's.

CHAPTER NINE

Mama sat so still in the rocker.

Nettie stood in the doorway, overcome by the stillness. Her mother gave a few half-hearted pushes with her foot, then stopped, as if that simple effort were too much. Her hands were clasped tight in her lap, her head bowed. Mama hadn't said but a few words since that terrible night Esther died.

Nettie couldn't shake the tight, closed-in feeling that had overcome her. She didn't know what to do to make things better, how to get back to normal. Nobody said much of anything. Recovered from the influenza, Papa and the boys stayed outside most of the day. When they came in to eat, their stone faces reflected empty silence. The house whispered as though it, too, recognized the deep sorrow that now lived within.

Esther's body lay frozen in a small pine coffin in a rear stall of the barn, and would remain that way until a spring thaw allowed Papa and the boys to dig a grave. Nettie could barely bring herself to go into the barn. When she did, she studiously avoided even looking in that direction. It was bad enough to feel the absence in the house. But out there, a presence of something unfinished weighed heavy on her shoulders. It was as if Essie's spirit waited, restless and uneasy.

Life was no longer the same. She'd never get to teach Essie to ride.

Nettie took another look at Mama and slipped outside. She closed the door gently so as not to startle her mother and walked out to the corral. On this bright, clear day the horses frisked about, tossing their heads and snorting, happy to be free of the barn after such a long cold spell. She stopped, leaned on the fence, and watched Toby run in the snow. He trotted up and nuzzled her hand. Tension flowed out through her fingers as she rubbed his soft nose and slid a hand up his blaze face to fondle his ears. He stood quietly for a moment. But when she offered him no treat, he turned and broke into another gallop around the corral.

Nettie watched him run, so free, so happy. She could almost feel herself in him, running, running, the wind washing her mind clean, leaving all the sadness behind. But the vision broke. With a long sigh, she trudged through the crusty snow back to the silent house. She had to stay home and take care of Mama.

It seemed to take forever for the deep cold to move out of Nettie's bones, but winter gradually melted into the softening air of spring. The temperature warmed and snowdrifts gave way to spidery rivulets running toward the lake. With each step she took, mud caked inches thick beneath each boot sole.

One morning Papa and Joe exchanged glances at the breakfast table. "Think we can dig today," Papa said. Joe stood up and they left.

The day had come. The bite of hotcake Nettie had just taken seemed to swell in her mouth. She stopped chewing. Mama sat hunched over the table as if her head were about to fall into her plate, her food untouched. Nettie couldn't swallow. She could barely move, her arms and legs heavy as logs. This was what they'd all been waiting for. And dreading. Time to put Essie's spirit to rest. Wasn't it?

She eased herself away from the table, spat the hotcake into the slop bucket, and came back to lay a hand on her mother's shoulder. It was as stiff and unmoving as a rock. Nettie went outside and sat heavily on the step.

Down by the barn, Ben mounted his horse. He rode up the slope and stopped in front of Nettie. "Gotta ride to Sunburst for the preacher, and then over to Margie's and Lola's."

Nettie nodded, dread's dark presence beside her.

The next morning Margie bustled in with her family. Floyd and Lola followed, Lola's abdomen rounded now with pregnancy. Although Papa had ridden to tell them of Esther's death as soon as he was able to travel, Nettie's sisters hadn't been able to come until now. With a shocked look at Mama's near-catatonic state, hugs and murmurs, they set to straightening the house. Their brisk efficiency and the laughter and cries of Margie's children created a brief stir of life inside. At least for a little while, Nettie could stand back and let her sisters care for and comfort Mama and Papa, something she had tried so hard to do, but didn't quite know how. For now, maybe she could put aside that helpless, lost feeling and absorb some of her sisters' tender care.

～～

A day after Nettie's sisters arrived, Reverend Mahler rode up; then neighbors began arriving with casseroles and pies and cakes. Nettie watched all this activity as though from far away. She had an odd sensation of looking down on herself, going through the motions of greeting everyone, setting the food on the table and on the cupboards, making coffee.

Margie's kids ran around the house, expending pent-up energy. Nettie froze, momentarily seeing Essie at play with them. She blinked and shook her head to clear her vision. Her eyes stung. Just wishful thinking. *Dear God, why did you have to take little Essie?*

On the afternoon of Saturday, March 19, 1921, they gathered under the willow trees near the lake where the little box lay in its hole, a gash in the earth like an open wound. Raw, moist dirt lay piled around it. Nettie held herself rigid, her body numb. She would not cry. She could not. Her face felt chiseled from stone. It would crack if she smiled. Or let a tear slip.

The minister held his Bible in one hand. With the other he adjusted his hat a little firmer in the frigid March wind. "We settled this country with hope. We had hope again, that our children's lives would be better than ours. We work the land, and it returns bounty. But sometimes it takes our children, our loved ones, from us."

A gust flapped his long black coat against his legs. "We ask why? How can God let this happen to us?"

A small mewling sound made Nettie turn her head toward Mama. Her mother and Papa stood close, almost touching. Their faces seemed made of stone. Mama reached for his hand.

"I don't have the answers." A look passed over the minister's face like guilt for not being able to offer more comfort. "I just know that God has his reasons for taking His children home with Him. And we can be assured that our little Esther Marie Brady is in a better place." He bowed his head. "Let us pray."

Emptiness filled Nettie. She would never see her little sister again. Never hear that delighted little chortle. Essie's own baby language. Nettie would never be able to teach her to ride. A sob gathered low in her chest. She swallowed hard, choking it back. *No. Not now.* She would not cry.

"Amen." The minister stepped back.

Papa stepped forward, picked up the shovel, and threw a scoop of dirt into the hole. The heavy, moist clods thumped on the wood. Joe added a shovelful, then Ben and Eddie took their turns. Little Chuck, one hand clinging to Mama's skirt, picked up a clod and tossed it in. Then they all stepped away, eyes lowered. Two neighbor men grabbed the shovels to fill in the grave.

Nettie paused at the edge, one hand searching her coat pocket. The damp, earthy smell filled her nose. She brought her hand out, gazed at the piece of blue satin hair ribbon for a moment, then dropped it onto Essie's coffin.

Inside the house, everyone filled plates and stood around talking about the toll from the influenza. Nearly everyone had lost someone or knew somebody who died. Nettie watched these stoic faces. Her family wasn't alone in their grief. She wasn't the only one who would miss a sister. But that didn't make it seem any easier to bear. Nettie held her fists tight to her sides. Baby Essie was precious. She should have lived.

"It got ol' man Franz over in the valley," one woman reported around a mouthful of potato salad.

"The Murdock family lost grandma *and* three kids." Another clucked in sympathetic disbelief.

"I was so sick, at first I was afraid I was gonna die." A man chuckled. "Then I was afraid I wasn't."

"My hired hand, Tex, brought it to us. We're all fine now, but we were laid up for three solid weeks," Jim Ferguson chimed in.

"I still have the cough." The echoes of loss and illness continued around the room.

Nettie shook her head in bewilderment. How could something like this devastate whole families, whole communities? And Tex, the one who'd started all this for them. He'd survived. *But he killed Essie.* Nettie felt a surge of anger, then stifled the feeling, just like the sobs that had threatened. She just couldn't wish death on anyone, even him.

She also couldn't understand why she and Joe had been spared. Perhaps because someone had been needed to care for the rest of the family. And she had done it, too. All the hard work that Mama usually did. But she hadn't been able to save Esther. Nettie bit her lip, the pain taking away the urge to cry.

Papa still had the cough. His lungs were weakened, and for the longest time when he exerted himself a little too much, he would double over with spasms, trying to clear his breathing. Nettie felt a queer flutter in her stomach and her hands shook when this happened. What if they lost Papa? She and Joe couldn't run this ranch by themselves. What if the sickness came back?

For the last three months, since Essie died, this formless terror had hovered just over her shoulder and roared its ugly threats in the dark wakeful hours of the night. Many nights she covered her head with her pillow and tried to shut it out by thinking of riding like the wind on Toby's back.

At dusk, Nettie slipped away from the gathering and walked down the hill toward the lake. She knelt by the little mound of fresh earth, and to the small wooden cross she gently tied the other half of the blue ribbon that had been Esther's birthday gift to her.

Little Essie was gone. She was in heaven now. At least that's what the minister had said. What was heaven like?

Nettie bit hard on her lower lip. Maybe it was like riding Toby, flying free in the breeze. Tears formed hot in her eyes.

Be happy, Essie. Be free.

———

As the days lengthened and sunshine warmed the air to bring forth the first green spears of grass, Mama awakened from her stupor. She threw herself into spring cleaning, seemingly determined to eradicate every spiderweb from every corner of the house. She hung the bedding out in the fresh breeze, beat the rugs within an inch of their lives, and threw all the winter clothing into the big copper tub to boil. Mama even got down on her hands and knees with a brush and a bucket of hot, soapy water to deep-clean the floors.

Nettie helped when she could, but mostly she stayed out of her mother's way. She felt an odd sense of lightness. A burden she hadn't known she was carrying had been lifted. And somehow she realized that Mama needed time alone with this backbreaking, bone-numbing, sweat-producing hard work to rid herself of the demons of death.

Even though Mama was closer to being her old self, Nettie knew that life would never be the same. Marie and Tom came to visit in April, full of plans for the new rodeo season. Marie clucked and murmured around Nettie's family, enveloping them in care and concern. Glad for Marie's womanly attention, Nettie felt another layer of heaviness peel away. She was caught up in the Gibsons' enthusiasm for the coming summer.

Over a supper of ham and beans one evening, Marie broached the subject once again. "There's a big rodeo in Miles City in June, and we'd be honored to take Nettie along with us."

Nettie caught a flicker of the old anger pass over her mother's face. Mama's lips thinned.

Marie set down her fork. "It would give her a good idea of what the life is like."

"That's really not a bad idea." Papa buttered another slice of bread. "She may find she doesn't even like it."

"We'll keep a close eye on her," Tom added.

Nettie gritted her teeth. "Why are you all talking like I'm not even here?" As if she was some little girl. She steeled herself with a deep breath. "Thank you, Marie, Tom. But I can't go. I need to stay here and help Mama."

Papa stopped in mid-bite. Her brothers stared at her, wide-eyed. Mama had a shocked look on her face, like a sage hen startled from the sheltering brush. She opened her mouth, then closed it, opened it again. "I don't need to be taken care of."

Nettie frowned. "But I—"

Mama interrupted. "Sure, make me the villain. You know how I feel about women riding in rodeos. But now it's 'Nettie has to give up her dream to stay and help poor ol' Mama.'" Her voice took on a sarcastic tone.

"Now, Ada," Papa began.

Her mother threw up her hands in exasperation. "Fine. Let her go rodeo. There's nothing we can do or say to change her mind. Maybe she'll find some cowboy willing to marry her and teach her some sense."

Nettie clenched her fists under the table until her fingernails dug into her palms, as if the physical pain could take away the hurt she felt inside. Her face blazed. "Moth-er. That is not fair and you know it."

A stricken look came over Mama's face and suddenly tears ran down her cheeks. She sat for a long moment, staring at the tabletop, then got up from her chair. "Go to the rodeo. I don't care anymore." She walked out of the kitchen to her bedroom.

Nettie felt all hollow inside. Mama had just given up on her, left her all alone. Right in front of everybody, in front of her hero Marie.

And after Nettie had volunteered to stay, instead of going to the rodeo. Isn't that what Mama wanted?

The conversation kept replaying in her head. What should she have done differently? She just didn't know what Mama wanted. Nettie thought her mother needed comfort and help since Essie died. Did she really not care about Nettie anymore? A sensation of darkness descended around her, like when storm clouds suddenly appeared out of nowhere on a summer day.

The conversation started up around her again, as if nothing had happened. Nettie didn't join in, but sat stricken with that sense of doom. When supper was over and the dishes were done, Papa reappeared from the bedroom. "It's all right with both of us if you go. If you want to."

Nettie stood holding the dishtowel, stunned. How could she ever begin to figure out what her mother wanted? "Of course I do." Marie winked at her. Nettie blinked and tried to smile. *Well at least I'll finally get to go to a big rodeo.*

CHAPTER TEN

Mama never mentioned the rodeo subject again, as if pretending nothing had happened and everything was back to normal. For the next month, Nettie walked through her chores in a trance. The black cloud hovered over her. She tried to summon up excitement about going to the Miles City Roundup, but Mama's outburst had dampened any enthusiasm Nettie could muster.

One day, she couldn't stand it any longer. "Papa, why did Mama get so mad at me and say she didn't care? Doesn't she love me anymore?"

The *swish-swish* of milking stopped. Papa turned his head from the cow's side. A puzzled furrow appeared between his eyebrows. "Why, honey, of course she loves you. More than ever." He stood and moved the milk pail out of reach of the cow's hind legs. "Losing Essie has been very hard on your mama."

Nettie puckered her face. "But that's why I said I'd stay home and help her."

"I know." Papa smiled and put a big hand on her shoulder. "It's hard to understand. I think it's because she wants you to be happy, to have your own life, not have to stay home and take care of her and the kids."

"That sure was a funny way to show it." Nettie scuffed her boot in the dirt.

Papa chuckled. "Yup. Us grown-ups ain't perfect either." Nettie shook her head as she took the milk pail to the house. *I guess they're not.* At least she wasn't the only one who felt lacking sometimes.

—⁓—

On a soft early Monday in June, Nettie stopped in the midst of packing her valise. Maybe she shouldn't go on this great adventure. What if Mama got so sad again that she couldn't cook and clean and take care of everybody? But if Nettie didn't go now, she might not have another chance. Hurriedly, she finished packing. *If Mama needs help, Lola or Margie can come over.*

She paused outside her parents' bedroom door. "Good-bye, Mama. I'm leaving for the train depot."

Mama stepped out and gave Nettie a long hug. "Have a good time, dear. Take care of yourself." She handed Nettie a cloth-wrapped bundle. "Some of the rodeo money you won, so you can eat and maybe buy yourself a memento."

Nettie could hardly believe what she heard. Mama was actually letting her go. She had just quit fighting the idea. Nettie reached out and hugged her mother back. "Are you sure, Mama? Will you be okay?"

Her mother nodded. "I'm fine. You go. Have a good time."

The black cloud of grief that had hovered over both of them lifted from Nettie's shoulders. "Thank you, Mama. If, when I win something, I'll pay you back."

—⁓—

On the train, Nettie settled in across from Marie and Tom and pressed her nose against the window to watch eastern Montana's changing vistas. A cowboy trotted his horse through a nearby meadow. An image of a train trip from long ago flashed across her mind.

She turned to Marie. "The first time I rode a train was when I was six, when we moved here from Idaho. That was the biggest adventure of my life, until now."

Marie's eyes sparkled. "Well, this is just the beginning of many more."

Nettie gazed out the window again. "That was when I saw a man riding a coal-black horse near the tracks. He waved at us. Then, he just kicked the horse into a gallop and raced alongside the train." Her focus softened, picturing the horse's muscles as they gathered and lengthened beneath its sleek coat, its long legs devouring the distance. "I knew then I wanted a horse like that. I've always known this. I have to ride."

"Of course you do."

Nettie couldn't help but grin. And now she was going to a big rodeo with her heroine. "Oh, I can't wait to compete. What events are you going to enter?"

"Well, I'll be doing some trick-riding exhibitions, and the saddle-bronc riding, and of course the races."

"You ride racehorses, too?"

Marie nodded. "Grew up riding my dad's racers. I'm one of only two licensed women jockeys in the United States."

Nettie raised her eyebrows. Her admiration grew. "Wow." She turned back to the window and watched the dusk fall gently over the rolling hills.

Trains brought exciting things into her life.

~ ✦ ~

In Miles City, they unloaded their horses from the boxcar, then rode to the rodeo grounds to set up their tents for the five-day roundup. Nettie felt like her younger brother in a candy store. It seemed like thousands of cowboys and horses were everywhere. And she'd thought the Browning rodeo was big.

"This is grand." She craned her neck to take in all the sights as she rode alongside Marie and Tom.

"You ain't seen nothin' yet." Marie laughed. "Just wait till you get to the Cheyenne Stampede."

Nettie grinned. This was already an adventure far beyond her hopes. "I can't wait." Anticipation fluttered like a bird inside her. Would she be able to measure up, make Marie proud? And Mama. Nettie had to bring home some money to impress her mother.

Marie reached up and undid the red silk scarf from her neck. "I want you to have this."

Nettie ran her fingers over the smooth fabric. "It's beautiful. Thank you." With a sense of grown-up pride, she tied it under her collar, just like Marie.

The next morning Marie knocked on Nettie's tent. "Ready to rodeo?"

Nettie stepped out. "Ready." Marie stood grinning, dressed in a voluminous brown divided skirt. Nettie stared for a moment. "Are you wearing a skirt to compete?"

Her friend gave a wry grimace. "I do feel so much more comfortable in a pair of Tom's denims, and that's what I usually wear around home. But it just ain't done in the bigger rodeos."

"Oh." Nettie nodded. She understood the difference a pair of pants made in how she felt, riding. But that meant she'd have to wear a skirt to compete, too. She grimaced. "Too bad. One of these days, we're gonna have to show them. If we're good enough to compete with men, we're good enough to wear denims, too."

"That's the spirit." Marie laughed and led the way to the corral for their horses.

The festivities began with a parade. A brass band played "The Beautiful City of Miles," and colorful floats, brightly dressed cowboys, and cowgirls rode through the downtown and out to the rodeo grounds. After a stagecoach holdup enactment, the rodeo began with a horse race. It was a huge, noisy affair, dusty and hot with jostling crowds, shouts, and cheers. Nettie even saw a camera crew taking motion pictures of the whole event. The excitement was contagious, exhilarating. She bounced on Toby's back as she rode alongside.

The end of the parade column broke into ragged lines, with riders hurrying to the arena to watch the horse races. Nettie found a spot near the track where she'd have a good view from Toby's back.

Marie and one other woman, clad awkwardly in their skirts, looked like children among the lineup of men.

"Who you bettin' on?" A deep voice spoke nearby. Another man guffawed. "How about a sawbuck on which woman comes in last?"

Nettie pinched her lips together and moved Toby away. How could they make such assumptions?

At the starting shot, the horses thundered down the track, two or three vying for leadership, the rest left behind in the dust. Nettie leaned forward in her saddle and squinted through the haze. Where was Marie? Yup, there she was, one of the three in front.

Nettie let out an encouraging yell. "Go, Marie!" Toby danced from side to side, as if sensing her excitement.

Around the circular track the horses galloped. First the man on the gray in the lead. Then the cowboy on the bay. Now the gray again. Marie, in third place, hunched her small body close to her black's neck. It looked like she was talking to him. Inch by inch, they gained ground. Excited anticipation skittered through Nettie like leaves in the wind. Yes, they were overtaking the bay. A couple hundred or so onlookers in the bleachers roared.

Nettie craned her neck to see where the other woman was, somewhere in the middle of the pack.

One lap to go. The gray's rider glanced over his left shoulder and flailed his quirt as he saw Marie closing the gap. His horse leaped ahead. Marie ducked closer to her horse's neck. Now they were nose to tail. Then the black's head was even with the gray's saddle. As the horses thundered down the track in front of Nettie, the man's face twisted in a terrible grimace. He slashed the quirt faster and harder.

Nettie could hardly stand it. *Is he going to hit Marie?* She whipped off her red scarf and waved it as she screamed, "Come on, Marie, c'mon."

Now they were neck and neck. The finish line loomed. The cheering thundered as the riders crossed and then sat upright, slowing their mounts. Who'd won? Nettie chewed on her lower lip. She peered across the track to see the judges' signals. Then came the announcement over the bullhorn. "And the winner is . . . Marie Gibson on Coal Dust!"

Nettie whooped. Whew, that was close. She trotted her horse toward her friend and slipped from Toby's back to give Marie a big hug. "You were great. What a ride!"

Marie waved her hat at the crowd. "Thanks. That was fun." As the groomsmen led the racehorses away, she turned to the other woman rider. "Alice Greenough, I'd like you to meet Nettie Brady. This gal's gonna give us a run for our money pretty quick."

The young woman smiled and dipped her head in greeting. "Good to have you with us. Come, sit with us in the grandstand."

Nettie flushed with pleasure. This Alice seemed real friendly, like Marie.

"Lad-ees and gentle-men," the announcer called out. "To give us a little break in the excitement, the next event is an espadrille, a square dance on horseback."

The women participants rode gracefully into the ring, dressed in sequined and beaded vests, with bright red, yellow, or blue silk scarves around their necks and waists. Some sported fancy feathers in their hats, and others showed a provocative peek of satin bloomers from under their skirts.

The audience showed their appreciation with whoops and cheers. Nettie watched the colorful, flashy show with Marie and Alice, clapping to the music. "That looks like so much fun." Maybe she could do that too, sometime. So much opportunity in rodeo.

Nettie leaned toward Alice during a break between dances. "Where are you from?"

Alice took off her white hat and shook out her shoulder-length brown curls. "Red Lodge, over by Billings."

Marie ducked her head sideways at the other woman. "She grew up on the back of a horse, just like we did."

"Yup. Dad always had a lot of horses around. Two, three hundred."

"Wow! What I wouldn't give for that many horses." Nettie could just picture the herd grazing in the Sweet Grass hills. On her very own ranch. "So you got to ride a lot?"

"Oh, yeah. Lot's of 'em weren't even halter-broke. Dad'd assign horses to me and my brothers." She let out a chuckle. "One of his favorite expressions was, 'If you can't ride 'em, walk.' That's how we learned to ride."

Nettie joined in the laughter. It was nice to know another woman who felt the same way about riding as she did. What a great family Alice must have.

"Tell her how you started bronc ridin'." Marie nudged her friend.

"Well, first time I rode in front of a crowd was a couple years ago, when I was sixteen. At Forsyth, not far from here. The fellas were teasing me, and first thing I knew, they had a big ol' gray bronc saddled up, I was up on his back, and they turned me loose in front of the grandstand. I didn't buck off, and I thought, hey, that wasn't so bad."

Nettie's face flushed with excitement. "Yeah, me too. Only, I rode a steer at a neighbor's ranch rodeo. Rode it to a stop."

"Welcome to the rodeo world." Alice patted her on the shoulder.

Nettie felt a warm glow of acceptance. She was a part of their circle now.

The announcer bellowed out the next event, so the young women sat back to watch the steer roping. The event would run two days, and anyone who roped and tied his steer in two minutes or less qualified to rope again in the finals.

"First prize is two hundred fifty dollars cash," Marie announced. "And a fancy silver-mounted saddle worth four hundred fifty dollars from the Al Furstnow Saddlery."

Nettie felt her eyes widen. *Wow! I might get rich winning.* If she could do that, Mama wouldn't have to take in mending any more.

Alice's face lit up. "I hope Tom wins." She laughed. "Only because my brothers aren't competing, of course."

The first four contestants missed tying their steers altogether.

Next out of the chute was Marie's husband, Tom. He had drawn a lightweight steer with small horns. Nettie sat on the edge of her seat with the other women, tension etched on their faces. She liked the Englishman and hoped he would qualify for the finals. Some of the older cowboys made fun of his clipped accent, but he could ride and rope as well as any of them.

The steer dashed for the open arena, Tom's horse right behind. Tom threw the rope and made a good catch. But when his horse stopped to jerk the rope tight, it slipped off the steer's short horns. Nettie grimaced.

"No!" Marie leaned forward, pounding her knees with her fists.

Tom turned the horse quickly, chased the steer back toward the starting point, and threw the rope again. The loop missed.

The crowd sighed, "Aaahhh." The seconds ticked away. Would he make it within two minutes? Nettie held her breath.

C'mon, Tom.

With no restrictions on the number of times he could try, Tom built a new loop. The steer turned and headed straight for the grandstand. When the animal came to the fence, he turned and ran to the right, just as Tom roped him and turned his horse to the left. The steer came to the end of the rope, snapped to a stop, and hit the ground. Tom was on him, wrapping his feet while they were still in the air.

Nettie let out her breath.

"O-n-n-ne minute, fifty-eight seconds-s-s." The announcer yelled the time. A cheer rose from the grandstands.

Nettie exchanged an open-mouthed look with Marie. He'd had to throw three loops to make his catch, but Tom was going to the finals. Nettie hooted with delight as the other two women jumped up and down and hugged each other.

"Well, nice to have met you, Nettie." Alice smiled as she took her leave. "I'll be cheerin' for you when you ride."

Nettie nodded. "Thanks." Alice seemed just a nice as Marie and genuinely willing to accept Nettie into the circle of "real" cowgirls. This could be a valuable friendship.

By late afternoon, cheers had faded, dust settled, and onlookers scattered, following the last event of the day. Nettie and Marie rode back toward their tents.

"Say, let's you and me go downtown and eat supper at the cafe. Tom's got other things a-goin' tonight, and I'm gettin' a little tired of beans in camp."

"Okay. I'd like that." Nettie hadn't really seen much of the town yet and this would be a chance to explore "city" life.

The two women unsaddled their horses and let them loose to eat and drink at the camp corral.

Then they collected buckets of fresh water from the cook tent to wash up. Marie brushed stray hairs from her face with the back of her hand. "Boy, is this gonna feel good. See you in a little while." She walked with a bow-legged stiffness toward her and Tom's tent.

Weary, but still atingle with excitement, Nettie stepped into her own warm, musty tent, closed the canvas flap, and filled her metal wash pan. She took off her grimy shirt and threw it onto her bedroll. Standing in her camisole and bloomers, she splashed the cold water on her face and arms. My, it felt good to rinse off the day's accumulation of dust and sweat. Her mind swirled with the events of the day. The exhilaration of Marie's close race. Tom's heart-stopping three loops in less than two minutes. The beautiful, colorful espadrille.

And tonight. Nettie could hardly wait. Eating in a restaurant, watching all the people. Oh, this was going to be such fun.

"Knock, knock." Marie stuck her head into Nettie's tent. "About ready to go?"

"You bet I am." She followed Marie's example and donned a clean white blouse and a divided skirt. Then they saddled their horses and rode into the heart of town.

~ ⌣ ~

The main street bustled with rodeo celebrants. Nettie and Marie tied their horses to the hitching post in front of the Range Riders Café. They stepped into the hubbub: the rhythm of clanking silverware, the buzz of a dozen conversations, and the sizzle of chicken-fried steak. Nettie's mouth watered.

Marie touched the brim of her hat at the cowboys sitting on stools at the long counter. She pointed toward the back of the room. "There's a spot." She threaded her way around tables full of rodeo riders who called out greetings.

"Howdy, Marie."

"Ol' Tom's a heckuva good roper."

"Who's this here purty gal you got with ya?"

Nettie blushed and stayed close to Marie.

They finally reached the table and ordered well-done steaks. A steady stream of Marie's old acquaintances passed by and stopped a moment to chat. Nettie savored each bite of beef and mashed potatoes with dark brown gravy. It tasted heavenly after several days of beans. They paid with tickets they'd received from the rodeo producer for being participants.

The lighted window of the Miles City Saddlery next door beckoned as they left the cafe. Nettie peered in. "It's still open."

Marie shifted a toothpick in her mouth. "Yeah, they stay open late to accommodate the rodeo crowd this week. Get half their business, evenings."

Nettie gazed at the hand-tooled saddle in the window. Intertwined roses were carved onto the flaps, set off by silver conchos. "Let's go in for a minute."

The sharp-yet-mellow smell of leather overtook her as she walked wide-eyed around the shop. Never had she seen so many brand-new saddles and bridles. The polished leather shone in the glow of electric lightbulbs. And the chaps: plain leather, some decorated with fringes or silver conchos. Even angora ones. A tingle raced up her spine. She glanced around to see if Marie was watching and slowly put out a hand to touch the white wool. So soft. So pretty. Maybe someday.

She could see herself, dressed in these chaps, a bright-colored shirt and hand-tooled boots, riding in a saddle like the one in the window. Maybe she'd be rodeo queen, or steer riding champion, or . . .

Marie grabbed a pair of soft leather, double-palmed roping gloves from the shelf nearby. "Better get yourself a pair. They work good for ridin' steers, too."

Jolted out of her dream, Nettie nodded. She had just enough money for new gloves. The shirt and chaps would have to wait. Besides, she wanted to get those boots first.

By the time they left the saddlery, new gloves in hand, the air was cooler, and darkness had drifted like fog over the town. Moths flew into the light from the store window that dimly illuminated the boardwalk. Down at the end of Main Street, music blared from Bennie's Bar. Despite Prohibition, the double doors swung constantly as noisy cowboys went in and out, some carrying bottles of bootleg whiskey, laughing, cursing, and whooping. Nettie couldn't help but stare. Next to the bar, men went up and down a set of stairs lit by a red lantern.

"Is that a store up there?" Nettie frowned and looked at Marie.

Marie chuckled. "That's the 'bawdy house.' Remember, we got some colored tickets when we signed up for the rodeo, like the green ones we used at the cafe? Well, the men get a red one that'll get them some lovin' at the red-light house."

"Ohhh." Nettie pursed her lips and raised her eyebrows. She'd never dreamed of such a thing. "You mean, men pay—?"

"Yup."

What kind of woman would do that for a living? What kind of man would take advantage? Nettie's mind raced. Pictures of the old bulls servicing their cows. Snippets of the stories she'd read in her dime novels. Whispered conversations between her sisters. So that must be what Mama meant when she talked about "loose women." How awful. Marie didn't seem bothered, though.

Nettie shuddered, but a sense of fascination kept her eyes focused on those stairs.

Just then, the noise from inside escalated as the bar erupted into a free-for-all. Nettie froze at the sound of breaking glass and the splat of flesh against bone. Two cowpokes rolled out the saloon door, fists flying.

Excitement and fascination kept Nettie rooted to the spot. Marie grabbed her arm. "Let's get outta here."

She turned and followed Marie across the street. Nettie stopped to watch. "Aren't they afraid of getting arrested? Isn't drinking illegal here, too?"

Marie chuckled. "That's the farthest thing from their minds. They're just lettin' off steam. Besides, you know how the sheriffs in Montana mostly look the other way on Prohibition."

"Yeah, the cowboys at home talk about what a ridiculous law it is and how several of them make extra money bringing in liquor from Canada." Nettie shook her head at the irony. Papa disagreed with the law, too, but Mama thought it was terrible to break it. Nettie couldn't quite understand what all the fuss was about. She'd tasted whiskey. Vile stuff. She shrugged. Drinking liquor must just be something men liked to do.

But these cowboys. They were a lot rougher than anyone she'd ever met. She shivered. She couldn't imagine her brothers being involved in a fight like this, even though they occasionally pummeled each other over some imagined slight.

A bottle sailed through the air and crashed in the street inches away from the women. Nettie gasped and took a step backward, as if she could hide behind her friend.

"Aw, it's all just in fun." Marie chuckled. "But that was a little close. Besides, the law might be arriving any minute to break up the fight. Let's head back to the tents." She turned away from the escalating melee.

Nettie hesitated, then followed, glancing back over her shoulder with a guilty sense of fascination and exhilaration.

They collected their horses from the hitching post in front of the cafe and soon the raucous sounds of nightlife in town gave way to the music of crickets and bullfrogs as they headed back to the campground in the cool evening air.

When Nettie eased herself into her bedroll, visions of red lights and fisticuffs flitted through her mind. Excitement and uncertainty churned through her. Is that what "city" life was all about? It was all so much, so fast, so violent. But that's where the rodeos were, and rodeos meant crowds of rowdy cowboys. If competing in rodeos meant traveling to cities, well . . . Nettie drifted off to sleep thinking of train rides, parades, and crowds yelling her name.

⸻

Five o'clock came too soon, the camp cook banging his big iron kettle with a spoon. Nettie splashed cold water, left over from last night, on her face. Then she pulled on a blouse and divided skirt and went with Marie on the short walk to feed and water their horses at the corral. Afterward, they joined others at the cook tent for flapjacks and coffee.

Following the morning parade, the crowd gathered early for the popular trick-riding exhibition. As soon as the spectators saw the women riders arrive at the arena they clapped and cheered. Marie would also take part in this event, so she left to go get ready.

Bertha "Birdie" Askin from near Miles City was the first to perform. She wore a fringed leather vest, a white blouse with flared sleeves, a leather skirt, high-topped boots, and ribbons that streamed from her hair. She warmed up the audience by riding while standing on top of her saddle as her horse galloped across the arena.

Nettie "ooohed" and "aaahed" along with the crowd as Bertha executed a vault. She slipped off one side of the horse, hit the ground with her feet, then vaulted back into the saddle. Nettie had never seen such spectacular trick riding. The woman certainly was strong and agile.

When it was Marie's turn, she added strap work, with specially designed holds on the saddle. These helped anchor her while she hung off the side of her horse, inches off the ground as he galloped around the arena. Nettie leaned forward on the bleacher seat, fearful with every hoofbeat that the horse would kick her friend in the head. When Marie's exhibition was over, she sat back, relieved. What talent that took. Marie must have practiced a lot.

With each performer, the audience's reaction grew louder. In the Roman race finale, the women rode two horses, one foot on the back of each. Nettie could almost feel the strain in her own thighs. This exhibition drew thunderous, stomping approval.

When her friend returned to the bleachers, Nettie could hardly contain herself. "Marie, that was fantastic. Could you teach me how to do that?"

"Sure, why not?"

Together they watched Bob Askin, Bertha's son-in-law, and Paddy Ryan, both local bronc-riding champions, compete. "Look't how he spurs." Marie pointed at Askin. "It's different from everybody else. He gets a higher reach in front. What a rider!"

Next came the bull riders, no saddle to help them keep their seat, just a surcingle and tightly clamped knees. Nettie watched several cowboys make successful rides. Others hightailed it for the fence when they were thrown while the rodeo clowns with brightly painted smiles tried to distract the pawing, snorting ton of fury.

Then, the next rider flew through the air and crumpled on the ground. Nettie gasped. *He's not getting up.* The bull turned, saw the man down, and charged, horns lowered. Running toward the beast, the clown jangled his bells and shouted. The pickup man galloped in, cutting between the animal and certain death. By now, the cowboy was on his feet and grabbed hold of his mounted rescuer.

The crowd exhaled a collective breath of relief, and the knot in Nettie's stomach released. *Rodeo is dangerous, too.* But she couldn't think of it in the same way as the drunken brawl she'd seen last night. That was different. Riding was a challenge, pitting your skills against the wiliness of the animal. That's why cowboys did it. That's why she wanted to.

Nettie scuffed through the dust as she followed Marie to the chutes where preparations were underway for the women's bronc-riding event.

Marie scoffed as they watched men saddle a horse and tie the stirrups against its sides with a piece of leather that ran from one stirrup to the other under its belly. "Dadgummed stupid rule that women have to ride with hobbles."

"Why do they have to?" Nettie asked.

A grizzled cowboy grinned through the poles of the chute. "It's just for your protection, ma'am. So's you don't fall off."

Marie humphed. "Oh, sure, I hate fallin' on the ground. But I can't spur with them things either. And if I was to draw a really rank horse, I wouldn't be able to get my feet free of the stirrups. That could be a darn sight more dangerous than gettin' bucked off."

The cowboy shrugged and bent back to his task. Marie made a face and turned away.

"Well, good luck with your ride." Nettie clapped Marie on the back and headed for the grandstand, where she watched the women's event with fascination, and compared it to the men's bronc riding. More pickup men seemed to circle the women riders than for the men bronc busters. The women couldn't escape their hobbled stirrups until these men came to their rescue.

Nettie rolled her eyes. This wasn't fair. What if the horse fell and rolled on its rider?

While the men riders could simply grab onto the pickup man's saddle and jump to the ground, a woman required a pickup man's arm around her waist to steady her while she kicked out of the stirrups.

Nettie tossed her head and sniffed. *They get to put their hands on us, play "hero," and sweep us off to safety.* She'd just as soon be treated the same as a man. *But maybe they don't want us to be the same.*

Nettie's palms broke into a sweat as the barker announced Marie's ride. She could feel her friend's every jolt and twist. But Marie performed well and drew an enthusiastic response from the crowd. *Whew.* This rodeo stuff was hard on the nerves.

The next woman rider drew a rough bucker that threw her up and down and from side to side in the saddle. Nettie gritted her teeth, fearing the worst. On one such violent lunge, the woman's blouse caught on her saddle horn. With the next trip skyward, the garment ripped open to the skin. Nettie watched in horror as the rider's ample bosom, now unfettered, received a severe lashing along with the rest of her body. Every time her head went down, her bosom heaved upward. As the bell sounded, a pickup man hurried to her rescue, just below Nettie's vantage point in the stands.

Nettie felt her face redden in sympathy for the woman's plight. But instead of blushing and stammering about her predicament, the woman just yelled at her rescuer, "For gosh sakes, somebody get me off this horse before I black both my eyes."

Nettie laughed with relief, along with the crowd. *Gosh, I hope nothing like that happens to me when I make my ride.*

For certain, *she'd* never ride hobbled when she had the chance. And, she'd make sure she wore something a little more binding under her shirt.

She went to find Marie. "Boy, you're right about those hobbles. They sure are dangerous."

Her friend turned to Nettie with a grimace. "We get scored same as men on how good a bucker we draw and how well we stay on. But then they tie our stirrups down and give us specially picked horses that 'buck high and show pretty' instead of the outlaws the men get. How are we supposed to compete fair and square that way?"

"It's not fair women have to have special rules. We can ride just as well as any man." Nettie gritted her teeth. "Maybe they're afraid we'll beat them."

"Yeah." Marie took off her gloves. "Maybe."

Nettie put her fists on her hips. "Well, I'm not gonna let them do that to me."

Marie turned to her with a grin. "You're a spunky gal. Maybe you've got something there."

That evening they all sat around the campfire. Someone strummed a guitar. Several voices joined in on "Tying the Knots in the Devil's Tail," and "Ridin' Ol' Paint." Others spat tobacco into the fire and swapped comments about the day and stories from past contests.

With a warm feeling of camaraderie and sense of belonging, Nettie sat down near Askin. "What's your secret to riding so well?"

He took off his wide-brimmed Stetson, brushed a weathered hand over his head, and thought a moment. "Well, ma'am. Ridin' a buckin' horse is a lot like dancin' with a pretty girl. Just get in step and the rest comes naturally."

Nettie smoothed back her hair. Like dancing, huh? That was a nice image. Not too scary. She liked to dance.

⚬~⚬

The sun beat hot on Nettie's back as the women's events continued the next morning. All too soon it was time for steer riding. Her stomach felt like a beehive that had been clawed by a bear. If it weren't for the twenty-five-dollar prize money offered, she'd be tempted to sit this one out. Too many people watching. But, this is what she'd come for.

Again, she noticed that women riders were given special stock: steers that weren't quite as wild. Or stags, old bulls that had been castrated. Anger coursed through her. *We can ride just as good as men.*

She tucked her divided skirt between her legs and eased her body down onto the reddish-brown steer, which was being eared down in the chute, its ears twisted to keep it from throwing up its head and bucking while she mounted.

Nettie snugged both hands under the rigging and pinched her knees into the animal's sides, thankful there were no stirrups so women weren't required to ride hobbled in this event. She spurred forcefully as the steer bolted from the gate. Its first few jumps weren't too bad, and she began to feel the rhythm of the "dance." *Askin was right. This isn't too bad.*

Then the animal changed its tune and began to twist in the air. Nettie tried to counteract, but lost her balance, tossed from side to side. Once more she thought she had regained her seat as the steer settled into a more predictable rhythm. But before she could even think about the next move, the steer twisted to the left as it went into the air and then to the right as it landed.

Hands scrabbling for a grip, Nettie felt herself flying in slow motion. Instinctively, she thrust out her left hand as she plummeted into the dust. Her wrist folded with a sharp, nauseating pop. She lay crumpled and dazed in the dirt. Dirt that had been churned loose by a hundred angry hooves. A blob of hot, wet saliva slapped her cheek. She heard the raspy breaths pass just inches from her head.

Nettie opened her eyes to look full into the steer's angry face as he bucked above her. Her limbs froze with fear. At that moment, a pickup man snatched her from the ground. His strong arms held her above the steer's fury and carried her to safety. "Acts likes he's part Braymer bull. They don't just want you off, they want to trample you once you're down."

Nettie gulped. At that moment, she had a new appreciation for pickup men.

Marie came running and encircled Nettie's shoulders with her arm. "You're hurt."

"Aw, it's nothing." Nettie winced through the excruciating pain that shot through her arm. She'd been bucked off calves a few times at home, but had never been hurt. Oh, maybe a bruise or two, but nothing like this. She straightened her shoulders. "I'll be okay."

"No arguments now. I'm taking you to get checked out." Marie steered her away from the arena, and Nettie couldn't find voice enough to protest.

At the first-aid tent, the doctor peered over his spectacles.

"I'm afraid it's broken, young lady. We'll have to put a cast on it. No more steer ridin' for you for awhile."

"No." Nettie slumped in her chair. She wouldn't be able to hide her injury from Mama. A sickening feeling of failure weighed her down. No. This couldn't be happening. Not now. Just when she was finally being allowed to do what she loved so much. *What will Mama say?*

CHAPTER ELEVEN

A miserable situation. Nettie stood in Lola's kitchen, a feeling of helplessness washing over her. First, when she came home from Miles City, there was Mama glowering at her, making her feel like she'd done something terribly wrong. Nettie winced. *You'd think I'm the only girl who ever broke her arm.* Then Lola asked if Nettie could come help cook for the haying and threshing crews and care for the baby. Although it was a chance to get away from Mama—ten miles away—Nettie dreaded the "I told you so" looks and remarks from her sister.

Now this. She wielded the rolling pin in her right hand and looked at the lump of piecrust dough in front of her. She tried to roll it over the dough one-handed but only succeeded in pushing the blob around on the counter. What if her wrist didn't heal right? She might not be able to go back to rodeoing.

"Drat!" She grabbed the rolling pin by one handle and pounded the shapeless mass into submission.

Lola turned from the apples she was peeling. "What are you doing?" Her tone carried a hint of irritation.

Nettie frowned. "Oh, this is going to be a fun summer if you're going to be after me all the time."

"What do you mean? You're the one who's grouchy."

Nettie slammed the rolling pin onto the dough. "I am not. You're acting just like Mama."

"Hmmph." Lola stood, arms akimbo, a frown deepening the furrow between her eyes. Then her mouth twitched. She started to laugh. Her paring knife dropped to the floor.

"What?" Nettie looked at her sister, hysterically doubled over. Suddenly a chuckle bubbled up out of her own resentment and erupted into a belly laugh. Soon both were sitting on the floor, hands on each other's arms, tears streaming down their faces.

"If you could've seen yourself." Lola pointed and collapsed into laughter again.

"Well, it is a little hard to use a rolling pin with only one hand." Nettie picked up a piece of dough that had fallen on the floor and threw it at her sister.

"All right, that does it!" With a shriek, Lola scooped a hand into the bucket of peelings and heaved the slippery mess at Nettie.

"No fair!" Nettie leapt to her feet and scattered a handful of flour at Lola, giggling. This was a lot more fun than cooking.

The kitchen screen door opened with a loud squeak, and Lola's husband stepped in. He stopped short, seeing the mess on the floor, the sisters laughing uncontrollably. A big grin spread over Floyd's moon face. Unwrapping the bandanna from around his neck, he mopped the sweat from his receding hairline.

"So, where's my pie?"

Still giggling, Lola jumped up to give him a floury kiss. "Here's part of it."

He shook his head. "I dunno. You two girls are just havin' too much fun. I don't think that hayin' crew's gonna have anything to eat when they get here tomorrow."

"Oh, pshaw. Look at all the bread we made. Ten loaves." Lola opened the pantry door. "And the three chokecherry pies we already baked. Don't you worry."

Still grinning, Nettie got down on her hands and knees to clean up the mess. Lola and Floyd were so cute together. She almost wished for something like that. A comfortable, loving playfulness with someone. Naw, she really couldn't see herself acting that way with any man.

"Lola, you sure have changed since you got married," Nettie said later as she helped her sister get supper ready.

"Changed? What do you mean?"

"Well, you don't seem so critical and 'uppity' anymore." Nettie grinned.

"Uppity?" Lola put her hands on her hips and tried to scowl, but a smile teased the corners of her mouth.

Nettie giggled. "Yeah. You're more like a friend now, like when we were little girls. This is more fun."

Lola squeezed an arm around Nettie's shoulders. "It is, isn't it?"

⌒‿⌒

Even though Nettie was limited in what she could do one-handed, they managed to work around it. And she helped with little Elizabeth, just weeks old.

The baby—everybody called her Betsy—was such a cute little thing. Nettie could have spent hours just watching the sleeping baby's expressive face. In so many ways Betsy reminded her of Esther. Such a good baby, always smiling and cooing. She had already wrapped her tiny fingers around Nettie's heart as well as her thumb. The aching emptiness that Essie's death had left became bearable when she held this warm little life. Maybe Mama's heart would be healed, too, when she got to know her granddaughter better.

Every day Nettie and Lola cooked and baked, preparing three full meals. As soon as they finished the breakfast dishes, it was time to start peeling potatoes for dinner. Nettie worked slowly, gripping a potato with the fingers sticking out from her cast. More often than not, she ended up dropping it several times, but eventually got it peeled.

Feeding five hungry men took mounds of mashed potatoes and gravy, hunks of venison or beef, and all the fresh vegetables the garden had to offer. Ordinarily she would have detested this hard, hot work inside the house, made nearly unbearable by continually adding coal to the cook stove. But surprisingly, she found herself looking forward to each new day. She made a wry face at the thought. *What am I doing, turning into a "housewife" after all?*

The best part of it, though, was when she and Lola laughed. Cleansing, healing laughter that washed away the sadness death had brought into their lives.

Midafternoons, Nettie headed out to the fields with jugs of cold water and a batch of fresh cookies to sustain the workers until suppertime. The summer sun baked the earth as brown as the piecrusts she and Lola made. Nettie blushed when she caught herself watching one young man's muscled arms bulge as he scythed the tall crested-wheat grass for next winter's feed. She couldn't help but stare at all the men again, though, when they pitched fork after forkful of the golden hay onto stacks that grew out of the prairie like anthills.

The month of haying passed quickly, and by August the grain fields turned russet. In the evenings Nettie and Lola, carrying the baby, walked with Floyd along the edges of the fields. Every night he strolled out into the middle to pluck a bearded head from its dried stalk. He crushed it in his hand, blew the chaff away, and popped the hard wheat kernels into his mouth to test their ripeness.

Finally he made his declaration: "Yup, we're ready for the threshin' crew."

❦

Within a few days Nettie watched a great steam tractor chuff into the field, towing a cylindrical grain separator, one wagonload of coal, and another with about a dozen men.

"Where'd all those men come from? I don't recognize any of them from around here," Nettie asked Floyd.

"Most of 'em are from back east." He took off his hat to fan his red face, his forehead white where the hat usually rested. "The railroads are running special 'harvest excursion' fares. They're comin' west by the thousands, just for the season." Floyd turned to go talk to the men hooking up the machinery, squirting oil into various holes, and checking the long, crossed belts and pulleys that joined the separator to the steam engine.

Nettie frowned. Hmmm. That was a long way to travel just for a summer's work.

Although the kitchen was even hotter, with all their cooking, Nettie was glad she didn't have to work out in the ninety-degree, dusty fields. That work probably would've been even harder to do one-handed.

"Why don't you buy one of these steam tractors? Wouldn't that be easier?" Nettie later asked her brother-in-law. She thought of all the farms around that were just waiting for the steam-powered machine to come help, rather than having to do it by hand, like Papa had always done.

"Well, they're purty expensive." Floyd reached into a sack and tossed a handful of wheat into his mouth. "And I'd have to be gone the whole summer, away from Lola and Betsy, traveling all around to make enough money for it to pay. Although, the feller who owns this one says he makes his yearly pot in just a month's time."

Nettie took a mouthful of wheat, too, and scratched at the chaff that settled on her neck and around the mouth of her cast. So this fellow made a whole year's wages in just one month. What would be so bad about that? She crunched the nutty kernels until they formed a gummy gluten in her mouth that she could chew on for a long time. Cowboys also tried to make enough to live on all year during the few months of the rodeo season. That was a lot tougher to do. She turned back toward the house. But a lot more fun than running this noisy machine and getting filthy and itchy with dust and chaff.

Ah, rodeo. Nettie grimaced at her cast, due to come off in a couple of weeks. How long would it be till she could ride in a rodeo again? It looked like the chance was shot for this summer. Besides, Mama was still so hopping mad, it'd be best to let some time go by before she broached the subject again.

꠸꠸꠸

In September, when the work was done at Lola and Floyd's, Lola brought Nettie back home. She and baby Betsy stayed for a few days.

From the moment they arrived, Mama sat in the rocking chair holding the little girl, chores, weather, and others now forgotten. She crooned lullabies, rattled a small jar with marbles, jiggled Betsy on her knee, bathed her, and changed her.

"I don't know if Mama'll let me take her home again," Lola whispered to Nettie with a small laugh.

With the baby around, Mama seemed to put all her sadness aside. All her love that was meant for Esther now shone through for this small being.

Nettie was glad it took Mama's attention away from her.

Her cast now gone and her wrist getting stronger, she often escaped to Toby's back for long gallops through the sage. She didn't dare broach the subject of rodeos, however. With winter coming up soon anyway, she figured she would just wait. Maybe her mother's edict of "no more rodeos" would be forgotten by spring. She sure hoped so. It would be a long, dismal winter without a rodeo to look forward to.

With Essie gone, things were not the same. A loneliness plagued her even with a large family around.

Papa worked as hard and long as ever. His weakness and cough from last winter's influenza had burned away with the summer sun and the sweat of hard work. He had a hound-dog sadness etched in the wrinkles around his eyes, though, and several times he surprised Nettie with a long and tender squeeze, his muscular arm about her shoulders. That felt so nice, so warm, and she longed for it to happen more often.

She looked forward to Papa or a neighbor going to town for the mail once a week. Every night, she reread the postcards Marie sent from her various travels. "Great fun at Cheyenne Frontier Days. Wish you could be here." The card showed a picture of a cowboy on the back of a rearing bronc.

Nettie sighed. *Oh, I wish I could be there too.*

On the back of one card that depicted a big city, "Calgary Stampede was a sell-out crowd. I won 'best woman bronc rider' again."

She lay back on her bed. *Good for you, Marie. Will I ever have that chance?*

Nettie itched to be there with Marie. Would she ever be free to go again, to feel the heady, blood-stirring excitement? Or would Mama insist that she stay close to home and marry an old farmer whose only interest in horses was how well they could pull a plow?

Her daydreams took her back to the Miles City Roundup: the pageantry of the parades and espadrilles, the adrenaline-producing excitement of watching the horse races and the bronc riders, the horror of seeing a cowboy flung from the back of a bull, crumpling to the ground as the bull came back to finish him off. Thank goodness for pickup men.

She'd never tell Mama about this part. Nettie's wrist gave her a twinge. Her injury had been nothing in comparison to what happened to some riders, but Mama'd sure been upset about it. Part of the lure, the excitement of rodeo, was defying the odds, escaping injury, besting that thousand-pound whirling devil of fury. Even after being injured, many a rider came back for more, ribs wrapped tightly, an arm in a sling or a white bandage peeking from beneath his hat.

She just hoped Mama would never find out about all this. It might be easier for Nettie to get her mother's approval to go rodeo that way. What she didn't know couldn't hurt her, surely.

CHAPTER TWELVE

As winter settled into a pattern of cold, snow, and long days cooped up in the house, Nettie wrote postcards and letters to Marie.

December 25, 1921
Dear Marie,

Christmas Day. Doesn't really seem like Christmas this year.
    Had a snowstorm two days ago. Margie and Lola couldn't come. Very quiet. Not many presents. Got another book to read, My Antonia *by Willa Cather. Mama thinks I should read something better than dime novels. Looks good.*
    Times are hard, Papa says. I think they're still too sad. Almost a year since everybody got sick.

Nettie put down her pen and went to gaze out the window. At the bottom of the hill, she saw Mama kneeling in the snow by Essie's grave. The wisp of blue ribbon Nettie had tied to the cross fluttered in the breeze. Something caught deep inside, a feeling that she might just stop breathing, and if she stood still enough maybe things would go back to the way they used to be.

Finally, Nettie willed herself to turn away from the window, to breathe again. *Mama and Papa never talk about it.* She sprawled across her bed. *I'm sad too.* Did that empty feeling ever go away? Did a person ever forget about someone who died? She didn't want to forget Essie, but when she saw her mother looking so sad, Nettie almost wished they all could forget.

January 1, 1922

Brand new year. Can't wait till spring. Sure hope I get to go rodeo again with you. It was so much fun last year, until I broke my wrist. I'm letting Mama forget all about that before I talk about going again.

Nettie looked at her journal calendar. Only five more months till June and the Miles City Roundup. This year, she would win.

April 9, 1922

In March we got a Chinook wind. Everything melted almost over-night. We've been calving two weeks and we got a spring blizzard. Been riding out several times a day to check for newborns dropped in the snow. Had to bring one in the house today to thaw out. Poor little thing.

Nettie warmed a bottle in a kettle of hot water while Mama rubbed the shivering red and white calf down with heated vinegar water, then wrapped him in a warm blanket. Nettie tested the milk on her wrist, let a bit of it dribble on the calf's mouth, and offered him the bottle. At first he fumbled with the nipple, then he drank greedily. After the milk was gone, he settled down for a nap. Soon he was up and scrabbling on the slippery linoleum floor, looking for his mama.

May 28, 1922

Went to a dance last night at the Demers school. So tired of silly young boys asking me to dance, drooling all over me.

Don't they get the hint? I'm not interested. Don't know why I go. I just like to dance, not the hands all over me stuff. One of them said I was pretty, though.

Boys. Nettie just didn't understand the girls at those dances and the way they acted, all twittery and giggly, with their sly smiles and heads cocked to the side. She rolled her eyes. Never would she act that way.

June 16, 1922

Toby is getting pretty old. Can't gallop like the wind any more. Papa says he heard of a new neighbor leasing the Davis place by Sunburst who has some good horses. Asked me to ride along tomorrow. Oh, boy. Can't wait.

Nettie rocked in the saddle, riding alongside Papa. A companionable silence rested between them in this rare outing together. A meadowlark trilled its spring welcome song, and all around her Nettie felt the buzzing of new life. She smelled the sweet scent of the lush grass that grew after the early June rains. Wildflowers burst onto the horizon in a cacophony of color. The sun shone warm and gentle.

She smiled, buoyant with excitement. She would get a new horse today. Then an arrow of doubt punctured her joy. She'd heard Mama arguing last night with Papa. Mama didn't think they should buy a new horse, since they didn't have a lot of extra money. Then Nettie heard Papa's firm voice through the thin bedroom wall. "Now, Ada, riding horses are not a luxury. They're a necessity. And we need an extra."

So, that was that, thank goodness. She put the memory out of her mind. But, good ol' Toby, her trusted friend. She reached down and smoothed the soft brown hair on his neck. Was she betraying him? He might be lonely if she rode another horse.

"Papa, do you think Toby will be mad at me for getting a new horse?"

Papa started to grin, then swiped his hand over his mouth and cleared his throat.

"No, honey. I think he'll be happy to retire, just laze around all day and eat grass and doze in the sunshine. Besides, you'll still ride him now and then."

Nettie nodded. Yes, Toby had worked hard all his life. He probably would be glad for a well-earned rest. And thank goodness, Papa hadn't said she'd have to sell him to get the new horse. Toby would still be around when she needed a friend.

About nine miles from home, she and Papa followed the trail over flat-topped rimrocks surrounding the green meadow pastures of the Davis ranch, named for the original homesteader. They rode by a two-story whitewashed house and approached the barn, where a young man brushed down his horse. He turned at the sound of their hoof-beats, tipped his gray felt hat back on his head, and strode forward to meet them. "Howdy."

Papa dismounted and met the cowboy with an outstretched hand. "Mornin'. I'm Charley Brady. This here's my daughter, Nettie. We've come to look for a horse for her."

"Jake Moser. Glad to meet ya." The tall cowboy, probably in his mid-twenties, removed his hat and ducked his head toward Nettie, and something lurched inside her chest. "That's dandy," he said. "I have plenty of horses. Now, what kind do you favor, an easy rider or a spirited runner?" His teeth shone white through his broad grin.

"Oh, I love to run. There's nothing I'd rather do than ride. That is, when my mama lets me out of the house. Ol' Toby here and I have galloped many a mile, and we help haze for my brother when he's working at Fergusons', but he can't go as far or as fast any more." Nettie blushed, then looked down at her saddle horn. Here she was, babbling away and feeling somewhat giddy.

Papa chuckled. "Well, that's the longest speech I've heard from you in awhile."

"C'mon, bring 'em in to feed. We'll take a look at what I got." Jake's blue eyes twinkled. He grabbed a halter and strode toward the pasture. Nettie slid off her horse and followed.

Papa fell in step with Jake. Nettie stayed by her father's side, sneaking glances at the well-muscled young man with the easy stride. A ruff of sandy blond hair glinted in the sunlight from beneath his hat brim, and his square jaw was bronzed from long hours in the glaring sun. Wait a minute. Wasn't he the same cowboy she'd seen thrown at Red Jones's rodeo last June?

"Jake, I wanted to ask you about the shipment of cattle going out from Sunburst to Chicago. When's that happening?" Papa talked as though Nettie weren't there.

Jake turned to answer the question and met Nettie's gaze. A jolt like a miniature lightning strike passed through her. Her face felt seared. She quickly looked off into the distance, as though she hadn't been paying a bit of attention to the men.

Then she spotted the multicolored herd of horses grazing the tender pasture grass. She inhaled sharply. Their smooth-muscled bodies undulated under sleek coats that gleamed in the sun. Almost as one unit, they raised their heads to gaze at the visitors. Nettie reached into her pocket for a carrot. A shiny black whinnied, trotted forward to the fence, and nuzzled Nettie's outstretched hand. His eyes sparkled like liquid coal.

"Oh, he's so beautiful."

"That's Blacky. He's special. Got a good easy trot, and he's a strong runner." Jake opened the gate and they stepped through. Jake patted the horse's back. "I think he likes you. He doesn't come up to just anybody." He winked at Nettie, and she ducked her head to hide her face.

Nettie stroked the gelding's neck and scratched the base of his ears, while Blacky nuzzled her pockets in search of another carrot.

Yes, it almost seemed like he was telling her how well he thought they would get along. She turned to Jake. "Can I ride him?"

He handed her the braided halter. Nettie drew the rope lead around Blacky's neck. The gelding dropped his head so she could slip the headstall over his nose and fasten it behind his ears. *Such a gentle horse.* He made no move to get away but bobbed his head as if to say, "Okay, I'm ready to go."

Nettie looked at Jake. "Is he broke to ride with a halter?"

He nodded.

Nettie grabbed a handful of mane and swung up onto his broad back. She glanced at the men, to see if they had noticed how easily she'd managed, even wearing a divided skirt.

Jake raised his eyebrows. "You don't want your saddle and bridle?"

With a wide grin, she shook her head, nudged the horse's ribs with her heels, and turned him away from the herd, through the gate, and toward the open spaces. His trot became a lope, then an eager gallop. She grinned. Riding Blacky was like fitting her hand snug inside a calfskin glove.

Nettie felt his strength beneath her as she gripped his sides with her knees and leaned low onto his neck. His ebony mane mingled with her auburn hair in the wind. She felt a freedom like never before. His smooth gait made it seem as though she were soaring on the back of a huge bird. The two men and the day, with its warm sun, bright flowers, and green grass, drifted into the periphery as she and the horse became one mighty flying animal.

They topped a small rise a half mile away before she eased upright and pulled back on the halter rope. *Whew! What a horse.* Blacky trotted to a standstill.

"Such a good boy. I hope you'll be coming home with me." Nettie patted his neck. "Now, you'll have to be nice to my old horse, Toby. He's retiring, but I don't want to hurt his feelings."

Blacky fluttered a breath through his nostrils and bobbed his head as if to say *okay*.

She sat, drinking in the beauty of this ranch beneath the rims of the Sweet Grass Hills. It was even prettier here than at home. She could see Papa and Jake back at the corral, each with a foot perched on the lower pole. They shared a flask, heads occasionally thrown back in laughter.

What a grand day. She allowed herself a smile and urged Blacky into a lope back to the barn.

"Well, what'd you think?" Jake stepped forward and offered a hand to help her dismount. She felt his taut muscles, and her arm tingled where he touched her. Her face flaming again, she averted her gaze. *What is this all about?*

She swallowed her confusion. "He is one fine horse." She turned to her father. "Oh, Papa, can we?"

"Yup." He chuckled. "We already shook on the deal. Looks like that horse was made just for you."

Her stomach danced an awkward two-step as she inwardly fought for a grown-up's composure. "Thank you, Mr. Moser. I'll take good care of him."

"No more 'mister.' Just call me Jake." He stuck out his hand to her. His warm, firm handshake made her fingers tingle, and she slipped them from his grasp.

Nettie held her breath, afraid she was going to gasp and embarrass herself. *Stop this right now, Nettie Brady.* She busied herself transferring her saddle from Toby to Blacky.

"You can keep the halter. I braided it myself." Jake's voice came from behind her.

She turned around and gave him what she hoped was a casual nod. "Well, thanks again, Mister, uh, Jake." Her throat felt tight. *Oh my, is he ever good to look at.*

"Well, we'd better ramble on back home so's we can get started early tomorrow roundin' up the steers. They're shipping sooner than I expected." Turning to Jake, Papa shook the young man's hand. "Adios for now. We'll be seein' you in a couple days."

The whole nine miles back home, Nettie rode on a cloud. Blacky was so beautiful, so shiny and sleek. Papa led Toby, who trotted along as if he hadn't yet realized he'd been replaced.

And Jake. She couldn't get his easy grin out of her mind. Her arm and hand still held on to that strange, yet thrilling sensation like a feather brushing lightly over her skin. Nettie shivered. She couldn't quite understand what had happened.

"With Joe working for Ferguson now, I'm gonna need some help with this shipping. Besides, I think your brother has eyes for that Ferguson girl, so we probably won't be countin' on him bein' around much any more." Papa tipped back his sweat-streaked hat and scratched his forehead. "Would you care to join me and Ben in the morning? Eddie's old enough to come, too. So with the four of us, we oughta be able to get the job done."

Nettie jolted back to reality. She couldn't believe her ears. She'd get to ride her new horse. "Oh, can I? Yes. Will it . . . is Mama going to let me?"

"I'll fix it with your Mama. I really do need your help."

Nettie couldn't help but grin.

❦

The dawn painted the purple hills with an orange wash. In the morning's coolness the horses snorted silvery steam and stamped with impatience. Nettie and Ben helped Eddie saddle up. Then they followed Papa across the gully, around the lake into the hills, to round up their herd.

"Well, I hope my gamble will pay off." Papa hadn't sold the calves born last year, but chose to keep them over winter, so they would grow and gain more weight.

"Do you think the prices are better this spring than they were last fall?" Ben's voice cracked, then deepened as he struggled to present a manly interest in the subject at hand.

"According to the week-old papers, they are." Papa pursed his mouth. "Just hope they don't drop between now and when the trainload gets there. Either way, we should be able to get a little more just 'cause they're bigger."

"They should be. They ate all that hay we put up last summer." Eddie urged his horse forward. At eleven, he was trying mightily to keep up with his teenage brother.

"I know." Papa scratched his forehead. "But at least we didn't have to buy any more to get through the winter. I figure that leaves us ahead of the game."

Nettie nudged Blacky past her brothers. By now she had learned ranching was always a gamble. She dreaded seeing her folks go through agony with such decisions every year. The discussions. The frowns. The questions. Should they sell the calves in the fall? Or wait until spring? What if the price got worse? And if they had to buy hay, they would lose any profit for that year.

She shook her head, glad she didn't have to make those decisions. During the long train trip to Chicago, the animals could lose weight and be less valuable by the time they arrived. And one or more of them might die.

Nettie inhaled the fresh spring air and smiled. It certainly wasn't a day for worry. She'd never seen a sunrise more spectacular nor heard so many birds welcome the first light. The horses' hooves released the tangy scent of green grass to mingle with the pungent leather and animal smells. Life in the saddle was good. Especially with her new horse. He was a dream.

They stopped atop a hill to look for the herd. Cows with their new calves and the yearling steers and heifers were scattered throughout the coulees. With few fences between neighbors, it might be hard to get all of their cattle rounded up without acquiring a few extras. Nettie wondered if the four of them could handle the task. Then she spotted a rider coming from the northeast, driving a small bunch before him.

As the cowboy came closer, Nettie caught a glimpse of blond hair trailing from beneath his hat. Her heart thumped like a tom-tom.

It was Jake Moser. "Howdy. Thought you might be able to use a hand."

"Help is always welcome." Papa grinned.

Nettie gripped her reins tight as if that could help her hang on to her composure.

Jake winked at her. "And how's that new horse workin' out for you?"

"Ah ..." Her first syllable cracked and she cleared her throat. "He's just dandy. I really like riding him." How embarrassing. She sounded like a little kid. Darn it, anyhow.

But he didn't seem to notice her tongue-tied predicament. "That's great. I know he's gonna be good for you." With a big smile, he wheeled his horse around and headed for another bunch of cattle.

Nettie turned Blacky in the opposite direction. Ben grinned at her, his eyebrows raised. She stuck out her tongue at him and rode on.

By evening they'd gathered a sizable bunch and pushed them home, toward the corrals. Threading through the milling, bawling mass of cattle, Nettie helped cut out the marketable yearling steers, separated them from the rest of the herd, and pushed them into pens. The cows and calves were let loose to graze their way back out into the hills. They'd have to be gathered again in a couple of weeks for branding. But for now, shipping was foremost on Papa's mind.

Nettie's mother invited Jake to stay for supper that night. He regaled them with jokes and stories about breaking horses for the various ranch outfits he'd worked with. Nettie sat back and tried not to seem as eager as Ben and Eddie, who listened wide-eyed.

"Where d'you hail from?" Papa took a gulp of his coffee. Jake accepted another slice of bread from Mama. "Oh, I been helpin' run my mother's ranch east of Sunburst. But she died last winter, and my sister and brother-in-law took it over. Heard the Davis spread was for lease. Figured it'd be a good place to raise rodeo stock and draft horses."

His easy manner, his grin, and the way he waved his buttered bread in the air to emphasize a point reminded Nettie a lot of her big brother Joe. Jake didn't talk down to her because she was a girl, but included her in the conversation, even asked her opinion from time to time. With relief, she found she was able to overcome her earlier clumsiness and answer with a certain amount of confidence.

The meal finished, he leaned his chair back on two legs and stretched. "Best be gettin' home to feed Pal, my dog. Thanks for the delicious supper, Mrs. Brady." He stood and offered a strong brown hand to Papa. "See you tomorrow for shipping." He reached for his hat, winked in Nettie's direction, and was gone before she could say a word.

She stared out the door for a long time, submerged in thoughts of those startling blue eyes, white teeth in that tanned face, and his muscular torso when he'd leaned back to stretch.

Mama finally gave her a nudge. "He's long gone. Better get the supper dishes cleared now."

Nettie jumped, and her face went hot again.

✦

The shipping pens at the railroad depot in Sunburst were in full concert with hundreds of steers bawling and snorting, cowboys shouting and whistling, horses whinnying and blowing. Ranchers from all over the area had brought cattle in for shipping day. The dust settled in Nettie's nose, along with the smell of green manure, animal sweat, and panic.

She rode Blacky with an easy air as he twisted and maneuvered their fifty head into the pens, where they'd be loaded onto cattle cars later. Clucking, whooping, and swiping her hat at the stubborn steers, she pushed them forward.

"Oops! Look out! That one's gettin' away," someone shouted above the din. Nettie nudged her horse with a knee. Without reining, Blacky was already after the rebellious yearling. It whirled and ducked. Her horse stayed with the steer, step for step. Then it bolted toward the open prairie and freedom, Nettie on Blacky close at his heels.

Nettie's hat flew off. The wind whistled through her hair. She bent above the horse's neck, urging him on faster. Her heart pounded. She couldn't let the men see her lose this steer.

She glimpsed a dark form closing in from the right. The steer veered as the other horseman cut off his path. Together they drove the animal back to the pens.

"Good ride." Jake's voice startled her.

She had been so intent on following the steer and making sure he didn't escape again, she hadn't even noticed who had ridden up to help her. "Uh, thanks for your help. He might've gotten away." Excitement and embarrassment warmed her whole body. *He thinks I did a good job.*

"Naw. I know Blacky. He'd never let that happen." Jake grinned.

"Blacky's just a dream to ride. He knows exactly what to do before I even tell him." Nettie's voice rose in excitement. "You did a great job of training him."

"Yup. He's a good horse. But you're a natural-born rider. The two of you looked like one, racin' across the prairie."

Nettie ducked her head to hide the flush rising up from her neck. *Again. Darn it. Why can't I talk to this cowboy without turning red?*

"Say, I could sure use some help keepin' my ponies rode down. What d'ya say? Would you like a job?"

Nettie's head jerked upright. Had she heard right? A job? Riding horses? "Would I? You bet I would. But . . . ."

"I know. You gotta ask your folks. That's okay. I think I can work on your dad. He can take it from there." He touched his hand to the brim of his hat and wheeled his horse away. "See ya later."

She could only sit and stare after his retreating form. If Papa and Mama would just say yes. It would be a dream come true.

"Our girl's got a job offer," Papa announced at the supper table that night. "From the new neighbor over on the Davis place."

Mama frowned. "Doing what?"

"Riding green-broke horses." Nettie couldn't keep the excitement out of her voice.

Without a word, Mama got up and busied herself filling the kettle with water to heat for washing dishes. With a nod toward the door, she stepped outside to refill the water bucket. Papa followed.

Uh-oh. Nettie stacked the plates and put them in the dishpan. The sun sank behind the distant hills, leaving the outside world in muted dusk. She stood by the open window, straining to hear her parents talk.

"What were you thinking? . . . work for this man?" Mama's voice was low but filled with an angry force.

" . . . work she loves. She'll be out on her own soon."

Nettie lifted clasped hands to her chest. Thank goodness Papa understood. She leaned closer to the window.

" . . . need her help."

The pump handle squeaked and water spurted against the metal of the bucket. "She can still do that." Papa's voice boomed over the noise. "She'll only be over there two or three days a week."

Mama was silent for a moment. "But to work for this man? It's hardly proper for a young, single girl. What do we know about him? . . . be all right with him? . . . send Ben along?"

Nettie rolled her eyes. Great. Just what she needed, her little brother tagging along.

The pumping stopped. "I need Ben to help me here. Eddie's too young yet. I really think we can trust Jake. His family's been around Sunburst a long time. I met his dad one time after he came down from Canada to homestead. And I've talked with Jake. I think he's an honorable young man. It's a good opportunity for Nettie to earn some money. That's gonna help us out."

Nettie peered over the edge of the windowsill to see Papa put his arm around her mother. "I know it's hard. But we're going to have to let her go sometime. This might be as good a way as any to let us get used to it gradually."

Nettie frowned. What did Papa mean? *"Have to let her go?"* They certainly didn't make this big a deal when Joe left to go to work for Ferguson. People really did treat girls different. *I can do anything the boys can.* And she wouldn't be gone forever, just during the day, a couple days a week.

Mama buried her head in Papa's chest. " . . . suppose so," came the muffled response.

~~

The next morning Nettie reined Blacky to a stop on the knoll over-looking Jake Moser's ranch. A white rail fence and a row of yellow-flowered Caragana bushes encircled the white-painted house. It was clear someone had taken care to make it a neat, cheerful-looking place. As she rode closer, Jake's border collie got to his feet, stretched in his sun-warmed spot on the porch, and trotted out to meet her. She dismounted, tied the reins to a rail, and ducked under the overhanging bushes to unlatch the nearly hidden gate.

"Hiya, Pal. Where's the boss?"

The dog wagged his tail and smiled.

The door squeaked. Jake stepped out. "Mornin'. Need some coffee before we head out to work?"

A warmth at the base of her neck told her that she was about to blush. Again. Nettie steeled herself. *Gotta act businesslike.* "No, thanks. Had some earlier. What're we going to do today?"

"C'mon down to the barn. I got some green ones I been breaking. If I don't keep 'em rode down, they want to go back to buckin'. That's where I need the help. I can't ride all of 'em every day."

The log barn was cool in the early summer warmth. Nettie blinked to adjust her eyes to the dimness inside. She caught a whiff of tobacco as Jake stepped by her. He gathered a bridle and saddle for each of them, and they carried them out into the corral where a small bunch of nervous young horses milled. Their wild eyes flashed over Nettie and Jake and they turned tail to run. But the rails held them in. Pawing the air and snorting, one buckskin tried to climb the fence. His hooves clattered ineffectively on the rails. Then he turned on the horse behind him and gave a vicious nip to its rear.

Jake cut the buckskin from the group and shooed him into an adjoining smaller corral. He shook out his lasso and walked slowly toward the horse, making low, murmuring noises. "Easy there, Bucky. This ain't gonna hurt a bit. Whoa, boy. Whoa, now."

The loop snaked through the air and settled around the buckskin's neck. Jake continued to talk as he worked his way down the rope to the horse. "Easy there. Atta boy." He stretched his arm out to the horse's muzzle, let him sniff for a moment, then stroked up the white blaze on its forehead to the laid-back ears. He rubbed one ear as the horse trembled, watching the man from the liquid depths of his brown eyes.

Nettie raised an eyebrow. Jake worked this horse nice and gentle, sensitive to the horse's fear, reassuring. Her stomach fluttered. She hoped she could do as well, and impress him.

Jake pulled the bridle from behind his back and smoothed the reins around Bucky's neck. Then he inserted his fingers into the side of the horse's mouth, slid the bit between his teeth, and slipped the leather straps over and behind the ears.

"There ya go. That wasn't so bad, huh?" Jake fastened the strap under the horse's jaw and patted the buckskin's neck. "Here's somebody I want you to meet."

Nettie took slow steps to the horse's head, her hand outstretched. She copied Jake's easy movements, let the horse take in her smell, and crooned in a low, soothing voice.

Minutes passed while Nettie savored the languid feeling of establishing a bond with this animal. Gradually the horse's trembling subsided. Hey, she must be doing all right. He turned his head to nuzzle Nettie as she rubbed his neck and passed her hand along his back where the saddle would lie. She stroked his legs, to let him get used to her touch and presence. This was fun.

Finally, with Jake holding the bridle, she picked up the saddle blanket, let Bucky smell it first, then smoothed it over his back. The horse switched his tail, and his back muscles quivered for a moment, but calmed as Nettie talked. When she thought the blanket was no longer bothering him, she picked up her saddle and swung it up. He shuddered a bit at the extra weight and looked back at this object. But with Nettie murmuring close by, he became calm again, only his eyes rolling to keep a watch on what this human was doing to him as she tightened the cinch under his belly.

Jake gave her the reins. In one fluid movement, Nettie inserted a boot into the stirrup and swung onto the saddle. She clamped her knees to his sides, ready for whatever he decided to do.

The horse threw his head back and blew, trying to escape the confines of his leather headdress. He pranced to one side, then the other, shaking his head up and down. His hindquarters snaked one direction as his front quarters twisted another, and he crowhopped few steps around the corral before he settled into a nervous trot. Nettie let out a pent-up breath. Good, he wasn't going to put on a big show.

'Round and 'round the corral they went, first one direction, then the other, until the horse responded to Nettie's gentle direction with the reins and nudges from her heels.

"Good job. Ready to take him outside?"

Jake's voice startled Nettie out of her concentration. She had been so engrossed with the horse that she'd forgotten he was still there. She looked at him standing by the gate, a lean, craggy presence, and smiled. *He thinks I did okay.* "Yeah. I think we're ready."

She nudged the buckskin forward. What a swell job.

CHAPTER THIRTEEN

July 9, 1922
Dear Marie,

Got to go to the Glacier rodeo for the big Fourth of July doings.
Missed seeing you. Went with Joe and Jake. Just ducky.
Like having two big brothers. They let me go along every-
where, never said, "This ain't no place for a girl." Jake even snuck
me in and signed me up to ride a steer! Rode to the end. Can hardly
believe Mama's letting me work for Jake!
I have Papa to thank for that. Love it, riding all those green
horses. And now that Joe's living and working at Fergusons', Jake
comes over a lot, to help Papa and Ben. Jake is quite a handsome
cowboy, a lot like Tom.

The summer flew by like Canada geese on their way south for the winter. Nettie threw herself into the chores Mama had for her. She cooked
and baked for haying and harvest, took care of little brother Chuck,
and helped Lola again when the threshing crew arrived at their farm.
But meanwhile, she fidgeted inside, waiting for the days she could go
help Jake.

He was often at the Bradys' now, too. He'd stay for supper and
many times helped Papa for several days when work was in full swing.
Although she told herself that he was just taking Joe's place, Nettie
was secretly pleased. She actually felt grown up when he was around,
not so shy and tongue-tied anymore.

Mama seemed to have warmed up to him, too. Nettie froze in embarrassment in the doorway one evening to see her mother bossing him around just like she did the boys. "Don't forget to wash up before you come in to eat. And take off those dirty boots. I just mopped these floors."

"Yes, Ma," Jake teased her back. "I just couldn't wait to get in here and get some of your wonderful cooking."

"Oh, pshaw. You get on outta here now. You're just looking for second helpings." Mama waved her hand to shoo him away.

Nettie smirked at her mother looking flustered.

Jake winked at Nettie as he stepped back outside to wash up.

"Very smart," she whispered. "Good way to stay on her good side."

Many an evening, Ben and Eddie sat wide-eyed at Jake's feet and Chuck on his knee as he told rodeo and roundup stories. Even Papa laughed and joined in telling tales. Nettie sat back with an inward smile, listening.

When the youngsters were put to bed, the men would play poker, betting with matchsticks. Sooner or later, Papa or Jake would bring out a bottle, and then they'd bet nickels or dimes. That was the cue for Mama to frown and announce she was going to bed. She'd jerk her head toward Nettie's room in a hint that she, too, should retire.

But Nettie ignored Mama. She just wanted to be near this fascinating man.

One morning as Nettie readied to ride over to Jake's, Mama turned from the stove, where she had just set a huge kettle of water to heat for the wash. "I don't want you to go today. I could use a little help around here for a change."

Nettie did a double-take. *What's this all about?* "But Mama, I've been home helping you the last several days. It's my day to go work for Jake." Surely Mama understood the importance of this work.

Mama's face flushed the color of rhubarb sauce. "That's men's work. I've put up with this long enough. People are going to talk. You need to be learning what it takes to run a household, and preparing yourself for the time when you have your own family."

Nettie forced herself not to yell. "I don't want my own family. I want to work with horses. I want to ride. I want to have a ranch of my own someday." She stood with arms akimbo.

"Hmmph." Mama's lips thinned. "Fine. Go on, then. You'll regret this one day."

Nettie flipped her braid over her shoulder. Things had been going so well. "I thought you were glad I have this job. I thought you liked Jake."

Mama just glared at her.

"You just can't stand to see me happy. That's it. You hate me." Nettie spun on one heel, ignoring her mother's protest, and stomped out of the house, the door-slam punctuating her anger.

She urged Blacky into a full-out gallop on the way to Jake's. The hard ride took away some of the steam inside her, but her thoughts still blazed when she arrived.

"Whoa, there, little gal. You're ridin' like the devil himself was after you." Jake greeted her with a concerned look. "Something happen?"

"Mama." Nettie dismounted. "You know, I just don't understand her." She unsaddled her horse and rubbed his lathered withers with a rag.

"Why? What's going on?" Jake's voice was soft.

"I don't know. It's not something I should concern you with. I'm sorry. Let's get to work." Nettie let Blacky loose in the corral with a swat to his rump and turned to catch the horse she was to work today.

But the horse wouldn't cooperate. He fought the bit, pranced sideways to avoid the saddle, and kicked, grazing her leg.

"Ow!" Nettie flicked her reins at the gelding. "All right, you devil-spawn, I give up."

"Hey there, little gal. Take 'er easy." Jake put a gentle hand on her shoulder. "Look, this thing's got you upset somethin' fierce. Why don't you tell me about it."

Nettie shrugged, her shoulder tingling where he touched her. "Just had a little set-to with Mama this morning. That's all."

"Doesn't sound that little to me. What happened?" Nettie rested one foot on the lower corral pole and took a deep breath of the manure-scented air. "She's always on me about learning to be a high-brow lady. I don't know why. Margie and Lola are doing just fine in that department."

Jake nodded. "Yeah? And you aren't?"

Nettie pushed out an exasperated breath. "It's about me doing 'men's work' instead of staying home. All I want to do is be out here, helping ride."

Jake swept his sweat-stained hat from his head and scrubbed his fingers through his hair. "Well, not everybody's good at the same things. You're certainly good at handlin' a horse and cuttin' cattle. And you're not too bad at cookin' and bakin' either. Those rolls you made the other night were wonderful. I think that's the perfect combination, myself."

Nettie's neck warmed with the compliment. She cocked her head and cut her eyes sideways at him. She hadn't really thought of things that way before. But Mama was so consarned stubborn. "The things she said, well, they just plain hurt." Nettie blinked against the sting in her eyes.

"Yeah, I can see that." Jake's voice was soft, soothing, like when he talked to his fearful horses. "But aren't you interested in settlin' down, gettin' married, havin' kids?"

"Naw." She scuffed her boot in the dirt. But maybe he was right. Maybe she didn't have to fight the idea of homemaking quite so hard. After all, she would probably be living on her own soon, although the possibility of marriage still seemed far away.

An odd feeling of comfort came with confiding in Jake. It was even better than talking to her brother. Till now, Joe had been the only one who really understood and appreciated how much she loved to ride and be out of doors. But when her brother left to work for

Ferguson and started courting their daughter, he no longer had time for Nettie. She had missed her only confidant terribly.

"I wouldn't mind running my own ranch someday." She waved her hat to create a breeze across her face and gazed at the prairie. "I suppose you're right. I gotta know how to feed myself and the work crews when that happens."

"That's right." Jake swept his arm toward the house. "I had to learn some of that myself."

"But sometimes, like this morning, I think Mama doesn't like me at all." Nettie ducked her head. "It felt like being kicked in the stomach by one of these green horses."

"Well." Jake reached for his tobacco pouch. "From what you've said, she's had a rough time of it since your little sister died." He shook the tobacco into the cigarette paper.

"Yeah, she's still pretty sad about that."

"Give her time, she'll come around."

Nettie watched Jake roll a cigarette. "How do you know this kinda stuff?"

He chuckled. "Well, I had a Mama, too. And two sisters." Nettie smiled back. *He has kind eyes. He really does understand.* So nice-looking, too. A shakiness began in her knees and worked its way into her stomach. She turned away. Her body kept doing these silly things. No sense thinking that way now.

❧

Nettie helped Margie lift the last of the empty wooden barrels onto the stone boat. The low sled mounted on runners had been built to haul rocks, but today would carry barrels of water. Nettie had ridden the eight miles to the Testers' ranch this morning to help her sister since Margie's husband was busy with haying. Without a well close to their house, the young couple had to make the five-mile trip to a nearby reservoir about once a month in the summer.

"Glen's going to try and dig a well again as soon as haying and harvesting is over." Margie wiped sweat from her forehead with a handkerchief she'd embroidered and patted her rounded belly. "This trip is getting to be a bit much for me, with the baby coming in a couple of months. And winter is just too tough to get to the lake very often."

Nettie's brother-in-law had twice tried the laborious process of digging a well by hand. Once, he couldn't go deep enough to hit water. The second time, he'd dug in a lower area only to find alkaline water they couldn't use. In past winters, her sister had been snowed in sometimes for as long as two months. Nettie grimaced. That must have been hard on her. She had to melt snow for drinking water and baths, then wash diapers in the bath water. When she washed dishes, she reused the rinse water to wash the next batch. With four-year-old Vera, toddler Madelyn—left with Grandma today for the water-hauling chore—and a new baby coming, those jobs would be even harder this winter. Nettie shivered, thinking about it, not the winter cold, but having three small children to care for.

She lashed the barrels securely with a rope, climbed onto the seat beside Margie, and clucked at the team. The big draft horses lifted their enormous feet and plodded down the track, pulling the sled behind in a cloud of dust. The summer sun beat down on their backs and the sweat coursed from Nettie's armpits.

"I hear you been seeing a lot of your new neighbor, Jake Moser." Margie took off her sun hat and fanned her face.

Nettie jerked her head back and wrinkled her brow in a questioning frown. Who had told her sister? Mama? And what had she said?

"Well, uh, I just been helpin' him keep his horses rode down, is all. He raises rodeo stock and draft crosses, and since he needed some help with the green ones . . . " She shrugged, feigning nonchalance, while her insides churned.

"Mama says he's a looker." Margie smiled over at her and winked.

A flush rose up Nettie's neck. "Uh, yeah, I guess. He's a friend. He's just . . . Jake's kinda like Joe. He doesn't treat me like a little girl." She grabbed her hat and reseated it as the wagon jounced over the ruts.

"Okay. Just checking. When Mama likes somebody, it bears looking at, that's all."

Nettie bit her lower lip. Mama told Margie she liked Jake?

Margie arched her shoulders and rubbed the small of her back. "You're going to be, what, seventeen this winter? Aren't you interested in getting married?"

"Maybe. Someday." Nettie stopped and gave an inward sigh. How could she explain to Margie, when she didn't understand her own feelings? Sometimes Jake's nearness made her all jittery inside. And those darn blushes she couldn't hide. But no. Jake was just a friend. Like a big brother. That was all.

Nettie couldn't express her dream to ride the rodeo circuit and then settle down with her own ranch, where she was the boss. No, her sister would just laugh. Best not to say anything. Right now, she was having a good time riding with Jake. Granted, with her job she hadn't been able to rodeo with Marie much this summer, but next year she would, for sure. And she'd ridden her share of broncs for Jake already. She smiled, thinking of the thrill those rides brought her.

"Well, it just seems like if there's an eligible young man around who's as good-looking as Ma says, you're probably old enough to be thinking about romance."

"Now, Margie, you just stop it. I'm not getting married and havin' a passel of kids. I want to ride and rope and, well, it's not something you'd understand!" She gritted her teeth and chucked the reins over the team's backs, urging them faster. Drat, Margie made her so mad sometimes. "Let's just go get the water."

"Well, you don't need to get so testy." Margie sat back against the hard wooden backrest, her mouth set in a grim line. They rode in silence the rest of the way.

Oh, sure. Now Margie is mad at me. Nettie set her face in an equally stony expression. That just proved her point. Margie still didn't get it. She didn't want to, that was the whole problem. Nettie's shoulders knotted as her tension seethed within. She occasionally glanced at her sister out of the corner of her eye, but quickly averted her gaze when Margie did the same.

At the sight of water, the team picked up its speed. The reservoir lay in a low spot, where several coulees converged. A natural dam collected runoff from snowmelt every year and if the summer wasn't too dry, the quarter-mile-long reservoir stayed relatively full.

Nettie rolled her shoulders and unhooked the horses so they could drink. Then the sisters grabbed buckets and sidestepped down the steep bank between scraggly willows to the water for the first round of barrel filling.

"What I wouldn't give for a well." Margie groaned and rubbed her belly. "You know, I guess I shouldn't complain. We got running water. It's us running up and down this bank."

Nettie stopped to stare, her brows raised. Now that had certainly come out of nowhere. In spite of her reluctance, a chuckle rose from deep inside. Margie giggled. Then they were both laughing heartily, their momentary tension eased. Panting, Margie put a hand on Nettie's shoulder to balance. "You know, it's nice havin' a man to love you, Nettie."

Nettie nodded. She'd wondered what that would be like. Maybe so.

Back at the stone boat, Margie anchored a sheet of cheesecloth, folded into several thicknesses, over the first barrel. They poured the water through the cloth to strain out the bugs, snails, and tiny water snakes that lived in the reservoir.

Margie grimaced and turned her face away. "Ugh, I hate knowing we're drinking water that had bugs in it."

Nettie snorted. "There's nothing in it after we strain it. It's perfectly clean." That just proved their differences. Margie preferred to work inside, and Nettie wanted to be outside.

By the time the barrels were full, their shirts were soaked through with sweat, and grime streaked their faces.

Margie rubbed her back again and groaned. "I'm not going to be able to do this much longer." She shaded her eyes and scanned the horizon. "It's hot enough to boil an egg. You know what? I don't care about the bugs. I'm going to take a swim." She peeled off her long skirt.

Nettie felt her eyes widen. Her straight-laced sister going to swim without a suit? Yep, there she went, stepping gingerly, sinking up to her pantaloons in the water. Gosh, maybe she wasn't such a stick-in-the-mud after all.

Margie submerged her bloated abdomen and gave a blissful sigh. "C'mon in, it feels wonderful. I'm light as a feather. I think I could float."

A swarm of gnats circled Nettie's head. She swatted them away and scratched at her tight, sweaty clothes. Then, scanning the horizon as her sister had done, she quickly stripped down to her camisole and pantaloons and ran, slipping and sliding in the mud, to dive into the coolness. She surfaced, blowing and splashing water at Margie, who shrieked and smacked the water back.

"Can't catch me." Nettie swam for the opposite bank.

"Don't bet on it." Margie's answer was close behind her. They reached the opposite bank about the same time, laughing and snorting water from their nostrils.

"Gosh. I haven't had so much fun since the time Glen and I . . . oops." Margie covered her mouth with her hand, her eyes dancing.

"You didn't."

"We did. No clothes, either."

"I'm gonna tell Mama."

"Oh, no, you're not!" Margie grabbed Nettie by a braid, then pushed her head underwater. Nettie came up sputtering.

"Promise?" Margie held onto the braid.

"No."

Down went Nettie's head again. And again until both were breathless with laughter.

"Truce." Nettie held up crossed fingers.

Margie made a face. "Besides, I'm an old married woman now, and I can do what I want."

A whinny from above and an answer from their team brought both up short. Nettie stared, frozen in mid-splash as her gaze swept the bank. A horseman sat slouched back in the saddle, his hat pulled low over his eyes.

Nettie gasped. Oh, no. Who . . . ? Was it Jake? She crossed her arms over her thin wet camisole. Darn, she'd never be able to look him in the face again. *Oh, my.* Where could she hide?

The cowboy pulled a grass stem from his mouth and chuckled. "Afternoon, ma'ams," he drawled.

Nettie thought she might faint. It wasn't Jake after all. Thank goodness. It was a stranger.

"I was just a-gonna water m'horse, but I see you've got the reservoir too riled up for 'im to drink. Have a good swim." He touched the brim of his hat, wheeled his horse around, and trotted over the rise.

Nettie swung her head around to her sister. Margie's eyes and mouth matched in perfect O's as she huddled in the water up to her shoulders. They stared at each other in shock. Then Nettie's mouth curled and a giggle formed down low and rose like a bubble to her lips. Margie's mouth creased into a smile, and soon, she, too, was laughing uncontrollably.

"I guess we'd better get on back home before that cowboy rounds up a bunch more to come see the show."

Still laughing, they dunked their dresses in the water to keep them cool on the trip back, climbed onto the stone boat, and urged the horses homeward. Water sloshed from the barrels with every bump and sway.

One morning in early fall Papa announced at breakfast, "I gotta go help Jake move Widow Thompkins's house into Sunburst today." He speared another bite of pancake and ham.

"Why's that?" Nettie asked.

"Mrs. Thompkins decided she's gettin' too old to live out here by herself. Wants to be in town, with people this winter. And she's kinda grown fond of her house, her and Elmer building it and all."

Nettie could understand that. Elmer had died two winters ago, and their children had all moved far away. Mrs. Thompkins must be very lonely.

Papa pushed his chair back. "Ben, I'll need you and Eddie to come along."

Nettie sat up straight. "Can I go too?"

Mama cleared her throat, but before she could object, Papa spoke up. "Well, I'll tell you what. Why don't you bring us a lunch 'long about eleven o'clock over at the widow's. We'll probably be needin' a little nourishment by then."

"Okay, Papa, I'll be there." Nettie jumped up to clear the dishes as he and the boys left. "What can we fix them to eat, Mama?"

Her mother chuckled. "There's some roast venison left over from yesterday. You can make some sandwiches."

Sandwiches. That wasn't a very impressive dinner for hard-working men. Nettie's brow furrowed. *Wonder what Jake would like.* "I know. Can't we fry up some chicken? The men are going to be mighty hungry after all that hard work."

"All right." Her mother brushed back a wayward curl. "But you'll have to go kill the chickens and get them ready. I have a mountain of ironing to do today."

Nettie bit back a protest. Killing and plucking chickens wasn't one of her favorite chores, although she'd done it plenty of times before. But this would get her out of ironing. So if she wanted to bring a chicken dinner to the men, she'd have to do it herself. Well, she could do it, all right. She put more coal in the stove. Outside the door, she lifted the five-gallon copper boiler from its nail on the wall, then carried a bucket to the well. When the boiler was full and on the stove heating, she grabbed an axe from the woodpile and headed toward the chicken coop by the barn. The plump white hens scratched in the dirt out front, crooning to themselves as they unearthed grubs and seeds.

Nettie searched the little flock for young chickens hatched last spring. She walked up slowly behind one and with a lightning-quick move grabbed it by the legs. Squawking bloody murder, the bird flapped its wings, tried to peck at her, and nearly loosened Nettie's grasp. Without a second thought about what she had to do, she plunked the hen's neck on an already stained stump and brought down the axe with a resolute thump. The wings continued beating as though the headless body were about to lift into flight. Finally after it stopped flopping, she went after another one. Then, careful not to get her skirts dirty, Nettie carried the chickens to the house.

She grinned. There, she'd done it.

Inside, she hoisted the big bubbling kettle and carried it out to the porch. Holding the chickens by the feet, she put them in the dishpan and poured the water over them, being careful to get the all the feathers wet. The wet feathers stank, but made the plucking easier. She used a glowing stick from the stove to singe the pinfeathers. Gagging at the smell, she gutted the birds, cut them up, and dipped the pieces in flour, salt, and pepper. Well, at least preparing them to fry was not so unpleasant.

As the mouth-watering aroma filled the kitchen, she cut thick slices of bread, slathered them with butter, and wrapped the pieces in waxed paper. Canned peas heated on the stove. A jar of applesauce from the root cellar would complete the meal. Nettie packed everything, plus a jug of iced tea and utensils, into leather panniers behind her saddle. Two hours from start to finish. She was ready.

"I'm gonna take dinner to the men. I left you a plate. G'bye." She didn't wait to hear a reply from Mama ironing in the living room, but swung into the saddle and urged Blacky into a trot.

She rode through the gray sea of sage toward the hunkering Sweet Grass Hills. The late morning sun was as warm as a summer day, and Nettie whistled as she rode along.

A covey of fat, ungainly sage hens flushed from under a bush. Blacky sidestepped for a moment as they chirred their indignation and waddled away.

━━◆━━

They crested the hill. A lone antelope bounced off over the next rise, its white rump flashing in the sunlight. Nettie smiled. It was a good day to be out riding. Below, Papa and the boys worked to get a single-story, two-room house off the ground.

Nettie blinked. She didn't see Jake. She pulled Blacky up short, her shoulders sagging. Shucks.

As she rode up, she saw that the men had taken a wagon apart. They had positioned its wheels on either side of the jacked-up house and had hung heavy beams beneath the axles with chains. The house now sat on the beams, and with a team of eight huge draft Percherons, they were ready to begin the five-mile trek into town.

"Just in time." Papa swiped a red bandanna across his moist forehead.

"Yeah, I'm starved." Eddie tackled the buckles on the saddlebags like a ravenous wolf.

Ben stood back and chuckled at his younger brother.

"Hey, slow down there. Let me get the food out and we can sit in the shade." Nettie rode to the other side of the house, unfolded a red-and-white-checked tablecloth on the ground and set the food on top. "Where's Jake?" She hoped she sounded casual. But darn, she'd cooked all this food.

"I'm right here. Need me for somethin'?" He rode around the corner of the house and dismounted. "Smells awful good." Nettie squeezed her eyes shut. Darn, he'd heard her ask about him. Then she smiled brightly. "Dinner's ready."

The men and boys sat, piled their plates high, and dug into the food. Occasionally they raised their heads for a breath of air, a second helping, or a belch. Unable to eat, Nettie drummed her fingers waiting for the verdict. *Sure hope it tastes all right.*

Jake set down a plate littered with bones. "That was the best durn chicken I've had in a coon's age. Thanks for comin' out here with dinner for us." His smile sent a warm rush up Nettie's neck to her cheeks. He liked it. Oh, what a relief. Now she could eat without worrying.

"Yup, good vittles, daughter." Papa lay back, his hat cocked over his eyes, hands folded over his stomach.

"You're welcome." She busied herself picking up the plates and repacking what was left of the food, sneaking sidelong glances at Jake's handsome profile as he and her father napped in the shade.

Late that afternoon the big horses strained, and the house groaned as it began to roll. Nettie watched the procession crawl down the road. She urged Blacky forward to trot alongside Jake, who drove the team. "It might be fun to have a house on wheels. Whenever you wanted to move to a new place, you could just pull it along."

Jake chuckled. "Well, maybe not exactly like this. It's a pretty big job."

"Have you done this before?"

"A coupla times." He swatted at a fly buzzing around his head. "Widow ladies like this who wanted to move into town. A school-house once."

"Wow! It is a lot of work. Looks like it takes a lot of know-how, too." Nettie's admiration for him rose another notch.

When they reached the dusty little plot on the edge of town, she watched the men place jacks under the house again to remove the beams and wagon axles. They set the building on a foundation of boards and poles, which they had already filled with dirt and manure from the ranch.

"That's insulation to help keep Mrs. Thompkins warm in the winter." Papa stood back to survey their handiwork as the hills threw lavender shadows in the wake of the setting sun.

Nettie stared at the little house, snug now in its new home. She wondered how much Mr. and Mrs. Thompkins had loved each other. She pictured the elderly couple sitting in front of a warm fire, sipping tea, content with their lives and each other, then the faces changed to hers and . . . Jake's? She swiped a hand over her mouth. Wherever had that thought come from? Doggone it. Things like that just kept popping into her mind. She spun around on one heel and headed for her horse before Papa saw the telltale look that must be written all over her face.

CHAPTER FOURTEEN

November 23, 1922
Dear Marie,

What a crummy Thanksgiving. Jake just up and sold his horses,
most of 'em anyhow, and went off to Oregon.

    Couldn't believe it. After all the work we did. Why? Said he
needs the money, can get work over there because the winters are
easier. Still has the lease on the Davis place so says he'll be back in
the spring. Doesn't make sense.

Nettie slammed the shovel into the snowbank that blocked the barn
door, broke off an igloo-sized chunk, and tossed it to the side. Here it
was, already mid-December and no signs of letting up.

"Shoulda snowed *on* Thanksgiving. Then he'd've been stuck here
just like the rest of us." Nettie's words kept time with each thrust of
the shovel into the hard-packed snow. She had heard nothing from
Jake since his surprise announcement the day before he hopped on the
train bound for Pendleton. The Bradys were boarding the half-dozen
draft horses he'd kept, with the promise he would return in spring.

Right now, spring looked like a long way off. She leaned on the
shovel, her shoulders slumped.

～～

On December 17, Nettie's seventeenth birthday, she awoke to another
howling blizzard. That meant no Margie and Lola. Drat. She pulled

157

on a heavy wool sweater and started to braid her long hair. Then she brushed it out and pulled it back into a bun. *More grown up this way.*

After a breakfast of warm maple syrup over apple-cinnamon pancakes, Mama brought out colorful wrapped presents, which included several new books.

Then Papa scooted a large box, wrapped in brand-new store-bought paper, across the table to Nettie. She opened her eyes wide. This was unusual. Mama usually saved any wrapping paper they had from year to year and reused it. Otherwise, packages were wrapped in newspaper, feedsack cloth, or a square of soft buckskin. Was it? Could it be? The boots?

"Oooh, it's so pretty." She took her father's proffered pocket-knife to slit the string holding the rose-strewn paper. Breath held, she opened the lid and gasped. Inside was the most beautiful high-crowned cream-colored felt hat she'd ever seen.

"Oh, Mama, Papa, it's beautiful."

Not the boots, but a hat to rival Marie Gibson's. Or even Prairie Rose Henderson's. She'd never imagined owning a hat like this. Conflicting thoughts flitted through her mind. They had spent a lot of money on this hat. *It's so pretty.* She didn't deserve it. But she'd look so grand at the next rodeo she got to go to.

Nettie looked up at last. "This is more than I ever dreamed of." *Are they starting to accept me as a cowgirl?*

Papa grinned. Mama had a flush in her cheeks. "Go ahead, try it on."

Nettie lifted the Stetson out of the box. She ran a hand over the smooth felt. She smelled the strong, pungent scent of the stitched leather hatband. Ah, better than the finest French perfume.

She set it on her head. The fit was perfect, as though it'd been custom made just for her. Mama brought her hand mirror from the bedroom and Nettie preened in front of it. *Wonder what Jake will think of it?*

"This is a wonderful hat. I just love it."

It wouldn't matter if she got absolutely nothing for Christmas. She had the best present she'd ever dreamed of.

CHAPTER FIFTEEN

Nettie pulled up the quilt to make her bed and plumped her pillow. Almost Christmas and no letter from Jake. As bad as Joe. Her brother never came to visit anymore. No note from Marie, either. *It's so lonely without them.* With a sigh she turned and flounced into the kitchen where her mother washed the breakfast dishes.

"Mama, we haven't gotten any mail for such a long time. What's the matter with J—?" She bit off her sentence, rubbed a peephole on the frosted window, and stared out at the vast whiteness. Out of the corner of one eye, Nettie saw her mother's raised eyebrows as she turned from the dishpan.

"Why, honey, we've been snowed in for weeks. Nobody's been able to make it into town to pick up the mail. Were you expecting something?"

"No, not really." Nettie jerked her heavy sheepskin coat from the nail by the door and stuck her boots into lined overshoes. Buttoned up tightly, she trudged out into a dry cold that instantly froze the hairs inside her nose. She gasped and drew her knitted scarf up over her face for the trek to the barn.

Inside, the damp warmth generated by the animals greeted her along with the musty smell of hay and manure. She walked down the row of stalls and stuck a hand into a feed sack for a handful of rolled oats. At Blacky's stall, she stroked his long face as he nuzzled the grain from her palm.

"You miss our rides, too, don't you, huh, big boy? Gee, I wish this snow would go away."

Nettie found the currycomb and brushed Blacky's shaggy winter coat. Then she fed the rest of the horses and the milk cow more hay and swept the aisles between the stalls. Her glance fell on a pair of angora chaps hung on the wall with the bridles and saddles. Odd, she hadn't really paid much attention to them before. They belonged to Jake. His dress chaps.

She reached up to stroke the smooth cream-colored wool. Wonder why he didn't take them to Oregon? Surely he'd have use for them there. The weather was supposed to be milder in the winter, but they'd keep him warm. Nettie shook her head. Who knew how men thought? Taking off like that, leaving all his friends, the place he was taking care of. Well, okay, she knew it was a chance for him to make some extra money during the winter, but still, why?

Nettie buried her face in the wool, breathing in the scent that lingered: summer afternoons, long heady rides through the lavender sagebrush, horsehide and sweat. Sack lunches in the shade of a lone cottonwood tree and the aroma of tobacco from the hand-rolled cigarettes Jake smoked.

She lifted her head, surprised to feel a hot tear trickle down the side of her nose. Wiping it away roughly with the back of her hand, she stomped her foot. Phooey! This was silly little girl stuff. She was just bored with winter, that's all.

Christmas would be here in a couple of days, and Miss Dorothy, the teacher, was staying with them because she couldn't travel and she'd run out of coal at the teacherage. They'd have a fun time anyway, despite being snowed in.

❦

"I think the snow has settled enough so's I can take the sled into town and pick up the mail and some supplies." Papa made his announcement the morning of Christmas Eve. "Everybody make up your list. If the weather hits again, this may be your last chance for awhile."

Mama's eyes lit up. "Oh, get something special for Christmas. I'll stuff the goose you shot, and we still have cranberries, and I'll make a plum pudding. In fact, let's have Christmas dinner tonight, instead of waiting till tomorrow."

One by one they all gave Papa their wish lists. He chuckled as he bundled up for the ride. "Well, I'm not making any promises, but I'll do my best."

Nettie watched the sled until it was just a speck on the blue-gray horizon. Ben and Eddie announced they'd go out to see if they could find a scrubby pine for a Christmas tree. "Wanna come?" Ben asked.

"Yeah." She thought of snowball fights and tromping through deep drifts to find just the right tree. But that was for kids. She was grown up now. "No, I guess I'll stay here."

But she wandered through the house, stopped in the kitchen, and fidgeted. Then she turned to her mother. "Can I help you? Should I skim some cream off the milk for the pudding? How about if we use your nice white linen tablecloth? Do you still have that red candle?"

Mama smiled. "Yes, let's make this a special Christmas."

Miss Dorothy began humming, "Christmas is coming, the goose is getting fat . . ." Nettie took up the chorus, and soon Mama joined in, their voices ringing loud and clear. " . . . If you haven't got a penny, then a ha'penny'll do. If you haven't got a ha'penny, then God bless you."

Brooms and mops flew. Water bubbled on the wood stove. Mama even risked opening the doors and a couple of windows that weren't frozen shut for a short time to air out the house. Nettie put the finishing touches on a needlepoint sampler that read "God Bless this Home" and wrapped it for the teacher. She'd been working on it with reluctance for a year, intending to give it to one of her sisters. But Margie and Lola wouldn't be here this year. She knew there wouldn't be many packages under the tree, other than what each of them had made in advance. And, of course, whatever Papa might bring back from Sunburst.

Late that afternoon, the goose was roasting in the oven and hot cider simmered on the stove, when Chuck shouted from his station at the window, "Here comes the sled. Papa's back!"

Nettie, Ben, and Eddie shrugged into their coats and ran out to help unload the wagon, unhitch the horses, and put them in the barn.

"Merry Christmas." Papa's cold-reddened face beamed as he carried armloads of packages into the kitchen a few minutes later. "Mmm, something smells good enough to eat." He kissed Mama on the cheek.

"What'd ya bring us?" Eight-year-old Chuck hopped from one foot to the other.

"W-e-l-l, some things have to stay a secret till later. But. You'll never believe this." Papa took out a blanket-wrapped package. "I found some fresh oranges at the mercantile, a treat for breakfast tomorrow. And, I have the mail." He dumped a sack on the table. Out tumbled a Sears and Roebuck spring catalog and an assortment of letters.

Mama thumbed through the stack. "Oh, we got Christmas cards from the Pooles in town, and the McDonalds, and, hmm, I wonder who this could be from. It has an Oregon postmark."

Nettie suddenly felt a weakness in her knees. She snatched the letter from Mama's hand. "Let me see." Then she stopped, her face suddenly hot. It was addressed to *The Moser Family*. "I mean, may I open it?"

"Of course, dear. Go ahead. I don't think we know that many people in Oregon." Mama's mouth curled up at the corners.

Careful to preserve the address, Nettie tore the end from the envelope, blew inside to open it, and extracted the letter. It was from Jake. Her heart beat faster.

Hi, Merry Christmas from Pendleton. Been meeting lots of nice folks here. Getting me a custom saddle made at Hamleys.

It'll be my good-luck saddle in the rodeos next summer. Hope you're wintering good. Happy New Year, Jake.

Disappointment crushed Nettie like a daisy petal under a horse's hoof. Not a word for her. Not even her name.

"What's it say?" Miss Dorothy had a smile in her voice.

Nettie tossed it on the table. "Oh, nothin' much. Just howdy." She turned away to stir the cider on the stove and hide the letdown that was surely written all over her face.

Then she forced a smile and turned back to the gathering. "Smells like the goose is done, Mama. Are we about ready to eat?"

With shouts and laughter, the family gathered in a flurry around the table.

The crisp brown goose skin crackled in Nettie's mouth, sending savory, delicious flavor messages over her tongue, mingling with the sweet-tart sensation of dried-cranberry sauce. If she closed her eyes and concentrated only on the smells, tastes, and warm, laughing coziness around the table, she could shut out the cold empty spot deep inside.

After supper, they all gathered in the living room around the little pine tree, decorated with popcorn and cranberries. Papa lit the candles, then read the Christmas story from the gospel of Luke. The younger children's eager shining eyes sneaked peeks at the parcels underneath the tree.

Nettie oohed and aahed with everyone else over whatever was in their surprises: knitted woolen socks and sweaters, little bags of store-bought candy. She smiled, grateful for the new diary Papa had gotten from the bank and wrapped for her. Miss Dorothy's delighted smile upon opening the sampler made Nettie glad she'd spent the hours of grueling needlepoint after all.

"Thank you, kind folks, for including me in your Christmas." The teacher's eyes glistened.

Afterward, Papa's sweet fiddle music wrapped her in the warm blanket of Christmas and family as they sang "Silent Night."

Late that night, thoughts of how Jake was spending his Christmas crept unbidden into Nettie's mind. She pounded her pillow, covered her head with the blanket, and tried to shut out Jake's image with memories of the goose, the presents, the music.

"... *Sleep in heavenly peace* ... "

Nettie found herself drawn to the chaps whenever she entered the barn. They hung, soft and warm, like a white beacon on the wall. She stroked the fur as though it were one of the barn cats that rubbed against her leg.

Whenever she closed her eyes, summer's bright, shimmery light shone behind them. Once again she was on Blacky's back, with Jake alongside, riding with the wind, hair streaming, laughter like fairy dust sprinkling the morning air. A warm glow spread from her very center, up around her heart, and flushed her neck. That's all she wanted, to be with her friend, feel that freedom again.

Wasn't it?

The barn door slammed open with a frigid gust. Ben came in carrying the milk pail and stomped snow from his feet. Nettie whirled away from the chaps. The winter wind wrapped itself around her, the warmth gone in an instant. She grabbed a pitchfork and furiously scraped bits of dirty straw together in a pile, averting her face as though she'd been caught robbing a bird's nest.

CHAPTER SIXTEEN

March 11, 1923
Dear Marie,

Chinook winds finally came. Went from four below to fifty above in just a few hours. Boy, am I glad to see those huge snowdrifts shrink! What a long winter. Of course, no word from Jake.

Thought Mama was going to go stir crazy with everybody cooped up inside so long. I think she still misses Esther. In a better mood yesterday though. Got on her overshoes, went outside without a coat, just sloshed around in the water puddles. Even loosened her hair when she thought nobody was looking and let it fly in the breeze.

One evening Ben banged the kitchen door open and stuck his head in. "That heifer's tryin' to calve and she don't look right." He turned and ran back toward the barn.

Uh-oh. Nettie fumbled into her coat and overshoes alongside Papa and slogged through the mud behind him. Ben held the lantern above his head, throwing an arc of light over the young cow. The heifer stared at them with wide, rolling eyes as she stood with her back arched, her tail held out straight. Just below, Nettie saw a pink nose protruding. Poor little cow, having such a hard time.

Papa knotted a makeshift halter around the heifer's head and snugged her tight against a post. He shrugged out of his coat and rolled up his shirtsleeve. "Ben, get some more rope. Nettie, hold the lantern closer."

Papa pushed on the calf's head until he got it back inside. Then he reached in up to his armpit to reposition its legs. The cow yanked against the rope, trying to get away. But she was worn out from trying to push all by herself and finally stopped struggling.

Ben brought the extra rope. Papa tied one around the calf's front legs, then braced his feet against the stall and pulled with all his strength.

The calf's legs straightened. Pretty soon Nettie could see its nose again. *Thank goodness.* "Push, girl, push!" She tried to will some of her strength to the first-time mother. The heifer moaned and raised her head against the rope to bawl. Her eyes rolled white with pain. Nettie gritted her teeth in sympathy. Was this what having babies was like for Mama? If so, Nettie didn't want any part of it.

Papa strained. Sweat beaded on his forehead. He paused, panting, then braced and pulled again. The head popped out with the forelegs, and then the rest of the body slipped out as far as the hindquarters and stopped. "Dang," he said, panting. "It's hiplocked. Need another rope."

Nettie reached around behind her, grabbed a lariat that hung from a nearby saddle, and tossed it to Ben. Her brother looped it around the cow's hind feet; then he and Papa pulled on the rope until she toppled onto her side.

Nettie chewed on the inside of her cheek. Losing a calf meant a loss of income, maybe twenty or thirty dollars. That was a lot of money to her family. And if the heifer died, too . . . she'd seen it happen before, and watched Papa's anger and sorrow afterward.

"All right, now, hold up her hind leg. Let's see if we can get 'im out." Papa sat, braced his feet against the cow's hindquarters, and pulled. "Dadgummit, c'mon out now."

The heifer bellowed, and then the calf slid free, slick and wet. Nettie ran forward to wipe its nose clean and clear its mouth. What a cute little thing.

"Maaaa!" A lusty bawl greeted her efforts.

Papa grinned. "A nice big bull calf." He clapped Nettie on the shoulder in his glee.

When the cow expelled the afterbirth, Ben untied her. She heaved herself to her feet, turned to sniff at the calf, mooed softly, and began to lick its red coat and white face.

Nettie smiled. Despite the pain the poor heifer had endured, she seemed to have forgotten all about it the minute she saw her baby.

After awhile Nettie and Ben helped the wobbling little creature to its feet and headed it in the right direction for its first meal. Nettie chuckled. "He knows just what to do. He'll be all right."

The three of them stepped out of the barn into the soft, cool air. Nettie could hear water running somewhere, the snow melting with the Chinook winds. A flash of light caught the corner of her eye. She turned northward and squinted. Papa did the same. "Douse the lantern, Ben, quick."

A faint glow quivered low on the horizon, silhouetting the meandering hills.

"Well, I'll be. Northern Lights." Papa took off his hat. "Ben, go get your mother."

The glow intensified into an arc. Its center stretched into the black velvet sky, like a cat awakened from a nap. Another followed, its tail waving white. Then another in green, and yet another in red. Eddie and Chuck ran out, and Mama joined them, clutching her coat close, her mouth open in awe.

Nettie watched as the arcs blended together, dancing, swirling, shimmering. The earth seemed to tilt. She felt as though she were looking down from heaven onto this giant glowing curtain as it undulated with waves of light that rippled through it like a gentle breeze.

The soft air enveloped her. Papa and Ben stood open-mouthed and dreamy. They turned toward her, smiling. Then the six of them walked in silence back to the house, basking in the light of miracles.

CHAPTER SEVENTEEN

Nettie touched her heels to Blacky's sides, urging him to the top of the hillock. He gathered his muscles and lunged upward. Nettie leaned forward over his neck. At the apex, they stopped and Blacky blew through fluttering nostrils. Below, a tide of new grass washed through the silvery sage. The low roll of hills beyond was spread with butter-yellow flowers. A meadowlark's song fluted over the warm breeze. A mate's answering "Oh-ho, look-at-me-now" trilled in return.

White wispy clouds feathered the crisp blue sky. Ah, springtime. Nettie smiled. What a great day to be out, even if it was fence-fixing time.

She slid from the saddle, took a hammer and a pocketful of U-shaped staples from her saddlebag, and walked along the fence, starting where she'd left off the day before. The snowdrifts last winter had knocked down a lot of fence. Where the wires simply drooped, she pulled them up tight with one hand and hammered a new staple into the green-and-rust lichen-covered fence post. Now and then she came across a post broken at the base and marked the spot with a strip of yellow rag she'd brought from home. Papa and Ben would be along later to reset the posts and splice any breaks in the wire.

As the sun rose higher in the May sky, Nettie shed her jacket and tied it behind the saddle. What a free feeling to walk along in shirtsleeves, leading her horse, reveling in the warmth on her back. How she had longed for a day like this last January when the only way she could venture outside was to bundle up so heavily she could barely set one leg in front of the other. An image of Jake's chaps hanging in the barn made her sigh. *Wonder if I'll be working his horses again this summer? If he comes back. That scoundrel. Not another word since Christmas.*

A hawk swooped low, cruising for dinner. Nettie stopped. The graceful bird dove straight toward the ground, then pulled up at the last moment carrying something—probably a mouse—in its talons.

She glanced at the sun directly overhead. Her stomach grumbled. It must be dinnertime. She loosened Blacky's cinch to let him graze, took a sandwich from the saddlebag, and walked up onto a low butte near the fence line. Nettie leaned back on a sandstone rock that dished like an easy chair. When she was younger and found funny-shaped boulders like this, she liked to pretend they were castles or even horses and go floating across the prairie like an Indian princess or a rodeo queen.

Her eyes drifted closed. The sunshine created red dancing flames inside her eyelids. She dozed.

Blacky nickered, and Nettie sat up, blinking. She heard hoofbeats and an answering whinny. Must be Papa and Ben catching up. She stood, walked to the edge of the butte to look down, and frowned. A single rider came along the fence she'd just ridden, about a quarter mile away. Skirting clumps of sagebrush and low gullies, the horse dragged a sled, fastened with ropes to the saddle. Nettie shaded her eyes and watched the rider come closer. Odd that Papa would come without Ben. Maybe he had her brother riding the other side of the ranch, doing the same thing she was.

But, no. That wasn't Papa's sorrel. It was a big buckskin. The rider caught sight of her and waved his straw hat, his familiar sandy-blond hair shining in the sun. Nettie lifted an arm tentatively, then let it fall as the realization swept over her. Despite the sunshine, she felt a chill, then a warm rush.

"Jake!" She stumbled over brush and rocks as she ran toward him. He jumped lightly from his horse, reached her in two long strides, encompassed her with his arms, and swept her around in a circle. His familiar tobacco scent penetrated her nostrils and the strength of his embrace dizzied her. Oh, this felt so nice. It was the first time he'd ever . . .

"Hey, little gal. Did you miss me?"

The spell broken, she pushed out of his arms, dusted herself off, and stood, feet apart, fists on hips. "And where the heck-be-gone have you been all these months?"

Jake laughed, took off his hat, exposing a two-tone forehead, and slapped his leg with the hat. "I'm glad to see you, too." He stood and grinned at her. His blue eyes twinkled.

Blacky ambled up beside them and touched noses with his old friend, Alsanger. Nettie watched the horses snort and bob their heads. She tried to keep her face stern and her mouth turned down, but mirth bubbled up inside, burst into her throat, and she had to laugh, too.

Nettie walked closer to stroke the buckskin's soft neck and to hide her scarlet cheeks. She hadn't wanted to admit it, but now that she saw him, that old empty ache seemed to be gone. "I didn't think you were coming back."

"Course I was." Jake put his hat back on. "This is home. I couldn't leave my horses now, could I?"

Horses? She frowned. *What about me?*

Jake gazed at her with a bemused smile. "I'll bet you missed me." The buckskin whinnied and tossed his head up and down. Jake chuckled. "See, even he knows you did."

Her knees shaky with his nearness, Nettie studied her friend. He looked thinner, his hair a little longer. "Okay. I guess I did . . . a little. I didn't have anybody to talk rodeo with all winter."

"Well, we can remedy that. I've come to help you." He turned and untied a bundle from his saddle. "Stopped by your place and your pa said you were out here working. I have the real McCoy for this fencin' job." He unrolled a metal contraption from a square of soft leather. "This here's a wire stretcher. Bought it in Pendleton. Some cowpoke in Nebraska invented this gadget. Works pretty slick."

Curious, Nettie watched him attach one serrated clamp to the end of a broken string of barbed wire and then onto the piece of wire that dangled from a post about a foot and a half away.

Pulling an attached lever, he ratcheted the two clamps toward each other, putting tension on the wire and bringing the broken pieces closer together. He snipped a short strip of wire from a roll on the sled and spliced the break.

"There. Tight as a fiddle string."

Hmm. How easily he'd fixed that break. How easily he'd made her emptiness go away. Nettie reached over and plucked the wire. She felt it thrum and imagined a giant fiddle bow playing over the fence, each wire tightened for a different sound. She laughed. "We make our own music out here."

"You can make music for me anytime, little gal." Jake winked and Nettie blushed.

They fell into their old easy partnership, working in a quiet, careful mood, saying little. Nettie sneaked sideways glances at Jake. His muscles rippled beneath his shirt as he stretched the wire and dug the postholes. She felt a little thrill that started at the base of her spine and traveled up her back.

They walked along the fence line that seemed to stretch into forever, and wiggled each post to test it. Now and then they found one that was broken off at ground level.

"So, did you get to ride in some rodeos in Oregon?"

"Yeah, a couple." Jake selected a new post from the sled, and Nettie dug the staples out of the broken one to free the wire. She untied a spade from alongside Jake's saddle and began to dig a new hole. Down about eight inches the shovel stopped with a shoulder-jarring clunk.

"Looks like you hit a rock." Jake took the spade from her and worked the blade around the stone until he could lift it out and finish digging the two-foot-deep hole.

"Did you win?" What was going through his mind? Was he glad to be back home? In a way, it was as though he'd never been gone.

"Once or twice. Nothin' big." He sank the new post and tamped the dirt tightly around it.

Nettie stapled the wires. Maybe he'd found a girlfriend in Oregon. She longed to hear what he'd been up to these long winter months, started to form a question several times, but was suddenly overcome by shyness and couldn't ask.

They walked a flat stretch of prairie, polka-dotted with the bright pink of cactus flowers and the pale, fragile petals of the gumbo lily. A sweet, tangy aroma rose from the new grass crushed beneath their footsteps. Up ahead, a prairie dog sat upright on his haunches. It stared bright-eyed for an eternal heartbeat at their approach, then gave a warning whistle and dove into its hole.

As the afternoon waned into dusk, they rode home in a companionable silence.

Back at her dad's barn, Jake grinned and crooked a finger. "Come look at my new saddle." He carried it into the light at the open door.

There it was, the famous Hamley. Its chestnut leather gleamed and she devoured its new, pungent scent. Nettie reached out a tentative hand and brushed her fingers over the engraved whorls and spirals of its rose-petal pattern. Silver conchos, inlaid stars, quarter-moons, and horseshoes glinted in the setting sun.

"Oooh." It was the most gorgeous thing she'd ever seen, and she had a sudden surge of envy. She looked up at Jake. "It's beautiful."

"Yeah, ain't it a beauty? When I saw the one Yakima Canutt won for the bronc-ridin' championship at the Pendleton Round-up, I decided I just had to have me one o' them for rodeoing." Jake stroked the green and white stitching that edged the saddle. "So I went to work for a hay-haulin' crew till I had enough for a down payment. Then, of course I had to stay till I had it all paid off."

He reached into his saddlebags lying by the door. "And I brought this for you."

Nettie stared at the bridle he held up, a hand-tooled rose design headstall with silver conchos just like on Jake's saddle. "For me?" Did he think something special of her after all? She trembled inside. Before she could find the words to thank him, Eddie burst through the barn door and threw himself at Jake.

"Yer home! Yer home!"

Laughing and untangling himself from the twelve-year-old's bear hug, Jake winked at Nettie. "And you thought I wasn't comin' back."

She had to admit to herself then how afraid she'd been that he wouldn't.

CHAPTER EIGHTEEN

The horses plodded through the sultry August heat, tails flicking at flies. Nettie's shirt clung to her back as she rode out to the horse pasture with Jake. She took off her hat and fanned it in front of her heated face.

If there were just one tree on this prairie, or even a tall sagebrush, she would more than welcome the shade. Maybe she would even be cooler sitting in the living room, doing needlework. Whoa. She had to smile at that thought. No. Even this breath-sucking heat was better than that, especially if it meant being with Jake.

Beside her, he rolled up his shirtsleeves. "What's Joe plannin' to do with his three-hundred-dollar first-prize money from the Canyon Ranch rodeo?"

Nettie chuckled, reseating her hat. "You won't believe it, but he's talking about buying some sheep. With prices the way they are, he could get about forty head." She turned toward him.

His mouth dropped open. "What? Sheep? You gotta be kiddin'."

"Nope. See, he's sweet on the oldest Ferguson girl, and he's thinking about getting married. Papa says he's crazy, but Joe wants his own place and a start on a cash crop with lambs first. He says he can't be a cowhand forever and support a family."

"Sheep, huh? I'll be. To each his own, I guess." With a wry grin, Jake scanned the horizon, looking for his herd of horses. "Well, if we can get these cayuses rounded up and closer to home, I can start working on plans for the rodeo in Sunburst come the end of the month."

"Are you nervous about putting on this rodeo?"

"Naw. Just hopin' I can find enough good stock for it. I'm invitin' cowboys from all over the country to come."

"That's great. I'll help if you want." Nettie chewed on her lower lip. Planning this rodeo with Jake would be so exciting. "Do you think some famous cowgirls might come?"

Jake threw her a glance from under his hat brim. "I dunno. We can try to track some down and ask, I s'pose. Want me to ask Marie?"

"Of course." Nettie smiled. It would be dandy to see her friend again.

They crested a low rise to see the horses in the meadow below. The herd had split in two. "I'll take the north bunch. You bring the other." Jake spurred his horse into a trot.

Nettie wheeled Blacky in the opposite direction, able to forget the heat now that there was work to concentrate on. She yelled at the horses, "C'mon now." Waving her hat in the air, she urged her group toward the bunch Jake pushed forward.

Blacky did a quick sidestep as a low rumble sounded behind them. Nettie jerked her head around to see the sky churning into a muddy charcoal swirl. Oh no. One of summer's sudden thunderstorms that came up out of nowhere.

The wind rose in just a heartbeat and slammed the grass flat in its first rush across the prairie.

Urgency stabbed her gut. *Gotta get the horses in.* "Yeehaw." She drove her bunch faster toward Jake. "Giddyup."

Jake waved and yelled, but she couldn't hear what he said. She dug her heels into Blacky's flanks. They'd have to hurry to make it home before the storm hit.

The air suddenly turned cold. The first big drop glanced off her hat brim. Then rain plopped onto the ground like fresh cow pies in the dust. It came faster and harder, with an ominous rumble. The horses milled around, tails switching. One bolted. Another took off after him, then another. Her heart beat faster. She swiveled her head. Where was Jake?

Jake galloped to her side. "Let 'em go. It's turnin' to hail. Head for that ol' house over yonder."

Blacky stretched to match the stride of Jake's buckskin as they raced for the abandoned homestead shack in the distance. Nettie's braid came loose and her hair whipped around her head. The hailstones grew in size and force, pounded her back, smacked her face, and blinded her. She yelped in pain as she struggled to hang on. Her hands were numb. Her boot slipped from the stirrup. "Don't think I'm gonna make it!"

Jake grabbed Blacky's headstall. Both horses skidded to a stop. "Get the saddles off," he yelled. "We'll cover our heads."

Nettie slid off and grabbed for the cinch, but an egg-sized hailstone thumped Blacky's flank. He reared and circled, trying to escape the abuse. She tried again and again, but her horse jerked away from her each time. He whinnied, his eyes rolling. A wild thrash of his head flung Nettie into the mud. Still hanging on to the reins, she pulled herself up hand over hand. "Please hold still, Blacky, please."

For just a moment the force of the stones seemed to let up, and Jake wrenched his saddle loose. "Here, grab one side." He hoisted it over their heads. The sky grew a shade lighter as the hail turned into rain that fell in sheets, driven diagonally by the wind. Nettie stumbled along with Jake, bumping into each other. Both held the saddle up with one hand and led their horses with the other, the storm pushing them from behind.

Lightning slashed through the murky sky. A thunderclap rattled her teeth. The horses shied and tugged at the reins. Barely able to breathe, Nettie could no longer feel her hands. Her whole body was numb. She felt the saddle slip. They wouldn't make it. She was going to fall. They'd both be hit by lightning. *Dear Lord, help us, please.*

"Hang on, we're almost there." Jake shifted the heavy saddle to take more of the weight himself. "It's okay. You can do it. Come on. Just a few more steps." Together they staggered the last few yards to the old shack. Jake dropped the saddle on the refuse-strewn porch and tethered the horses under the roof overhang on the lee side. Then he pushed the door open and helped Nettie through the opening. She nearly fell into the room, relief flooding over her.

He pushed the door shut against the gusts of wind and rain and struggled to latch it. Then he knelt beside her, his wide eyes examining her face. "Are you all right? Are you hurt? Anything broken?"

"I'm okay." Nettie looked up at him, gulped and blinked. "Oh my gosh, your eye." She sat upright and reached up to caress the rapidly swelling bump.

"I'm just fine."

"Jake, we coulda been killed." She shuddered as the realization washed over her, then broke into great hiccupping sobs.

He encircled her with his long arms and drew her face to his chest. He smelled like horsehair and tobacco. It didn't matter that his sodden denim shirt stuck to her cheek. She closed her eyes and snuggled close inside his embrace as he stroked her wet hair.

The rain beat a vicious tattoo on the roof. Just like those hailstones on her head and back. Her skin still stung, and her hands were raw and tingling. She shivered again. The ice seemed to have penetrated her blood. Her teeth chattered. Never in her life had she been so scared. They were lucky to be alive. Safe in his arms now, her sobs gradually subsided.

Jake hugged her closer, his face only inches from hers. She felt his warm breath on her cheek.

He rubbed a hand up and down her back, sending warm shivers through her body. "I have to let you go for a minute and see if I can get a fire going."

Nettie clutched at him. She didn't want him to go, even a few feet away.

Murmuring in her ear as if soothing a skittish colt, he eased out of the embrace and off the floor. He picked up an old horse blanket from one corner of the nearly empty room and shook the dust off. Gently, he wrapped the worn, dirty wool pad around her shoulders.

Nettie glanced around the room, wallpaper peeling in strips, cobwebs strung over the windows, the floor rotted and splintered. *Wonder what happened to the people who lived here?* A wooden chair slumped on its side, a leg missing. Jake stomped on the remaining legs to break them, then the rungs and the back, into pieces. He pried up a loose floorboard to add to the pile of firewood

Nettie watched him squat before the fireplace, moving with such confidence. *Gosh, he knows just what to do.* He whittled shavings from the wood, then struck a match from a little tin canister in his pocket. *He's so handy. And so caring.*

He protected me.

Jake blew on the flame, coaxed it to catch. Above the sunburned line on his forehead where his hat usually rode, his skin was fair. His reddish blond hair shone softly.

The flame caught and grew, its flicker kindling a spark of hope in her. She heard the snap as it spread to the other shavings and sticks of wood.

Jake added more fuel to the fire. He coughed as it smoked, but then the smoke drew up into the chimney. He sat next to her again, cradling her in the curve of his arm. He took out a small flask from his pocket. "Here, have a slug of this. It'll help warm you."

She coughed at the harsh fire that ran down her throat. But it did warm her, and her shivers diminished as her clothes dried.

"Thank you for saving my life." Nettie raised her face to his and kissed the corner of his mouth. Then, to hide her blush, she leaned against his strong body. He tightened his arm around her shoulders.

They'd made it. Together. They were together, and that was all that mattered right now.

~ ~

Nettie brushed her hair back into a bun and chose a red bandanna to wrap around her neck, her aches and bruises from the hailstorm two weeks ago now a fading memory. Then she slipped into a crisp white shirt Joe had left behind, tucked it into Ben's cast-off denims, and sat on the bed to pull on one boot. She shivered with anticipation. Jake would be here any minute. The two days she hadn't seen him seemed like two weeks. Today they were going to Browning to watch a rodeo. She could hardly wait.

A strange sound brought her up short. Was someone running a threshing machine outside? But the threshers weren't due for weeks yet. The engine noise grew louder. The horses in the corral whinnied. Then a series of loud pops propelled her to the window. Who was making that noise? Her folks were in town, and her brothers had gone to the pasture. Were they back, shooting at something?

With one boot on, the other hanging from her hand, Nettie could only stare, her mouth open wide. Here came Jake, driving an open-air Model T over the dusty wagon track. His grin reached from ear to ear, and he waved his hat in the air as though he rode a bucking bronc.

Nettie nearly forgot to breathe. She couldn't believe what she was seeing. Jake driving a car? Not riding a horse?

He squeezed the horn bulb, sounding a raucous squawk, and whooped when he saw her run out of the house, swinging her empty boot.

"Hoooeee. Lookee here what I got."

"Jake, what in the world?"

The engine cut out with a jerk. Jake jumped over the side and swept his hands toward the car. "Ain't she a beaut? Sure got her cheap, only two hundred fifty. Even has an electric starter. Guess we can go places now."

Nettie's hand flew to cover her mouth. Her eyes felt as wide as full moons. "It's really nice." She limped around the machine in one boot, looking at the hard, thin rubber tires, the gleaming black running boards, the pinstriped upholstered seats, excitement building. "We're really going to ride in a car?" She'd never ridden in a car. In fact, nobody she knew even owned one.

Jake followed her, chuckling. "Yup. If you wanna finish dressing, I guess we could go on to the rodeo."

Nettie looked down at herself, realizing that she was still minus a boot. Her mouth twitched upward into a smile. "Okay, big shot. I'll get my boot on and you can take me for a ride." Jake opened the passenger door, gave her a hand up onto the running board and into the seat. Then he ran around to hop over the doorless driver's side. He turned a key and adjusted one lever on the steering column for the spark and another for the gas.

At the same time, he worked a pedal on the floor with his foot. The engine fired up and Jake revved it with the gas lever. The Model T lurched forward, a cloud of dust spinning from beneath its wheels. He wrestled with the steering wheel as the vehicle snorted and bucked over the rough trail. Nettie clung to the side with both hands and whooped.

"Ain't this fun?" Jake looked over at Nettie. The car swerved and jounced.

"Look out." Nettie slid down in the seat and braced her feet against the floorboards. "You're hitting every pothole in the road." At last the bouncing slowed as they entered a more traveled roadway. Jake pulled to the side, stopped the car, and turned off the engine.

"Scare ya?" He grinned like a banshee.

"Have you ever driven a car before?" The words spewed from her lips.

"Heck no, but it can't be any harder than tamin' a good bronc, can it? 'Cept for shiftin gears."

"Well, can I try it then?"

"Let me get the hang of it first." Still chuckling, he hopped over the side and reached into the back for a gas can and another filled with oil. As soon as the refueling was done, he jumped back in, fired up the engine, and popped the gearshift. The exhaust sputtered and threw up a plume of acrid oily smoke behind.

Nettie grabbed onto the edge of the seat with both hands. Does he really know what he's doing? Good land, and she'd been afraid of being killed in that hailstorm. That was nothing. She giggled. If she survived this trip, she'd be ready for anything.

As he drove, Jake seemed to tame the creature and the ride smoothed. Nettie admired his chiseled profile, his arms rippling as he gripped the steering wheel. "Wow, you're good at everything, breaking horses *and* automobiles."

Jake grinned. "Of course. And young fillies, too." Nettie stared at him and blushed.

Then she saw a cloud of steam erupt from the front of the automobile. She pointed. "Oh, my gosh, what's happening? We're on fire."

Jake laughed and coasted to a stop. "Naw. That's the radiator. It's boilin' over."

Every few miles the radiator bubbled and steamed, and they stopped to let it cool and pour in more water. Jake also added more oil. The farther they drove, the hotter it ran and the more often they had to stop. They finally pulled into a fuel station in Prairie City.

The owner peeked under the hood and chuckled. "Well, I think ya need to drain some o' that there oil out. It shore shouldn't be needin' that much."

After performing that chore, they were once again on their way, with a lot less smoke. But a few more miles down the road, Nettie heard a pop, then the Model T lurched and swerved. Now what? She looked at Jake with raised eyebrows.

"Flat tire." He grimaced, climbed out, and went around to the back to get the jack and a spare inner tube. Nettie got out to stretch her legs.

Inserting the tire iron as a handle for the jack, Jake pumped until the wheel raised off the ground. He unfastened the entire assembly from the hub, and pried the flat tire from the rim with the iron bar. "This jalopy didn't come with a spare tire," he grumbled.

"No wonder you got it for only two hundred fifty dollars."

Jake merely grunted.

"Let me help." Nettie grabbed the spare tube. "Show me what to do."

"Okay. I'm going to replace the flat inner tube with the good one, like so." Then he attached a hand pump to the valve. "You can pump it up."

Nettie pushed the handle down and up repeatedly until the tire was inflated.

Jake wiped the sweat from his face, prodded the tire onto the rim, and released the jack.

Easing the automobile back down, he kicked at the tire. "Okay. We're ready to go. This'll probably happen a couple more times. Got two, three more inner tubes, and a patch kit, too, just in case."

Nettie dusted herself off and twisted her mouth into a wry smile. "We probably could have ridden the forty miles on horseback just as fast, with all these stops."

"Aw, where's your sense of adventure?" Jake grinned at her. "Wanna drive now? There's a nice straight stretch of road comin' up."

"Yeah. I bet I can do better than you."

Jake helped her into the car and showed her which levers to push. Nettie revved the gas lever and lifted her foot off the clutch pedal. The Model T jerked forward and stalled.

"Oops. What did I do?" Nettie grimaced. Maybe this wasn't so easy after all.

"You didn't do anything wrong. Just let your foot off slowly . . . there ya go." Jake chortled as the car roared down the highway. "You're doing great."

"Whoopee!" The wind blew Nettie's hair just like galloping on horseback, but the car went faster than a horse. At least downhill. It would chug up the incline, and then the pit of her stomach dropped as they swooped over the crest and picked up speed on the way down. Nettie giggled. Every day with Jake was an adventure.

Browning teemed with color and motion. Indians dressed in full rega-
lia, cowboys in their finest, and ladies in their Sunday best all gathered
at the rodeo arena. Jake zoomed toward an empty space between rows
of black Model Ts like theirs, then had to slam on the brakes just
before meeting the back end of another jalopy. Nettie braced her feet
again, waiting for the next jolt. Her legs ached from tension. "I think
horses are easier to handle."

"She doesn't corner like my ol' buckskin." Jake ground the gears
into reverse and tried again. After several tries, the Model T was
wedged so close to the next vehicle that Nettie had to climb over the
gearshift and brake lever to get out on Jake's side.

"We made it." Jake mopped his forehead with his bandanna and
grinned down at her.

She couldn't help but smile at the endearing way he had of making
the best of any situation. "I swear, Jake, cars sure are ornerier than any
horse I've ever seen."

"Aw, they're no worse. Just gotta know how to handle 'em." He
winked at her.

She rolled her eyes. "It's fun, though."

Nettie caught herself watching Jake throughout the day. The way his
eyes crinkled at the corners when he smiled. The way the muscles in
his arms rippled under his shirt. The way he walked, tall and sure,
broad shouldered and slim-hipped. The way his smile melted her
heart.

Things hadn't been the same since the day of the hailstorm. On
one hand, they still worked comfortably together. But on the other, she
would start to tell him something, think of his touch, and then become
tongue-tied as a hot flush rose from her chest, across her shoulders,
and up her neck. She'd never had this happen before.

Nettie barely noticed anyone else around—the cowboys and cow-girls who waved or hollered hellos at Jake. She closed her eyes and lost track of the rodeo, of who was riding and how the rider was doing. Leaning close enough to feel the heat of Jake's arm, she relived the warmth of his embrace in the shack.

A shiver ran through her at the memory of the hail, the rain, the wind, and the lightning that had sneaked up on them that day. Then she tingled with the pleasure that just being by his side brought her.

Nettie blinked rapidly to bring herself back to the present. All these new conflicting feelings. Would she ever get this out of her sys-tem? Did she want to? What did this mean? She could hardly bring herself to think the word. Love? *Wonder if he's thinking the same things?*

After the rodeo, as they strolled back to the Model T, Jake took Nettie's hand. She could feel the ridged calluses on his warm, dry palm. This simple action seemed so natural now, made her feel so secure, so cared for.

The car Jake had parked so close to was gone, so he opened the door with a flourish. "Your carriage awaits, my lady."

My, how poetic. How romantic. Just like the men in her dime novels.

He smiled at her. "Have a good time today?"

She smiled back and clung to his arm just a moment longer than necessary before settling into her seat. "I sure did. Did you?"

"You bet." Jake fired up the engine and drove away from the rodeo grounds in a slightly smoother manner than he had come in.

Sunburned and heady with the sensations and excitement of the day, Nettie looked forward to the ride home. "So, you think you got a handle on this smoking, bouncing iron monster? Or do I need to show you how?"

"Hey, this is a little like tamin' broncs. It just takes practice." Jake chuckled.

"I don't know." She teased him back. "I think riding broncs might be easier."

"Well, this ol' jalopy gets us there a little faster when we have a ways to go, but it sure ain't gonna help us with our work." Jake reset his hat and gunned the engine.

"No, I can just see the herd scatterin' to the winds when they hear all this noise." Nettie laughed to herself, picturing this snorting, popping beast tearing across the pasture. The horses would jerk their heads high, eyes rolling. One look at the smoking hunk of metal would send them hightailing it into the farthest reaches of the pasture.

No, that wasn't the way Jake worked. He was calm, quiet, and patient with his horses. She stared out at the pastureland speeding by in the deepening dusk.

For a while Jake talked about the rides he'd seen that day—the ones she hadn't noticed—and ideas he had for his upcoming rodeo. Then he fell silent as he wrestled the steering wheel.

The cooling evening air caressed her arms. She longed to reach out and touch Jake, to have him hold her. Instead, she snuggled into her corner of the seat and sneaked glances over at him. How she enjoyed looking at his handsome, square-cut face, so intent now on driving into the growing dark. *Better not distract him.*

What would it feel like to bury her face in Jake's silky hair? She closed her eyes and allowed a delicious shiver to race through her body. Her eyes flew open. Thank heavens it was getting dark and he couldn't see her flushed face.

CHAPTER NINETEEN

The Sunburst Sun
August 28, 1923
Program
1:00—Parade of cowboys and cowgirls, headed by Cut Bank brass band.
1:30—Roping and bronc busting.
2:30—Nettie Brady will enter competition with entire field, riding wild steers with only one hand on surcingle.
8:30—Roundup dance at Sunburst hall. Hammond's famous Glacier Park orchestra. Dance continues until it stops.

Dust from the corrals hovered as approaching dusk painted the sky with yellow-crimson hues. Snorts and an occasional whinny from one of the horses still in the pens echoed off the empty bleachers. Nettie felt a strange hollowness after the spectators were gone, as if they'd taken all the energy and intensity with them.

She helped Jake pay off the winners with money collected from entry fees. "See you at the dance tonight, Jake," one woman called as she joined the men headed into town to celebrate.

Something in Nettie's chest lurched. Did other women expect to dance with him, too? She frowned. Well, of course. He was the kind of gentleman who would dance with the wallflowers.

She put on a smile and looked up at his grimy face. "Your rodeo was a grand success. Nobody got seriously hurt, everybody had fun, and the winners sure are happy." He had pulled it off. Produced his first big rodeo without a hitch. What a guy.

"Yeah, it came off purty good. And you." He grinned back at her. "I'm so darn proud of you, the way you rode that steer and beat Marie. You've come a long way."

Nettie grinned. Yes, she did feel pretty proud about winning. And Marie had been genuinely happy for her.

Jake stretched his tall frame and grimaced. He must ache from his own winning ride. Nettie reached out in sympathy to touch his shoulder. "Are you all right?"

"Oh sure. Just a little sore's all. Let's stop by the Stockman's and buy the champs a drink before we go over to Beulah's for supper."

"Great." Too excited to acknowledge how tired she was, Nettie jumped on her horse for the short half-mile ride into town. A thought of Mama's reaction to her daughter going into a saloon flitted through Nettie's mind, but she brushed it aside. She wasn't about to let anything spoil her fun today.

When they reached the Stockman's Bar and stepped into the dimly lit room, her body seemed to vibrate, alive with fiddle and guitar music, shouts of laughter, and glasses clinking. Cigarette smoke hung in the air. She smelled the sharp tang of alcohol. This was the first time she'd ever been in a saloon. With a buzz of excitement, she slipped onto the only available stool at the long mahogany bar. On the back wall hung a painting of a woman stepping out of a bathtub, a towel not entirely hiding her nakedness. Nettie let her mouth drop open and raised her eyebrows. She glanced at Jake, but he apparently hadn't noticed her shocked reaction.

Below the picture, a wall-width mirror reflected the animation in the room. Despite Prohibition, Stockman's had drawn a shoulder-to-shoulder crowd, and whiskey, probably smuggled in from Canada, was plentiful.

"Two whiskeys." Jake waved at the barkeep.

Nettie glanced around. "Doesn't the sheriff object to the bar serving alcohol?"

"Nah, small town. He don't care." Jake shrugged. "Only time he gets involved is if somebody gets too rowdy and takes it out to the street."

Nettie pictured the rough crowd in Miles City the night she'd been there with Marie. Montana didn't seem to march in step with the rest of the country. She grinned. *Kinda like me.*

She took a sip of her drink. It burned its way down her throat and she coughed. This wasn't as harsh-tasting as the moonshine she'd sampled before, though. It had a smooth, smoky flavor.

Jake stood behind her, greeting the cowboys one by one as they stepped up to congratulate him.

"Darn good rodeo."

"Best I've been to in a while." This comment from an old-timer.

"Congratulations. You pulled it off, you ol' sonovagun." Jake's brother-in-law Roy pumped his hand.

"Another round for Jake and his purty lady." Another cowboy slapped him on the back.

His lady. Hmm, that has a nice sound to it. Nettie, flushed and a little dizzy from the attention and the whiskey, pushed the second glass away. One was enough for her. She looked around the crowded room. Too bad Marie and Tom had to leave for home early. She would have loved to talk to her friend about the events of the day.

Dusk had settled when they finally escaped the overzealous crowd and rode to Jake's sister's house on the edge of town. Suddenly she was bone-weary. All she wanted to do was lie down and sleep.

"About time you two got here." Beulah motioned them inside. "Been waitin' supper on ya, but I had to feed the kids already. They were hungry enough to eat their saddles." She gave Nettie a motherly hug. "Heard you won steer riding. That's great."

"Thanks." Nettie smiled at Jake's older sister. She could get to like this woman.

Fried chicken and mashed potatoes had never tasted so good to Nettie. Gradually the victuals refueled her and the tiredness began to ebb.

Beulah's husband, Clem, grinned at Nettie. "That was quite a ride you made today, young miss. You're gonna be beatin' the spurs off ol' Jake here pretty soon." He poked a knobby elbow at him.

Blood rushed to Nettie's face. She sneaked a look at her cowboy out of the corner of her eye. Gosh, would he be worried about that? "Not if he keeps drawing horses like Dynamite."

Jake winked at her. "Aw, shucks, I just happened to stick. He probably wasn't buckin' his best today."

Nettie left the warm laughter to take a short rest in Beulah's bedroom before she dressed for the dance. She crawled under the thick quilt and settled into the feather mattress on the iron bedstead. But she couldn't sleep, thinking of the fun she'd had today. And now she was going to a dance, with Jake, for the first time. Butterflies tickled her ribs. But those other women would want to dance with him.

She got up and shook out the clothes she'd packed behind her saddle that morning. Donning white gloves so as not to run her stockings, she smoothed them on and fastened them to a garter belt. With a sigh, she pulled and tugged to get the seams straight in the back.

She fumbled with the buttons on her red blouse, finally getting them fastened just right, then slipped on a gray wool skirt. What if she didn't look as nice as the other women? Now she wished she had paid more attention to Mama and her sisters. She turned from side to side in front of Beulah's mirror. Well, it would have to do.

Now her hair. Her usual braid wouldn't look right. First she pulled it back into a bun. No, that wasn't festive enough. She shook it loose, brushed and rearranged it, trying to get the waves to fall to her shoulders just right. Would Jake think she was pretty? She pursed her mouth. Was this lipstick too bright? It was one Lola had left. She hoped he would want to dance with her once or twice at least. There were so many prettier girls who would probably vie for his attention.

She'd seen how they fawned over him at the rodeo. A dagger of jealousy sliced through her. Then she giggled. *Oh, stop being silly, Nettie Brady.*

Her legs trembled in the unaccustomed high heels, also Lola's. Nettie finally descended the stairs into the living room, her hands icy. The joking and laughter hushed. Jake stopped in midsentence and blinked. He smoothed a hand over his hair and, adjusting his bolo tie on his clean white shirt, stepped toward her.

Nettie tried to swallow but her mouth was as dry as corral dust.

"Wow." He stood at arm's length. She felt the heat of his gaze travel from her head to her feet. Then he gave a low whistle. "You are one pretty filly tonight. Let's go dancin'." *He thinks I'm pretty.* Her whole body felt as much on fire as her cheeks. She certainly hadn't needed to put on that rouge. She forced her trembling lips into a smile. "All right. Let's go."

They walked, arm in arm, the few blocks to the town hall, which blazed with lights. As they entered, the orchestra greeted them with a familiar Great War song, "How Ya Gonna Keep 'em Down on the Farm, After They've Seen Paree."

Jake grabbed her hand and swung her into a fast cowboy two-step. The same sensation of freedom she felt when galloping in the wind came over her as he swung her in a wide circle, then swooped her back into his embrace. She caught a whiff of his familiar tobacco smell, mingled with a clean soap scent. Finally, a handsome, wide-shouldered, slim-hipped cowboy to dance with, just like she'd dreamed. This sure was different from dancing with the sweaty, awkward Porky Conners back at those schoolhouse dances.

The upbeat tune ended. Laughing and brushing back stray tendrils of damp hair, Nettie turned away from the dance floor. Fun while it lasted, but Jake would surely want to ask some other girl to dance now. She brushed aside the pang of disappointment that threatened.

The band set a slower pace with "If You Were the Only Girl in the World." Jake caught her hand and drew her close. Warmth that had nothing to do with the exertion of the previous dance flooded her body.

Nettie settled into happy enchantment, swaying with the music, at home in Jake's arms. Oh, she could stay here forever. As the last chord died away, his deep blue eyes gazed into hers and he squeezed her hand.

"May I have this dance?" A husky female voice shattered the spell. A slender hand with long painted nails rested on Jake's arm. Nettie looked up. The young woman's black hair was bobbed stylishly. She wore a shimmery beaded dress that skimmed straight down her boyish body and ended in fringes just above her knees. She stood with her other hand on one cocked hip, balancing a long black cigarette holder between two fingers.

Nettie gaped. Who was this? Her hands turned cold and dropped to her sides as the woman drew Jake toward the crowded dance floor. "Hey, cowboy. Want me to teach you a new dance?"

Nettie turned away and closed her eyes as if she could shut out the world from witnessing her embarrassment. She didn't want to see Jake sweep this woman onto the floor. A flush consumed her entire body. How dare that woman steal her cowboy away?

Suddenly the great care she had taken in choosing her outfit and fixing her hair and makeup seemed harebrained, absurd. It was all a sham. She could never measure up. She was just a cowgirl. Men didn't want women who were their competitors. They wanted women who were competent in the kitchen, or beautiful, sexy women like this one, to flatter them and make them feel like kings. Nettie knew how to gentle a horse, rope a calf, fix fence. But she didn't know how to be flirtatious or charming and sexy. She would surely lose Jake's attention now. What a fool she was. For a moment she was torn between running out of the dance hall or marching up to that woman and—

She felt a gentle hand on her shoulder. Oh, no. Some poor cowpoke, feeling sorry for her, trying to ask her to dance. She didn't want to dance with all the short, bandy-legged old bachelors, desperate for any female companionship.

Nettie shrugged and opened her eyes. "No, thank—"

It was Jake. "I ain't up to no dance lessons. You're my girl tonight."

Her heart trip-hammered. *My girl.*

From one dance to another they swayed and twirled. When someone tapped his shoulder to cut in, Jake just grinned and swept her away. "Pardon my rudeness, ma'am, but I ain't lettin' you go for nobody." His deep blue eyes held hers.

Weightlessness enveloped her body. Her feet barely skimmed the floor, high heels or no.

After the dance, Nettie changed back into riding clothes and rode side by side with Jake along the Saddle Horn trail over the rims toward home. A silver-dollar moon brightened the rolling hill country. Shadows sharpened in the deep coulees filled with tall grass. All was still except for their spurs jingling, the horses' clopping footsteps, and an occasional coyote's howl in the distance. The pure night air washed over Nettie. A lilting tune of cowboy romance ran through her head. She was filled with the joy of the music and dancing. Sheer magic. Jake had chosen her to dance with, all night. She wanted to hold on to that bubbly, dreamlike happiness forever.

The hairs on her arm tingled when her horse brushed her leg against Jake's. She turned to look at him at the same moment he swiveled in his saddle and leaned toward her. As if the horses, too, had fallen under a spell, they both stopped at once. Jake reached out to pull her closer. She leaned toward him. His lips found hers.

A delicious shiver ran through her. She melted into euphoric dizziness. Let her never come back to earth again.

Jake broke off the kiss with exquisite slowness. His lips brushed hers once more. Then again. His warm breath caressed her cheek. "I love you, little gal. Think you could learn to love me?"

Nettie struggled for a reply. "Oh, Jake." Love. The word whirled through her mind. The soft warmth of his kiss enveloped her. Could she love him? Did she love him?

"I mean, will you marry me?"

"Yes." She looked deep into his eyes, crinkled at the corners. No need to think. She knew.

~~~

Nettie crouched low over Blacky's neck. She'd said yes. For three interminable days the impulsiveness of her answer had haunted her. Her first instinct when she arrived home that night—had it been only three days ago?—was to awaken everyone with her shouts of joy. But a prickling of doubt subdued her and she sat, trance-like, studying the moon until its light faded and the glow of the sunrise took its place. She'd said yes to Jake. But now she wasn't so sure.

She dug her heels into Blacky's flanks, urging him faster, faster. The wind loosened her hair from its bun, and it whipped around her face like the horse's mane.

At last she let Blacky slow, his breath coming in grunts. The tension in Nettie's legs eased. Her arms relaxed as her own breathing slowed. She reined him in to a trot, then a walk to cool down the lather bubbled on his shiny black withers.

They came to a stop in a meadow. Nettie slid from the horse's back, let the reins drop, and sank into the knee-high grass that rippled golden in the breeze. Shivering despite the late August heat, she put shaky fingertips to her lips. She still felt Jake's kiss as though it had been branded on her mouth.

He'd asked her to marry him. And she'd said yes.

She didn't understand this urge to run away. And here she was, trembling and shaking like a newborn calf in February.

He loved her. Her golden cowboy, gentle and understanding, square of shoulder and lean of hip. But he was her best friend. She couldn't marry him. Could she? But these feelings he aroused in her. It had to be love.

Aw, darn. She wasn't ready to be a wife. Cooking, cleaning, sewing. All those things she detested. What about rodeo? If she were stuck at home doing domestic chores, she wouldn't be able to travel. *I'm only seventeen. There's lots of time before I have to settle down.* She doubled over in the grass. Her stomach felt like she'd swallowed a rock.

Nettie raked her fingers through her tousled hair. All these conflicting thoughts. She stood and buried her face in Blacky's mane. Who could she talk to? Not her mother. Mama'd be thrilled when her wild daughter married and "settled down like a proper wife."

Margie? Lola? No, her sisters didn't understand her urge, the compulsion to ride, to compete, to win.

She gazed out over the rolling hills. Oh, how she wished Marie were here. She would know how Nettie felt. She could tell her what to do.

But Marie lived a day away by train or two days on horseback. The next time they'd likely meet would be at the Havre Roundup in September, still three weeks away. She couldn't keep this secret from her family that long. Mama kept giving her sidelong glances, as if she knew something was up. Torment shot through her.

She couldn't avoid facing Jake and her doubts that long. Nettie watched a meadowlark flit through the sagebrush.

But wait. Jake loved to rodeo, too. He wanted to travel. When they were planning his rodeo, they'd talked about the big exhibitions they wanted to go to: Pendleton, Cheyenne, Calgary. Yes, he did encourage her riding. She smiled. They could do it together. That would be fun.

Nettie rubbed her hands together as if to warm them and closed her eyes.

That kiss. The warmth returned to her fingertips and tingled up her arms, then down through her core.

It was awfully nice.

❦

Nettie leaned against the corral fence and watched the rider approach, dark against the clear afternoon sky.

It was Jake. Her heart thudded like a trapped rabbit's. Maybe she could run to the house and hide in her room. She swiveled her head frantically. Or the barn. It was closer.

"So you *are* home." Jake dismounted, dropped the reins, and walked toward her. "I was beginning to wonder. Haven't seen you since the dance. A week ago. Is everything okay?"

Heat rose to her face. She stared at the toe of her boot, drawing circles in the dust. Finally she lifted her head and forced a smile. "Well, Mama's been keeping me pretty busy helping with the cooking."

"Uh-huh?"

"Well, you know the threshing crew will be coming soon."

Just then Alsanger moved forward, holding his head out toward Nettie, nostrils fluttering softly. Jake looked at her with his intense blue eyes. "See, Al missed ya, too. Look at 'im."

Nettie rubbed the buckskin's soft nose. She stepped to the horse's side, put her arms around his neck, and buried her burning face in the warm mane. She felt the heat of Jake's body as he came around behind her. He put a gentle hand on her shoulder.

"Is something wrong? Have you changed your mind about marrying a no-good cowboy like me?"

Here it was. The question. She wanted to crawl under the cover of Alsanger's mane. "No." Her voice was muffled against the horse's neck.

"Then what?"

The anguish in Jake's voice made Nettie turn her head slightly. She looked at him with one eye. Oh, how that voice soothed her, just like the wild horses he gentled. She gulped. She didn't mean to cause him any hurt.

"Oh, Jake, I was just . . . scared." She turned fully now. He encircled her with his arms and they stood that way for long minutes. Nettie took in his familiar horsehair and tobacco smells, felt his strong arms holding her. She wished this would last forever. The cold hard lump of fear inside began to melt.

Jake grasped her hand to lead her to a rock nearby. "Tell me."

Nettie sat. She planted her boots in the dust to still her shaking knees. She took a deep breath, held it, then let it out. "You've been my best friend, since Joe moved away. And you understand me. I mean, you know how important riding and rodeoing are to me."

Jake nodded.

"But, if we get married, oh, you know how much I hate cooking and cleaning and sewing and—"

She broke off when she saw the corners of Jake's mouth twitch. "And, you know, isn't that what being a wife means? I'd rather be out riding with you than embroidering pretty tablecloths to serve you dinner on."

Jake's smile widened. A low chuckle rose and burst forth into a hearty laugh.

Nettie looked at him, astonished. Her cheeks felt ready to burst into flame.

"Oh, my sweet little gal. If that's all that's worryin' ya." He turned toward her, took her face between his palms, and peered into her eyes.

"You're my best friend, too. We'll be partners. You don't have to do any more cookin' or cleanin' than you want to. Heck, I been batchin' long enough. I know what to do to keep the mice from takin' over. I'll help you, and you'll help me with the ridin' and the horse breakin' and whatever your heart desires. How's that?"

Nettie's eyes brimmed with tears. "Are you sure?"

"I'm sure."

"But aren't women supposed to take care of the house and all those things?"

He squeezed her hand. "We'll be partners. Heck, we're already a great team."

Her shoulders relaxed. What a guy. He was so understanding. What more could a girl ask for?

She grinned. "It's a deal."

Jake leaned forward and brushed her lips with his. "Sealed with a kiss. Now, would you like me to go ask your father's permission?"

"Yes." She jumped up from the rock. "No. Let's go tell my family together."

CHAPTER TWENTY

September 25, 1923
Dear Marie,

I can not believe Mama. I've been in prison the last two weeks.
Sitting in the house all day, embroidering. Got to fill my hope chest.
What for? That's what I want to know. Sun's shining outside.
Blacky's racing back and forth along the fence. Jake's got work for
me to do. But no. Mama says I have to get ready for my wedding.

Nettie's underarms were sodden, her back ached, and she'd pricked
her finger for the umpteenth time that day. She grimaced and stuck it
into her mouth. Her linens were going to be speckled instead of white.
She wadded the half-finished pillowcase and threw it to the floor. The
weather was too nice to spend indoors. Darned if she was going to put
in another day on this drudgery.

She peeked around the corner into the kitchen. The house was
quiet, save for the clock ticking. Good. Mama was outside, raking up
the dried remnants of the garden. A sense of mischief tickled inside as
she dropped her skirt onto the bedroom floor and slipped on a pair of
soft, worn denims.

Now, to sneak down to the pasture. Heart thrumming, Nettie eased
the door open without a squeak and let it clunk softly closed. Once
outside, she stopped at the musty root cellar to grab a carrot. Then she
slipped down the other side of the hill past the barn, to the meadow
where Blacky stood, his ears pitched forward. He gave a welcoming

whicker as Nettie bent under the barbed wire. She fed him the carrot, opened the pasture gate, then vaulted onto his bare back.

"Let's go, boy." Suppressed laughter erupted when the horse broke into a lope. Her lungs filled with the warm fall air. She clung to his mane and pressed her knees into his sides. No more bondage for her today, or for Blacky.

They raced along the familiar trail over the rims to Jake's, both knowing instinctively the destination. Reflected sunlight winked from the windows of the white two-story house. Pal got up from his spot in the shade and trotted out to greet them, tail wagging. Blacky whinnied. From the barn came an echoing reply from Alsanger.

Jake strode around the corner and stopped short as they galloped toward him. "Whoa, there, little gal. You're gonna run me over."

Nettie slid off the horse's back, still brimming with laughter. She flung her arms out wide and twirled in a circle, her head back and hair swinging loose. "Free at last."

Jake grabbed her hands and spun with her until she collapsed into his arms. His strong hug sent an oh-so-delicious tingle up her spine.

"Oh, Nettie, I've missed you. Your dad sent word that your mama had you tied to the sewing machine. How did you manage to get away?"

"I escaped." Nettie stepped back from his embrace but couldn't stop laughing. Joy kept popping up like little bubbles. "Oh, honestly, Jake. I can't stand another day of sticking that nasty needle into cloth and making tiny little Xs. I have as many holes in my fingers as in those pillowcases." She held out her hands. "Just look."

Jake cupped her hands in his, bending forward to kiss each finger, then her palm. "There. That'll make 'em better."

Nettie giggled again. "Oh, stop, Jake. That tickles."

❧

Nettie slipped through the kitchen door, making sure it didn't slam, and tiptoed to the living room. Mama sat, rocking in short little bursts.

She held Nettie's pillowcase, stabbing it with the needle. Her mouth was set in a firm, grim line. "So."

Nettie paused, her heart full of the sun-drenched happiness of the day. "Hi, Mama."

Her mother laid the sewing on her lap. She folded her arms, looking at Nettie through dark gray slits. "Are you not taking this seriously? You have made a commitment to marry this man, and it is your duty to bring a proper trousseau to your new home."

Nettie looked down at her pinpricked fingers. "But, Mama."

"But? But what? You think you're still a child, running off to ride and play while there's work to be done? You don't yet have a decent set of bedclothes, never mind tablecloths. And what about your wedding dress? Have you even set a date? There'll be baking and cooking to do." Mama stood up, her hands on her hips. "And you'll have to learn how to cook properly first."

Nettie's jubilation collapsed like wilted daisies after the first frost. "Mama, I do know how to cook. But Jake and I, we're not fancy folks. We're not going to put on dinner parties that require all this embroidered stuff."

Her mother sniffed. "Ha." She picked up the pillowcase and thrust it at Nettie. "Well, if you think that getting married is just 'playing house' and that you're going to be outside riding all the time, you'd better think again."

Playing house? Housework was a dirty word. It wasn't "play." Nettie didn't want to be inside. She couldn't stand it. Outside was where her freedom lay. With her horse. With Jake.

"I know that, Mama." Nettie sat. The needle may as well have been made from a ton of lead. The pillowcase a hard leather oxen yoke. "I'll finish this set and that's it. If you want to give me a gift of more, that's fine. But this is all I'm doing."

"We'll see about that." Her mother huffed and stalked from the room.

Nettie didn't remember Mama being so demanding of her sisters when they got married. Of course, *they* were ladies. *They* did things right. Why couldn't Nettie have the kind of wedding she wanted? After all, she was the last of the girls.

She closed her eyes against a rising tide of tears.

───

The days stretched into long, dull hours of needlework, wedding dress design, and cooking lessons. Nettie told herself that every pie and pot roast, and each frill added to the dress, brought her closer to marrying Jake. Her jaws ached with tension over all the tiny stitches, but she nevertheless forced herself to smile and agree with every little detail her mother brought up.

Mama was so excited it almost seemed to be her own wedding she was planning. She would stop in mid-stitch with a glow of delight on her face. "Oh, we could make those English scones and have choke-cherry jelly at the reception." Or she'd get Nettie pinned into the satin dress so tight she couldn't move, then run to look through an old cook-book for a recipe she'd just thought of, leaving Nettie to stand straight and tall, hardly able to breathe. But her legs twitched and her fingers closed and opened at her sides. How much longer would this suffocating task last?

She hated this dress. It was all poufy and lacy, so . . . girly. She imagined herself dressed in Ben's old cast-off denims. Wouldn't it be wonderful if she and Jake could sit on horseback up on the rims over-looking Jake's place, the traveling preacher intoning the vows before them. That would be a perfect wedding.

The need to talk to someone rose up in her like a storm cloud. If only Marie lived closer. Not even her married sisters were sympathetic when she had broached the subject. They teased her, the tomboy. "Let Mama have her fun. You'll love being a good housewife after you're married. You'll look back on all this someday and be thankful for it."

Nettie sighed. The Indian summer of October had been blasted by the freezing winds of November, and she was getting no closer to a wedding date. Mama insisted that everything be "done up good and proper" before she would allow her daughter to go off on her own. Now she talked about renting a hall all the way down in Cut Bank for the event. Would these notions never cease?

"Papa, you've got to help me." Nettie pleaded with her father during evening chores. "Can't you talk some sense into Mama? She's trying to make a princess out of me, and I'm just a plain ol' cowgirl." She was nearly in tears by now.

Papa simply pursed his lips and shook his head. "You know your Mama, when she gets an idea in her head." He plied his rake to the stalls. "But those weddings sure do cost a lot."

Nettie's shoulders slumped. Not Papa, too. If anybody was on her side, she'd've thought he would be.

Papa stopped and leaned on the rake. "I think it's 'cause your mama didn't have a proper wedding."

"She didn't?" The realization hit Nettie like horse's kick. So that's why she wanted her daughters to have fancy weddings.

❦

Jake came to visit nearly every evening, since Nettie was unable to get away during the day. On this night they walked in the frosty air toward the barn. Jake reached for her hand, but she snatched it away and stomped her booted foot. "Thanksgiving's coming soon. It's going to be winter any day now. We could get snowed in and never have the wedding until spring. What am I going to do? I can't sew any faster. I can't stand that dress, and I don't want a town hall full of people I hardly know."

Jake cupped her face in his hands. "This sounds serious, little gal. What's more important here, keeping the peace with Mama, or doin' it the way you want to?"

"Oh, Jake." A tear slipped down Nettie's cheek. "I don't want to disappoint Mama. She never had a big fancy wedding for herself, and I'm her last daughter, since Esther died." Her lip quivered. "Lola had a nice country wedding, but they couldn't afford to put on a big, modern 'town' kind for her or Margie. I still don't see that they have any more money now. But it's her big dream."

Jake stepped back, pulled out his tobacco pouch and papers, rolled a cigarette, twisting the ends, and flicked the bits of tobacco from his tongue. He struck a wooden kitchen match on his boot heel, cupped his hand around the flame, and dragged deeply until the tobacco glowed. He exhaled the smoke slowly.

"Could we just go away, just the two of us?" Nettie's voice was barely a whisper.

"Why not? I got some business in Great Falls in a few days. We could take the train, make a week of it."

Nettie's mouth dropped open. A spark of hope leaped inside. "Really?" Remorse clutched at her heart. "I don't know. Mama will be awful disappointed."

"I think your mama will get over it." Jake flicked his ash onto the ground. "What do *you* want to do?"

She swallowed hard. "You think we really could?"

"Absolutely. We can do it."

This was it. Her chance to avoid all the drudgery and falderal of a fancy wedding. She was different, unique. She wasn't going to be like Mama. Or Margie. Or Lola. She was Nettie, a cowgirl and partner with Jake. They didn't need much to be happy.

"Then let's." The joy returned, lifting the heavy yoke of wedding preparations from her shoulders. She threw her arms around Jake and smothered his face with kisses.

❦

"Mama?" Nettie folded yet another pillowcase into the trunk filling with her wedding trousseau.

Her mother looked up from her needlework. "Yes, dear."

"Couldn't we just have a really small wedding, just the family, maybe on Thanksgiving, when everybody's here anyway?"

Mama peered up at Nettie, lines furrowing her brow. "What? After all the plans we've made? Honey, that's absurd. This is your *wedding*. You deserve a big send-off, a party, with lots of people wishing you well."

"That's not what I want, Mama."

"Yes it is. You just don't know it. You'll regret it always if you don't. I know I've always wished—" Mama waved her hand as if to shoo the thought away. "I want you to have this beautiful wedding."

"That's right, Mama. It's your wish. Not mine." Nettie turned and stomped out of the room.

❦

Nettie lay under her covers still fully dressed. She listened to the night sounds gradually settle: the final whimper from her eight-year-old brother in his room, her mother's last firm "Good night. Now go to sleep."

Her parents murmured in the next room, talking over the events of the day as they usually did. Weren't they tired? She squeezed her eyes shut and willed Mama and Papa to go to sleep. The murmurs gradually died away, and she heard Papa turn over on the squeaky bedsprings. She wondered what time it was. The house creaked and settled into the night.

The enormity of what she was about to do held her rigid in the bed. If Mama had been furious when Nettie sneaked off to ride in that first rodeo, her mother would be livid when she discovered that Nettie had evaded all the big wedding plans. She set her mouth into a firm line. Darn it, anyhow. This was her life, not Mama's. And she was about to realize her dreams. How could her mother begrudge her this? Mama had dreams once, too. She'd wanted to go to the city and study music. Nettie tried to relax her stiff arms and shoulders.

After what seemed like hours, Papa's breathing slid into deep, contented snores. Then she heard Mama's softer whistling breaths. Nettie flung back her covers. She lit a candle and tiptoed to where she had stashed the pillowcase behind the door. It contained her folded gray skirt and red blouse she'd worn to the dance the night Jake proposed, along with a satiny nightgown Lola had given her for the wedding night. As her fingers lightly caressed the soft fabric, a tiny giggle rose into her throat. She had to clamp her hand over her mouth to keep it from escaping. This flimsy garment wasn't about to keep her warm this time of year. The next bed she'd crawl into would be with Jake. What would that be like? She shivered in the growing chill. Well, she just wasn't going to think about it right now.

Her whole body vibrated with an expectant nervousness. Avoiding creaky floorboards, Nettie stepped out to the kitchen. She set the pillowcase by the back door, slipped one arm into her heavy winter coat, and bent over the table to scrawl a note.

Dear Mama and Papa,

Jake and I are going to Great Falls to be married. I'm sorry, Mama, but I have to do it this way. I don't want you to spend all of your extra calf money on me. Thank you for all of your work. I know you love me and just want the best, but I can't face a huge wedding. Please don't be angry.

Love, Nettie

She eased out the door into the frosty darkness to the barn. Panting in her nervous haste, she saddled Blacky, packed the bundle into her saddlebag, mounted, and let him have his head toward the rims. He needed no urging, but broke into a trot down the familiar path.

They'd traveled at least half a mile before her heartbeat slowed. Nettie blew clouds in the cold moonlit November night air. A shiver swept through her despite her warm clothes. Couldn't she ever get things right with her mother?

Mama was so stubborn. Appearances were so important to her. She wanted everyone to know that the Bradys had proved their homestead and made a go of it, to boot. It wasn't Nettie's fault Mama hadn't had a fancy wedding. She understood how her mother would want things better for her children. But Nettie couldn't replace Essie. She couldn't take on the burden of Mama's loss.

And Papa. She frowned. He hadn't stood up against Mama's ideas. But he did mention how much money a big wedding would cost. So why wouldn't he be on Nettie's side?

Lantern light glowed in the window of Jake's house. Nettie felt a flutter in her chest. It would soon be her house, too. Well, if Mama was so worried about appearances, she should be happy that her daughter would be living in the only painted house between Cut Bank and Sunburst. She smiled. That should count for something.

Jake greeted her with a hug. "Hello there, little gal. You're a sight for sore eyes. I wasn't sure if you would still want to go through with this."

Nettie burrowed into his warm, comforting arms. "I had some whim-whams on the way over. They're gonna be so mad."

"Are you sure you want to, then?" He held her at arm's length and studied her face with his piercing gaze.

A lump rose in Nettie's throat. He really did care about her. And her family. She blinked back moistness in her eyes. All she could do was nod.

"Okay. But you tell me if you change your mind. All right?"

Nettie shook her head. "I won't."

Jake packed her saddlebag into his larger valise, and then they were off. The close proximity to the man she loved and the gentle, rocking gait of her horse soothed Nettie. A comfortable silence accompanied them on the hour-and-a-half ride into town. Her thoughts kept returning to Jake's house. She was surprised to find that she was mentally putting out the dishes and doilies her mother had collected for her. Well, that wouldn't take long. And then there was the barn. She could already see her saddle hanging next to Jake's. Satisfied contentment washed over her.

They left their horses at the livery near the train station in Sunburst. Climbing aboard, Nettie settled next to Jake on the hard-cushioned seat. He slipped his arm around her shoulders and grinned down at her. "So, we're off. Still sure this is what you want to do?"

"You bet." She squeezed his hand.

"Tickets, please." The conductor shuffled down the aisle toward them.

Even though Nettie had ridden the train several times to rodeos, a childlike excitement came over her. This is what she'd felt as a six-year-old on that train ride when her family moved from Idaho to Montana. Trains really did bring exciting things into her life.

Jake grinned and reached for her hand. The train swayed and rattled over the tracks, clicking off the miles.

She watched the landscape lighten with the approaching sunrise. The whorls of frost outside the train window refracted the soft pink that suffused the edge of the crisp gray-blue horizon. Then the tufts of hoary-laced prairie grasses began to glow with gold as the sun pushed itself up and awoke.

"Nice herd of cows." Jake looked out across the pastureland. "One of these days, we'll have to get some cattle, too."

"Our horses. Our cows. Our ranch." The words rolled off her tongue. They sounded so nice. Nettie squeezed his hand. "Now I'm glad I'm a girl."

Jake leaned over and kissed her. "I am too."

The aroma of fresh-brewed coffee wafted into Nettie's senses, and her stomach rumbled, reminding her it had been hours since last night's supper. She turned to Jake at the same moment he spoke. "Wanna go to the dining car for breakfast?"

In the dining car, clinking china on white linen tablecloths and napkins folded into intricate angles greeted them. "Oh, how lovely."

Nettie hadn't eaten in a dining car before. The rodeo gang had carried their lunches.

The heady scents of bacon, pancakes, and maple syrup accompanied the quiet morning conversation and laughter of those already eating.

Nettie and Jake found a table for two and faced each other with an easy, anticipatory silence. He reached across and folded her hand into his. A momentary spasm of shame for what she was doing to her family sent a shudder through her. But then the sun glinted through the window, highlighted his reddish-blond hair, and warmed their hands and her heart.

This was right. So right.

❦

That evening the train chugged into the Great Falls station. The depot bustled with more people than Nettie had ever seen in one place before. She stared at the women, attired in a wide array of fashions: from older ladies in long skirts and hats with feathers to young girls in tight-to-the-head cloche hats and dresses that hung straight from the shoulders and ended in beaded fringes just above the knee. A knot formed in her stomach. They were so stylish. She brushed at her rumpled divided skirt and her hand-me-down wool coat.

"Hey, Jake. Over here."

Nettie turned to see a young man with coal-black hair, dressed in a dark gray banker's suit, waving at them. Beside him stood a girl about Nettie's age, her dark hair bobbed straight just below her ears. She wore a fox-fur stole over a short, spangled dress, the latest "flapper" style Nettie had seen in a magazine.

"Snooky." Jake grinned and strode toward the couple, pulling Nettie alongside, as if he was leading his horse. He pumped the young man's hand and tipped his hat to the woman. "Mr. and Mrs. O'Haire, I'd like you to meet my lovely bride-to-be, Nettie Brady. Nettie, my good friends, Snooky and Ruth. They're going to stand up with us."

Nettie nodded a how-do-you-do to the couple. *My, how formal Jake sounds*. How out of place she was.

Ruth took a drag from a cigarette in a long holder, blew the smoke from the side of her mouth, and offered her cheek to Jake for a kiss. "Hi, handsome."

Nettie gulped. Jake must have had girlfriends like her before.

Then Ruth's smiling eyes swept Nettie from head to toe. "Nice to meet you, Nettie." A rich contralto voice wove itself amidst the smoke streamers.

The knot in Nettie's stomach grew tighter. *I'll never fit in with these people.*

Snooky took Nettie's hand, bowed low, and brushed a light kiss on the back of it. "So pleased to meet you finally. We've heard so much about you." He turned to Jake, still holding her hand. "I think you've got yourself a keeper here."

Nettie's face flamed.

Ruth linked her arm with Nettie's. "Come on. You two have to stop at the courthouse and get your marriage license and blood test. Then we'll take you to your rooms at the folks' hotel. Jake's been burning up the telegraph lines all week, getting this all planned." She had a mischievous twinkle in her eye. "We've been friends with him for a long time. Snooky and I grew up in Sunburst, you know. Jake is such a great guy, and we can tell he's crazy about you."

Nettie felt drawn to this woman's exotic looks and sophisticated manner. It might be fun to dress up like that. And Ruth was actually a small-town girl. Maybe she wasn't so unreachable after all.

The O'Haire Hotel rose tall and imposing against the low horizon. A doorman stood under a canopied entrance and ushered them inside. They followed a porter who carried their bags through a plush carpeted lobby filled with leather-cushioned chairs. Several men sat talking, smoking cigars, or reading newspapers. The porter stopped in front of a metal-grated door in the wall. He pushed a button and stood watching a bank of lights above the door. Nettie frowned, looking for a handle, but couldn't see one. Then a bell pinged and the porter pulled the grate aside to let them enter.

Nettie stood next to Jake inside the small, boxlike room, feeling a bit woozy as her stomach swooped downward. She grabbed onto his arm and closed her eyes.

Snooky chuckled. "First time in an elevator, huh?"

She opened her eyes a mere slit and nodded. The box shuddered to a stop. The porter opened the grated door to let them out. Relief washed over Nettie. She'd felt so closed in. Like she was about to suffocate.

Ruth led her down a long hall and opened a door with a key. "I'll help you get settled in here, while Snooky shows Jake to his room." She stepped in, flipped a switch next to the doorway. Electric light flooded the room.

Nettie stared. Dark red and gold brocaded paper covered the walls and maroon velvet curtains framed the tall window. A marble-topped chiffonier, like the one Mama admired in the Sears catalog, stood to one side, and in the far wall a door stood open to a gleaming white bathroom. The bedspread matched and blended with the wall covering, big pillows fluffed up against the brass headboard. Nettie blinked. It was so fine, so beautiful, so rich. How did she deserve this?

Ruth chuckled. "Pretty stylish, huh?"

Nettie blinked again. Gosh, Jake really had made plans. She'd had no idea he knew people who had such influence. It was all a bit dizzying.

❧

The next morning, Ruth woke Nettie with a knock at the door. She came in, carrying a tray with a boiled egg, buttered toast, jam, and a pot of coffee covered with a knitted cozy. "Here's some breakfast for you. Then let's get you dressed. We've got a church and a minister booked for you this afternoon."

Nettie stood before the ornate full-length mirror. As she buttoned the red blouse, her hands shook even more than they had the night she'd gotten ready for the dance. If only she'd had time to buy something new, something more stylish. She smoothed the fitted gray skirt along her hips and turned to survey her image.

"You look lovely. That outfit becomes you." Ruth put out a hand and brushed Nettie's hair behind one ear. "And you have such beautiful auburn hair." She reached behind her to where her charcoal cloche hat lay on the bed. "Would you like to wear this?"

Oh, how nice of Ruth. Nettie placed it on her head. She turned from side to side, examining herself in the mirror, and smiled. She could almost see herself in bobbed hair, wearing a short, shimmery dress. "I like it. Do you mind?"

"Not at all. I have others in my room. Shall we go?" Ruth turned, her spangled dress glinting in the light. They grabbed their coats and stepped into the hall, where the men already waited.

Jake's eyebrows lifted. "Golly, do you ever look nice, little gal. Ready to go get married?"

Nettie linked her arm in his. "Yes, I am."

❧

Snooky stopped his Model T in front of a white steepled church, and he and Ruth went inside. Jake leapt out, and offered Nettie his arm. "You are so beautiful." His whisper brushed her ear. The side of her face tingled as she stepped down onto the running board and into the street.

Beautiful? She'd never thought of herself in that way. But the way he looked at her, his kind, handsome face filled with light, his touch gentle on her shoulders. Even though she was dressed in an ordinary gray skirt and red blouse he'd seen before, suddenly she felt like a princess in the flowing white gown she'd scorned at home. Light-headed, she smiled up at him.

Nettie watched as he turned back toward the car, his broad, strong shoulders stretching the back of his black suit coat. *How handsome. He dressed up special, for me.*

Jake reached behind the seat and, with a flourish, brought out a huge bunch of flowers. "Your bridal bouquet."

Nettie gasped. White roses, framed in soft clouds of baby's breath, gave off an iridescent glow. She bundled them in her arms and buried her face in their fragrance. She thought she had smelled something light and fresh in the car, but figured it was Ruth's perfume. Tears momentarily overwhelmed her. She'd never seen such flowers, much less dreamed she'd ever receive any. Was there more to life than simple wildflowers in the pasture? She suddenly knew she would have many new and wonderful things to look forward to with this man who was about to become her husband.

She found her voice. "Jake, they're lovely. Thank you."

A plump, rosy-faced minister, wearing an ankle-length black robe, greeted them at the church door. "Come in, come in. I'm Pastor Swanson. I'm so glad you've arrived. Mr. and Mrs. O'Haire made all the arrangements. We've been waiting for you." He ushered them into his office, where he explained the ceremony. "I understand my good friend, Reverend Mahler from Sunburst, comes to your schoolhouse for monthly services."

Nettie's mouth opened in surprise. This minister knows another one clear over in Sunburst? "Why, yes. He does."

Pastor Swanson steepled his fingers. "So you know what the holy bond of matrimony means."

She blinked. Was this a test? "Y-yes, I think so."

Jake spoke up. "Both of her older sisters were married by Reverend Mahler."

"And you, Mr. Moser, have you also been brought up in the church?"

Jake shuffled his feet. "Ah, yes, I attended Reverend Mahler's church in Sunburst when my mother was alive."

"Fine. Good. Well, then. My wife will play the organ. Nettie, would you like to walk down the aisle?" The pastor looked at her.

She wondered if she could actually walk. Her legs didn't seem a part of her. "Yes. That would be nice." She caught Jake's approving smile. "Could we walk together?"

"The two of you?" The minister raised his eyebrows. "Well, uh, certainly. I don't see why not, since you have no one here to give you away."

Nettie suddenly had a sinking feeling as she thought of Papa. He should have been here. And Mama too. But they wanted too much. Nettie had to do it her way. She had made her choice.

The minister stood. "Let's get started, shall we?"

They stepped out of his office. The minister escorted Snooky and Ruth to the front of the church. The red runner carpet stretched out forever between the echoing, empty pews. The altar seemed a mile away. A hopeful ray of sunshine glowed through a pair of stained-glass windows in blues, reds, and greens. The minister nodded at his wife.

The swell of music filled Nettie's soul. She walked, suddenly light as air, down the aisle beside Jake. She sneaked a sidelong glance at him, tall and strong, achingly handsome, his light hair slicked to the side. A wayward lock hung over his forehead, making him look boyish. A black silk ascot contrasted with the stark white shirt under the black suit. As they came to a stop in front of the altar, she kept a tight hold on his arm, afraid that if she let go, her shaking knees would betray her.

"Dearly beloved . . ."

Nettie slipped out of her skirt and blouse. She gazed around the bathroom, with its huge porcelain claw-footed tub and an actual flush commode. Such luxury she had never seen before. Never dreamed she would want or even enjoy such things. Hadn't wanted a fancy wedding, didn't dream of a house filled with modern conveniences. Well, this was certainly a lot fancier than she ever could have imagined. But, to her surprise, she liked it.

She twisted the shiny brass faucet. Warm water ran into the deep white sink. She didn't even have to heat it first. She splashed her face. Reaching for the soft white towel, she patted her cheeks dry and stared into her own wide eyes in the mirror. Beautiful. That's how Jake thought of her. That's how he made her feel. Yes, for the first time she could look at herself and think that she was beautiful.

Nettie shrugged out of her underthings and slipped the white satin nightgown over her head. It slithered over her naked skin with a delicious fluttering smoothness. It left so much bare. She shivered in the cool tiled room. Taking another glance in the mirror, she squared her shoulders and stepped out into the ornate bedroom. It now seemed huge, the bed a long way from the bathroom door.

This was it. Her wedding night. She was Mrs. Jake Moser. Already in bed propped against the thick pillows, Jake wore his hat but no shirt. He grinned at her, pulled the bedspread up to his chin in mock modesty, and winked. Nettie couldn't help but giggle. Leave it to Jake to try to make her feel more comfortable.

He took off his hat and patted the blankets folded back on her side. "Come here, beautiful." His voice was low and husky.

She could feel his appraising eyes on her as she walked slowly across the wide expanse of room. She hoped her icy hands and feet wouldn't shock Jake when she touched him. Her teeth chattered.

It was their first night together. Would she know what to do? Giggled conversations with her sisters really hadn't prepared her for this moment. Why hadn't she asked more questions?

She hesitated, then smiled and slipped between the soft cotton sheets. He turned to her with open arms and kissed her on the forehead. Caressing her cheek, then her arms, he helped her slip the nightgown off. Then he drew her tight against his chest. She could feel both their heartbeats. His tender kiss sent hot tingles into her head. Warmth spread down her spine and into her belly. She moved closer, against his warm, dry skin.

They fit together just right.

CHAPTER TWENTY-ONE

Cut Bank Pioneer Press
November 30, 1923

*Nettie Brady and Jacob Moser put one over on their many friends
and relatives Nov. 22 when they left for Great Falls and were
married in the Electric City. Mr. Moser is a rancher and cattle-
man with a place under the rims. Congratulations, Mr. and Mrs.
Moser.*

December 1, 1923
Dear Marie,

*A fabulous week. Thanksgiving. Our wedding day. Truly thankful
for my wonderful husband. And Snooky and Ruth, great friends.
Our week at O'Haire Hotel, their wedding present to us. Shopping
with Ruth. Latest fashions, short skirts, cloche hats, a fox-fur stole.
Didn't think I'd like those things, but feel so grown up, sophisticated. Jake said I was beautiful.*

*Dressed up, took me to dinner at the Speakeasy, danced, played
cards, drank whiskey. I even tried to smoke cigarettes with those
long-handled holders. Talked, made plans. We'll hit the whole rodeo
circuit next year, produce another big one in Sunburst, raise rodeo
stock, maybe even a racehorse.*

Can't wait.

The weather turned bitter cold the day Nettie and Jake returned. The next morning Nettie was up by dawn, a suspenseful excitement setting her nerves afire. She poured Jake a cup of coffee. "I can't wait. Can we ride over to see Mama and Papa today?"

"Sure, little gal. Let's go get saddled up."

The horses blew frosty steam clouds in the crisp November air as they trotted along the path toward her old home. Nettie couldn't help smiling and sneaking glances over at Jake. Her husband, this warm, loving, handsome man. Her whole world had been transformed in the past week. She rode as if floating on a pillow of air.

A twinge of apprehension pricked her. How upset would Mama be? But surely when she saw how happy Nettie and Jake were . . .

As they topped a rise and she saw the house and barn, a lump rose in her throat. This wasn't her home anymore.

Papa was pitching hay over the fence to the horses. The boys were nowhere in sight. Probably out riding the pastures. Papa greeted them with a crisp nod and a grunted "Hello."

Nettie slid off her horse and gave his stiff shoulders a quick hug. "Hi, Papa." She ignored the stab of a tiny nettle in her conscience and ran up to the house, while Jake stayed outside with her father.

Mama half-turned from the stove as Nettie stepped into the kitchen, glared at her with thin, set lips for a long moment, then turned back to stir a large pot. Nettie's euphoria faded like wisps of steam. Suddenly she was a little girl again, caught doing something wrong.

"Hello, Mama." Her voice came out choked. Mama continued stirring the soup. Nettie tried again. "I'm sorry."

"Sorry?" Her mother whirled to face her. "That's the poorest word in the English language."

"Mama, I—"

Mama pointed to the half-finished wedding dress crumpled in the corner of the living room. "The wasted fabric. The wasted time. And worst of all, the rumors. I could deal with almost anything but stories

216

that my daughter got herself in a family way and *had* to get married quick."

She threw down the spoon. Drops of broth sizzled on the stovetop. "How will I ever be able to hold my head up in this community again?" Mama sank into a kitchen chair and buried her head in her arms, sobbing.

This was what Nettie had feared most. She rubbed the shiny gold band on her finger, then closed her eyes.

"Mama, I'm not having a baby. Those rumors will pass quickly. I just didn't want you to spend all your extra money on a big party I really didn't want. Don't you understand? I'm not like everybody else. I'm a simple cowgirl. I love Jake. He loves me. We both love to ride. That's where I want to be, where I need to be."

"So now you're going to become one of those rodeo floozies and gallivant all over the country with a bunch of men." Her mother's voice was raw.

Nettie squeezed her eyes closed for a moment. "You know I'm not that kind of woman. You told me once you followed Papa here to homestead, because you love him. That's what I'm doing."

She put a gentle hand on her mother's rock-hard shoulder.

"Mama, listen to me. I know you wanted a big wedding because you never had one. But I'm not you, Mama. I need to live my own life. Please try to understand."

Mama raised her head, her eyes narrowed. "You're no daughter of mine. Get out!"

Glass shards seemed to pierce Nettie's heart. "I love you. Jake loves you. You're welcome to come visit us any time, but I won't come here again unless I'm invited." Nettie turned and walked outside to where Papa and Jake silently kicked at dirt clods.

Papa looked at her from under his hat brim, gave a little half-smile and reached out to squeeze her shoulder before turning back toward the barn. The lump that rose in her throat nearly choked her. Wasn't

Papa happy for her either? Or maybe it was just that he couldn't side against Mama.

Jake's face was grim. They rode homeward without speaking. Nettie could barely hang on to the reins. Her heart felt like it had been stomped by a half-ton steer. She had known Mama would be upset, but really hadn't anticipated this heaviness, this feeling of irreversible wrongness. But, darn it, she hadn't done anything wrong. Mama wanted her to be someone she wasn't. She couldn't live up to an ideal that only lived in her mother's imagination in a city somewhere. She shuddered. That just wasn't her.

In this country, women had to be strong and work hard alongside the men. She was old enough to make her own decisions. And this is what she wanted, more than anything. She was happy being with Jake. She had made her choice to elope. Then why this shame, the burning in her stomach, the hot dampness in her eyes?

Fat snowflakes drifted slowly from the sky and melted as soon as they touched the horses' warm bodies. Nettie tilted her face upward to blink back her tears and opened her mouth to catch the feathery softness on her tongue. She turned to see Jake smiling at her.

He reached out to take her hand. "It'll be all right. Your papa's not holdin' a grudge. He says it's just that your mama's never quite gotten over losing Esther. She'll come around."

Nettie sucked in her lower lip. *Oh, dear Lord, please let it be so.* She just couldn't stand it if her family disowned her. When they reached the corral, Jake stopped her just outside the gate. "Wait here a minute."

Puzzled, she sat on Blacky's back, watching the snow collect on the roof. Jake took Alsanger into the barn. He rustled around inside, then led out a dark chestnut Hambletonian mare. She stepped high, muscles rippled, liquid brown eyes flashed, and she tossed her mane like a beautiful lady.

Nettie's mouth dropped open. "Who is this?"

Jake grinned. "This is Tootsie, your wedding present from me."

All the air seemed to leave her body. This horse must have cost a fortune. "Jake, where . . . ? How did you . . . ?"

His face beamed with a self-satisfied look. "I traded one of my draft horses to Ferguson. Had him deliver her this morning while we were gone."

Nettie slid out of her saddle. "Oh my gosh, she's beautiful. Jake, you shouldn't have." She approached with her hand outstretched for the spirited mare to sniff. She ran her palm up the fine-boned face to stroke the ears, then along the arched neck, over the curve of the back and down the muscular hindquarters. *This horse is magnificent.*

Jake was so good to her. Just like Papa, when he got Blacky for her. She felt her eyes sting. Memories flooded in. This was the end of the world as she had known it. Papa wasn't speaking up for her. Mama had lashed out, looked at her with such cold eyes. Nettie was a disappointment to them.

She chewed on her bottom lip. And yet, this horse . . .

"Jake." At a loss for words, suddenly she was in his arms, sobbing.

Jake's arms tightened around her. He stroked her hair, murmured soft words in her ear. Just like the horses he gentled, she gradually stopped shaking and her sobs diminished. He was her world now. The world she wanted. She eased herself from his embrace, sniffed, and wiped away the moisture on her cheek with the back of her hand.

She looked up at him, her smile trembling. "Can I try her out?"

He chuckled. "Why, Mrs. Moser, you sure can. I'd be proud to go with you." He transferred her saddle and bridle from Blacky to Tootsie.

Smiling now, Nettie stepped into the stirrup and swung herself onto the horse's back. The mare tossed her head and danced lightly in place. Excitement zinged through Nettie's body. She could feel the mare's power and energy beneath her. Loosening the reins, she pressed her heels against the horse's belly. Tootsie moved ahead, her ears forward. Jake rode alongside on Alsanger.

The mare's pace, the fastest trot Nettie had ever experienced, was energizing, an almost electrifying experience. She urged the horse into a gallop, the snow now only a minor nuisance, the rift with her family momentarily set aside.

By the time they rode back home, evening had set in, along with a steady snowfall. Nettie and Jake hurried through their outside chores. Then, while Jake laid the fire in the coal stove, Nettie opened a jar of canned venison to heat, cut thick slices of bread, and covered them with slabs of butter. They sat down at the square wooden table to eat by lantern light.

The warm food, the circle of light, and Jake's closeness filled Nettie with a rosy glow. The energy of that fine horse still coursed through her veins. She looked across the table at Jake and couldn't keep the grin from spreading across her face.

"What's ticklin' you, little gal?" He grinned back.

"Oh, nothing." She glanced down at her plate and back up again. "Everything. I can't believe that horse, and being here with you. I just love you."

～●～

Over the next few weeks, when Nettie awoke in the mornings, her first thoughts were of Jake beside her: his warmth, the excitement of the love they shared. Then, the icy whistle of the December wind would jolt her from her security and remind her of Mama's coldness, her new life broken from her past.

Praying that Mama would someday come around, Nettie slipped from her warm marriage bed into the frigid room and crept downstairs to stoke the fire.

Jake trudged down the steps just as the coffee bubbled. He sat across the table and reached for her hand. "Such a sad face, little gal."

His commiseration only added to the dammed-up tears in her heart. She couldn't speak, afraid she would cry. This was no way to start a marriage. She forced a smile and a light tone. "Hey, after breakfast, what d'you say, we go for a ride? I can't wait to get on Tootsie again."

And so, despite the snow, Nettie gave in to her compulsion to be out riding. The crisp air and hard gallops erased the pain that overwhelmed her when she thought of Christmas without her family. It also eased her remorse over replacing Blacky as her favorite. After all, they would keep him to add to their saddle string.

December 25 loomed, a cold, dark date ahead, with no word from Mama or Papa. She bit back her disappointment and threw herself into the role of Jake's wife. He was her life now. His happiness was the most important thing to her.

"Beulah and Clem want us to come for Christmas," Jake announced after making a mail run into Sunburst one day. "Emma and Roy will be there, and all their kids. It'll be fun."

Regret pierced Nettie like a knife. As much as she liked Jake's sister, Beulah, and as funny and teasing as Clem was, it just wouldn't be the same. Nothing would ever be the same again. Maybe she had made a mistake by eloping. Maybe she should have let Mama have her way, gone along with the big, fancy wedding, just to keep peace in her family.

No. She couldn't have done that. She was Nettie, the simple cowgirl. She loved Jake, cherished their wedding trip, and now their marriage, their partnership. That was the plain truth. She wouldn't have it any other way. If Mama couldn't accept that, then she had lost another daughter. Nettie's heart contracted. *Oh my gosh, how could I think such a thing?*

She looked into Jake's kind, concerned face. He was really trying to make things all right for her. And his family had accepted her. The least she could do was accept them, as well. "Sure. Let's go. It sounds like fun."

On the afternoon of Christmas Eve, Nettie and Jake bundled up, harnessed the draft horses, and took the sled into town. She snuggled next to him as the runners squeaked over the snow. In Sunburst, windows glowed with candlelight in the growing dusk. She heard bells tinkling as other families arrived in their sleighs.

Jake's nieces and nephews were building a snowman in front of Clem and Beulah's house. "Uncle Jake!" One young boy scooped a handful of snow, formed it into a ball, and tossed it at them. Jake leapt out of the sleigh and returned fire. Nettie joined the fracas, laughing and shrieking as the snow pelted her face and slid down her neck.

"Good heavens, what a warm welcome." Beulah opened the door and beckoned them in. The smell of hot cider and cinnamon wafted through the open door.

Nettie ducked another snowball and dashed inside, Jake close behind. Beulah hugged them both to her plump bosom. "Take off your coats and stay awhile."

Clem pumped their hands. "Merry Christmas. Glad you could come." He took cups of steaming cider from Beulah, poured in a dollop of whiskey, and ushered them into the living room, where a fragrant pine stood bathed in candlelight.

Jake's other sister, Emma, offered a cool, slim hand to Nettie and a cheek to Jake. Roy clapped Jake on the back and encircled Nettie with his arm. "Welcome, you two. Come, set. We're ahead of you on the cider." His ruddy cheeks shone in agreement with his statement.

Nettie shut the door on the memories of Brady Christmases. She let the warmth of the spiked cider and the family atmosphere overtake her. For a little while, anyway, she forgot the cold emptiness in her heart.

CHAPTER TWENTY-TWO

On a heavy gray afternoon just before the new year, Nettie heard horses whinny. She roused herself from an equally gray daze and looked out to see a sled pulling up to the house. Now who could that be? It wouldn't be Marie. She'd sent a card saying they were going to Canada for Christmas week. Nettie frowned and squinted through the frosty panes.

Two men jumped down from the high seat. One strode forward to take care of the team, the other reached up to help two women to the ground. Heavily bundled against the cold, they waddled toward the house.

Nettie opened the door. "Hello?"

One of the women unwrapped the scarf from around her face and stepped forward, her arms open. "Is that our baby sister?"

Nettie screeched. "Margie."

"Naw, she's no baby sister. This is *Mrs.* Jake Moser." Lola giggled and threw her arms around Nettie, too. The sisters danced in a circle, hugging and laughing and crying at the same time. Nettie hadn't seen them since weeks before her elopement.

She finally turned to the men who stood back with bemused expressions. "Glen, Floyd. What a great surprise. Jake's in the barn. Run your team on down and then come to the house."

"Yeah, we brought that oats Jake wrote us about." Floyd reached for the team's lead line.

"He wrote you about oats?"

"In the Christmas card," Lola said.

Nettie stared at her, puzzled. "Hmm. He didn't mention anything. Maybe I just forgot." *That tricky guy. He did this for me.* She smiled at her sisters. "What're you standing around in the cold for, come on in." Suddenly the drab sky didn't matter anymore.

Nettie put the teakettle on while the women shed their heavy clothes and hung them near the stove. The smell of wet wool mingled with the faint smokiness of the fire.

The sisters all spoke at once. "Oh, I'm so glad you came." "What a cozy kitchen." "Nice window right by the table."

Nettie laughed. "Come, let me show you the house."

"Ooh, doilies on the sofa." Lola giggled. "See, that crocheting and needlework Mama made you do paid off."

Nettie cuffed Lola's arm in mock annoyance.

Margie just smiled. "I love this blue vase on the windowsill. I can just see yellow daisies in it this summer." Even though Nettie always scoffed at such "girl things," a warm sense of pride welled up in her. "Come, look at the upstairs."

In the bedroom, Margie smoothed the patchwork quilt. "This is lovely. I don't remember seeing it."

"A wedding gift from Jake's sister Beulah."

Lola flopped onto the bed. "Nice and soft." Her face crinkled with a teasing grin. "So, our little sister is married." She winked. "Tell us, how is married life with Jake?"

Nettie faced her sister with a grin. "It's just great. You should've told me."

Lola rolled her eyes. "We did! But you wouldn't listen. 'No, I'm never getting married. I only want to ride horses.'" Her voice mimicked.

Nettie shook her head. "Jake is just right for me. I wouldn't trade him for all the horses in Montana." The sisters laughed and hugged again.

Margie gazed out the window where distant purple rims ringed the white lakelike expanse of snow. "This is the nicest house in the valley. You're lucky to live here."

Gratitude and happiness swept Nettie like a warm wind over snow. "Let's go back to the kitchen and have tea."

They sat at the table near the stove, clutching their steaming cups close to their bodies for warmth. Margie reached across and put her hand on Nettie's arm. "It's so nice to be together again."

Nettie ducked her head. *Yes, and it's all because of my wonderful husband.* She looked up at them. "I'm sorry I didn't have a wedding you could come to."

"Well, I did miss—" Lola stopped short when Margie elbowed her in the ribs.

Nettie bit her tongue. Just like Lola to throw a wet blanket on the mood.

"My goodness. No use cryin' over spilt milk. That doesn't matter now. What matters is that she's happy, right, Lola?"

"Uh, yeah. Sure. That's right." Lola looked chagrined. Margie patted Nettie's hand. "Christmas just wasn't the same without you, though."

Nettie blinked back tears. "I can't tell you how much I missed you." She traced a curlicue in the oilcloth on the table. "Is Mama still upset?"

Margie ducked her head and sighed. "She hasn't said much. But I could tell she didn't feel right about you not being there. You think so, too, Lola?"

Their sister nodded.

Nettie took a deep breath. "How about I come back with you and talk to her?"

❧

A warm amber light shone from the window of Nettie's childhood home. The glow reached into her heart, a welcome-home sight she'd seen so many times before. But would it be, this time? Nettie sat in the sled after everyone had jumped down, bracing herself. She could barely breathe. How could she make it up to Mama, bridge that cavernous gap that had grown between them?

Perhaps she'd been wrong to come. Oh, why hadn't she brought Jake?

Papa opened the door and peered out. "C'mon in. Don't just stand out there in the cold . . . oh." He stepped outside as he saw Nettie, strode forward with a big smile, and reached up to help her down. "Welcome home."

Nettie hugged him. "Thank you, Papa," she murmured against his chest.

They all trooped inside, her sisters laughing and teasing their husbands. Mama turned from the stove. "I have some venison stew all ready. You must be hungry." She stopped and stared.

"Mama." Nettie's lips trembled. *Is she going to kick me out in the snow?*

Her mother blinked. "Nettie!" Her arms opened wide and Nettie fell into the embrace.

"Welcome home, dear." Mama's murmur was warm against Nettie's hair. "I was wrong. Forgive me?"

Nettie thought she might just melt into a puddle on the floor. *An answer to prayer.* "Oh, Mama."

Her mother held her at arm's length. "Would you and Jake come over for New Year's and celebrate the Christmas we missed together?"

"Yes, we will. Thank you."

Her sisters grinned and Margie flashed a thumbs-up.

A happy spark leaped in Nettie's heart. Now the packages she'd been carefully wrapping in secret wouldn't have to be hidden away until next year.

Her mother went into the bedroom and returned, carrying a white-wrapped package. "For your eighteenth birthday."

Nettie tore the wrapping from the heavy box, blinking at the large "J" on the side. Her hands shook. Slowly she lifted the lid. All she could do was stare. Inside were highly polished black leather boots with spirals of bright green stitching decorating their high tops. Just like the ones she'd admired in the catalog since she was fifteen. A dark cloud lifted from her shoulders as though a summer sun had just dawned.

⸺ ⸺

Nettie watched Marie Gibson finish her ride to loud cheers from the audience. Bending down, Nettie brushed the dust from her shiny black boots. Then she turned to Jake to accept a leg up onto the back of the big red steer and snugged her hand under the surcingle rope.

Jake clapped her on the back. "Ready?"

Nettie took a deep breath. For the first time, her whole family, even Mama, was there to watch her ride. A warm rush of love and excitement coursed through her body. She tightened her knees against the steer's back, grinned, and nodded at Jake.

She was ready for anything.

About the Author

Heidi M. Thomas grew up on a working ranch in eastern Montana. She had parents who taught her a love of books and a grandmother who rode bucking stock in rodeos. Describing herself as "born with ink in her veins," Heidi followed her dream of writing with a journalism degree from the University of Montana and later turned to her first love, fiction, to write her grandmother's story.

EPIC Award-winning *Cowgirl Dreams* is the first in the Dare to Dream series about strong, independent Montana women.

Heidi is a member of Women Writing the West and Professional Writers of Prescott, is also a manuscript editor, an avid reader of all kinds of books, and enjoys the sunshine and hiking in north-central Arizona, where she writes, edits, and teaches memoir and fiction writing classes.

Married to Dave Thomas (not of Wendy's fame), Heidi is also the "human" for a finicky feline, and describes herself primarily as a "cat herder." Visit her at heidimthomas.com.

LOOK FOR THE NEXT CHAPTER OF NETTIE'S LIFE,
WILLA AWARD–WINNING *FOLLOW THE DREAM:*

Nettie Moser's dreams are coming true. She's married to her cowboy, Jake, they have plans for a busy rodeo season, and she has a once-in-a-lifetime opportunity to rodeo in London with the Tex Austin Wild West Troupe.

But life during the Great Depression brings unrelenting hardships and unexpected family responsibilities. Nettie must overcome challenges to her lifelong rodeo dreams, cope with personal tragedy, survive drought, and help Jake keep their horse herd from disaster.

Will these challenges break this strong woman?

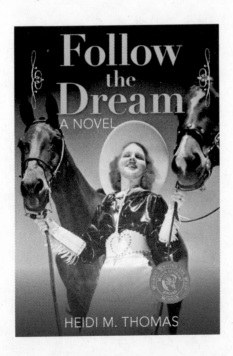